Ghosts on the Red Line

A Novel

PETER DAVID SHAPIRO

PenLane Press
11 Wachusett Drive
Lexington, MA, USA 02421

This book is a work of fiction. References to real establishments, organizations, technologies, or locales are intended only to provide an air of authenticity, and are used fictitiously. All characters, and all procedures, processes, incidents and dialogue, are products of the author's imagination and are not construed to be real.

MBTA system map in the Preface is used with permission (MBTA 2011).

For information please write: PenLane Press, 11 Wachusett Drive, Lexington, Massachusetts USA 02421

www.ghostsontheredline.com
www.peterdshapiro.com

ISBN 978-0-9839244-0-1 (pbk)
ISBN 978-0-9839244-1-8 (ebk)

FIRST EDITION 2011

ACKNOWLEDGMENTS

My sincere thanks to Bernadette Nelson, muse to aspiring authors, John Amiard, Elizabeth Shapiro, Stu Lipoff, and Janet Reid and her "trusty minion" for their generous help and advice. Also to Walter Nelson for his anecdotes about his adventures as a police officer.

Since we must understand whether ghosts and spirits exist or not, how can we find out? Mo Tzu said: The way to find out whether anything exists or not is to depend on the testimony of the ears and eyes of the multitude. If some have heard it or some have seen it then we have to say it exists. If no one has heard it and no one has seen it then we have to say it does not exist. So, then, why not go to some village or some district and inquire?

— Mo Tzu (470-391 BC), translated by Yi-pao Mei, www.book-of-thoth.com/thebook/index.php/Ghost , GNL Free DOC License

Preface

A RED LINE TRAIN DEPARTS Alewife Station every nine minutes during the commuter rush hours and every eleven to thirteen minutes during other times of the day and evening, until the last train completes its run shortly after midnight.

From Alewife, the subway terminus where the City of Cambridge borders the western suburbs, it journeys 17.6 miles inbound through Cambridge, across the Charles River into Boston, through Boston, and down to the Town of Braintree. Meanwhile, another Red Line train leaves Braintree for Boston and Cambridge, terminating at Alewife.

Red Line passengers can change in Boston for the Green, Orange, Silver, or Blue lines. These five color-denominated subway lines, along with buses, commuter trains, and ferries, are kept in sync by the Massachusetts Bay Transportation Authority, or MBTA, known locally as the T, subject to inclement weather, accidents, equipment failures, signal malfunctions, traffic, driver errors, computer glitches, and passenger emergencies.

Over 240,000 passengers ride the Red Line every weekday.

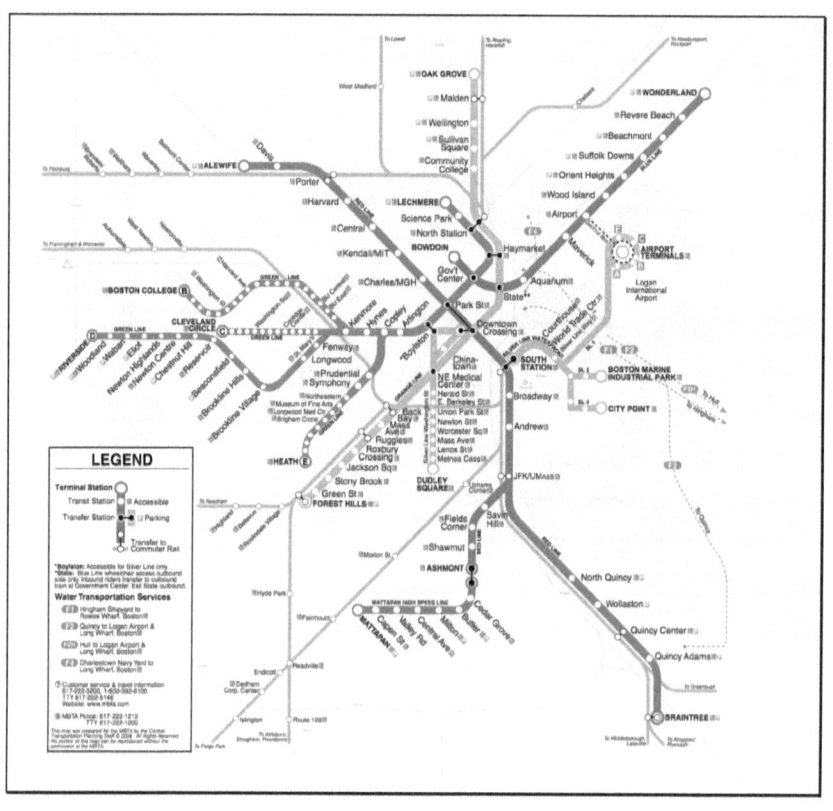

MBTA 2011

PART ONE

ON THE RED LINE

One

BILLY DELAHUNT BOARDED A RED LINE TRAIN with his mom at Boston's Downtown Crossing station heading towards Harvard Square in Cambridge for his piano lesson and then afterwards, she promised, to shop for a new skateboard. Because their train car was almost empty, he and his mom had no problem finding seats.

Billy loved to observe the other passengers. Sitting across from him, for example, was an Asian lady, her long dark hair carefully brushed and all in place, tidily dressed for work in matching clothes, intently checking her BlackBerry. A young woman standing near a door was gripping a pole with one hand and the handle of a baby stroller with the other. Also standing near the same door was a grey-haired man in a blue blazer and red tie, white trousers, and brown loafers. At the far end of Billy's train car, a young man chatted with two women, all three of them probably students based on their ages, casual dress and backpacks. The women laughed at something that the man said, which Billy was unable to overhear above the *basso profundo* rumble of the train's steel wheels and the creaks and shrieks from the train car's undercarriage as it braked and swayed around turns, noises that were amplified in the reverberant Red Line tunnel.

Billy stared unblinkingly at his fellow Red Line passengers and being only eleven, he did not glance away even when one of them caught him staring. However, their faces revealed little beyond the obvious external clues; they were non-threatening, non-welcoming, and frustratingly for Billy's research purposes, blandly non-expressive.

Suddenly shattering the spell and causing Billy almost to jump out of his seat, the neatly-dressed Asian woman right across from him screamed, "Oh my God!"

She lurched sideways and stared transfixed at the empty space beside her and exclaimed again, "Oh my God!" and then, "Robbie! You've come back to me! Is it really you?" She began to sob, causing her eye make-up to run, which smeared glistening smudges on her formerly immaculate cheeks. "Oh my God!" she repeated. "I can't believe it!"

But Billy saw no-one sitting next to her, nor standing in front of her. There was no-one there, no "Robbie" nor anyone else.

He checked whether the woman might be communicating with someone – her Robbie – through a Bluetooth headset hanging off one of her ears, perhaps hidden under her dark hair, but her ears were ornamented only by small gold hoop earrings. Her hand clenched as if it were taking hold of something. "I've missed you so much!" she said, and then paused, looking at the space next to her, seeming to listen.

As their train approached the Central Square station in Cambridge, the woman stood up from her seat and pleaded, "Come with me, Robbie. Promise that you'll stay with me!"

The grey-haired man and the baby-stroller woman sidled aside to give her extra space at the train car door. They let her get out first, and then followed several paces behind. After the door slid shut, she turned back towards the train car. She looked surprised, and then distraught, and cried out, "Where are you?

Robbie! You promised you'd stay with me!" Billy could hear her calling frantically, as the train began to move, "Will I see you again?"

Billy's mom was flipping through a free Metro newspaper that someone had left on a nearby seat. "Did you see the woman crying?" Billy asked.

"Yes. She was very emotional."

"Did you hear what she said?"

"Not really," Billy's mom said, "I was reading the paper."

"She was talking to someone."

"So?"

"But she was alone!"

"Maybe on her cellphone."

"No cellphone. No Bluetooth. I checked."

"Sometimes people just talk to themselves."

"Well I thought it was weird."

"You're weird yourself," his mom said and added, as the train slowed to enter the Harvard Square station, "This is our stop."

Once they were on the platform, Billy repeated to his mom, "She was really sad when she got off the train." When his mom did not respond, Billy pointed to an official MBTA sign attached to the red-tiled station wall, "See Something? Say Something!"

"That's for security. It's not about ladies on the train who were crying."

"I want to report it."

They approached a man wearing an MBTA uniform, including the official logo, a black T inside a silver circle, stitched on the right shoulder of his jacket. "My son wants to make a report," Billy's mom said.

The MBTA man listened attentively as Billy described what he saw. He asked for all the details that Billy could remember and took notes as Billy talked. He thanked Billy for his report and assured him that he would pass it along to the proper authorities.

"Satisfied now?" his mom asked, once they were on their way again. They were going to be late for Billy's piano lesson with Mrs. Fiona Lewis, who was a stickler for starting on time, so his mom hustled him to keep up with her as they climbed the steps out of the station to street level in Harvard Square.

After Billy's piano lesson, he texted his friends about the lady he saw crying on the Red Line, about how she was talking with someone who wasn't there, and about how the MBTA man in the Harvard Square station seemed really interested when Billy reported what he saw.

One of his friends responded, "Sweet!" and another replied, "Woo! Maybe she was talking to a ghost!"

Two

MOLLY LU BARELY glanced up when Harry West, co-founder and Managing Partner of Blair West International, management consultants, arrived for work at their offices on the fourth floor of the Andleman Building in Central Square.

"Hi Molly," Harry said.

She responded with a listless "Hi, Harry," and held out to him a manila folder, "Couple of admin forms for you to sign, also an applicant's bio for one of our new analyst positions." Her eyes were red and puffy, and she seemed pre-occupied, even disengaged, quite unlike the Molly Lu who worked tirelessly to ensure that their office functioned perfectly, with everything in its place and everything being done that needed to be done.

Harry noticed, but he chose not to comment. Whatever Molly's problem was, and apparently something *was* bothering her, it wasn't his business. She could deal with it. Anyway, he had to check his emails, look over the documents that Molly had just given him, and lead a conference call that was scheduled shortly with a major client. He had enough to do, managing fourteen consultants in Cambridge, plus generating revenues for the firm by selling, serving, and tending to clients, plus coordinating with Stephen Blair, his co-founder and business partner, who managed another twenty Blair West International consultants in Hong Kong, halfway around the world.

After the client conference call ended, Jerry Seligman appeared in Harry's doorway. "That went well," he said. "As I predicted, if I may say so."

"Jerry, you were right, as usual," Harry said.

At forty-three, Harry was almost as wiry as he'd been twenty years earlier, while Jerry, now in his mid-fifties and the oldest member of the Blair West International staff, carried the rounded physique of a person who appreciated a good meal. Unlike Harry's full head of curly brown hair, Jerry's dome was almost entirely bald, fringed on the sides and in the back by long grey strands that tumbled haphazardly over his shirt collar, except on formal occasions when he tied it in a ponytail in the style of the hippie that he might have been if he hadn't missed the Summer of Love by a decade or so.

On first acquaintance, Harry came across as cool, and distant, while Jerry was everybody's instant close friend.

But, despite their superficial differences, they had been friends and colleagues for years, since before the founding of Blair West International, and had worked together on more projects than Harry could count.

"Did you notice Molly when you came in?" Jerry asked.

"I did, but I didn't want to pry."

"She's sitting at her desk weeping like her heart is breaking."

"Christ!"

"I asked her what was wrong and she blew me off."

"Alright, I'll talk to her."

"I'm fine," Molly replied, when Harry asked if she was OK.

"Look Molly, you don't usually cry at your desk. I may not be Mr. Sensitive but even I can tell that something's going on."

"You wouldn't understand."

"Try me."

"I saw Robbie."

"Where?" That Molly's fiancé had died was not in doubt. Robbie had been killed a year earlier in Afghanistan by a roadside bomb. His memorial service was attended by all of Molly's colleagues at Blair West International, including Harry.

"On the Red Line, on my way into work this morning."

"That's not possible, Molly. You know that."

"I don't care what's possible," Molly said, defiantly. "I saw Robbie. I talked with him. I held his hand."

"People don't come back," Harry said. "No matter how much we wish they would."

Harry restrained himself from adding that when your life ends it's no less over for you than it is for the chicken that finds its way into your chicken salad sandwich, thereby proving that he wasn't nearly as tactless as some people said.

Jerry brought over a cup of tea and laid it gently on Molly's desk. His bushy salt-and-pepper eyebrows jumped and bounced like Groucho Marx's as he told her, "Made the way you like it, one tea-bag in hot water."

"Thank you," Molly said damply, taking a sip.

"Don't worry about Harry," Jerry said. "We all know he's a cynic."

"I'm not a cynic," Harry said. "I'm a skeptic. I don't accept what I hear on faith just because everyone else is a believer."

"Nothing wrong with that, Harry," Jerry said. "But it could get lonely out there."

"So be it," Harry said. He marched to the beat of his own drum, and always had. The caption under his headshot in his Palo Alto High School yearbook put it nicely, "Harry is the *individual* of Paly's senior class."

Jerry asked Molly, "Why don't you tell us what happened on the Red Line?"

"What's the point? Harry has already told me basically that he doesn't believe me."

Harry protested, "Molly, I don't doubt that you saw something, even if…"

"I did see Robbie," Molly insisted. "All of a sudden there he was, right beside me. He said, 'Hello, Molly.' I was so shocked. I couldn't believe it. He was sitting right beside me as real as either of you. He was all spiffed up in his uniform, as crisp as on the day he left for Afghanistan. He took my hand, and told me not to be afraid, and said that he loved me. I started crying. I couldn't help it." Molly's voice broke and tears welled in her eyes.

Jerry handed her a paper towel, and asked, "What happened then?"

"I was so grateful to see Robbie again and to hear his voice, but I didn't know what to say. Finally I asked, 'Is it really you?' He said yes, that he was really Robbie and that he had come back to me. There was so much I wanted to ask him but our train was approaching Central. I was so stupid, so unbelievably stupid, I should have stayed on the train with Robbie but I was sure that he would come with me. He promised that he would. He held my hand as we walked to the door. The door opened, I got off first, and I thought he was right behind me. But he'd disappeared. Our time together was so brief! Now I've lost my only chance to have Robbie with me again, and he's gone forever and it's all my fault!

"No wonder you're feeling shaky," Jerry said.

"Do you think I'm crazy?"

"No, Molly, of course we don't think you're crazy," Harry replied firmly, although in fact the notion *had* crossed his mind that she may have come unhinged.

In a fatherly tone, Jerry said, "We understand, Molly, it's been a year since the awful news about Robbie. Maybe you should take the day off."

"I have a lot to do here."

"You're not in the greatest condition to work right now," Jerry said.

"Will you be alright if I go?"

"Sure," Jerry said. Turning to Harry, he asked, "Do you agree? Shouldn't Molly take some time off?"

"Yes, we'll manage," Harry said. "Go home, Molly. Come back tomorrow when you feel better."

After she left, Jerry said, "Poor Molly! The anniversary of Robbie's death must have hit her really hard."

"She's not herself," Harry agreed. "She's usually so level-headed."

"What do you think about her story, about seeing Robbie?"

"As you said, it's the first anniversary. She's probably been thinking about him a lot. When a person's upset, the mind can do strange things."

Three

JIM CUDDIHY'S EMAIL to Harry later that morning adhered to his usual terse style, "Call me."

Cuddihy, the Chief Operating Officer at the Massachusetts Bay Transportation Authority, was a former client. Blair West International had recently completed a project for him to help structure a deal with ClearCell, a mobile telecoms provider, to improve its cellphone service in the MBTA's subway tunnels.

Lately disputes had erupted concerning ClearCell's plans to install its system and although Blair West International was no longer involved, Cuddihy felt free to contact Harry to vent his frustrations. Harry anticipated hearing more on this topic when they talked.

When Cuddihy answered his phone with a gruff "Cuddihy here," Harry took the initiative, "Hey Jim, how are things going with ClearCell?"

"Same as always," Cuddihy growled, "and every day I have to fuck around with those SOBs, Harry, I think of you."

"Jim, you cut us loose to save on our fees," Harry said. "We were ready to help you work with ClearCell."

"Yah, I know," Cuddihy said. "Whatever. That's not why I contacted you."

"You have more work for us?"

"Maybe. Despite ClearCell, I still like you."

"And we're fond of you, too, Jim."

"I've heard that you guys have a history handling funky stuff that's out of the usual for consultants, not like your job for us on ClearCell."

"We call them our special projects."

"Like that money laundering thing in Hong Kong, where the murder happened, and the telephone company exec who went missing up in Vermont."

"Like those projects, and others," Harry said. "We just get drawn in. What's going on?"

"Not on the phone," Cuddihy said. "Come to my office this afternoon. Around 3:00 P.M."

At 2:55 P.M., Harry and Jerry cleared security at the entrance to the MBTA headquarters in the State Transportation Building in Boston. When they got off the elevator on Cuddihy's floor, they were greeted by Marla Johnson, his executive assistant, with a cheery, "It's the dynamic duo!"

"Hey Marla," Jerry said. "How're things?"

"Just peachy-keen, Jerry. How about with you?"

"Keeping busy."

"And you, Harry?"

"Me too."

After leading them into an empty conference room, Marla said, "Gentlemen, help yourselves to refreshments," gesturing towards a side table. "As usual, you have your choice of coffee, tea, bottled water and juice in the ice bucket, and our delicious plain cookies."

"I love it when Marla calls us *gentlemen*," Jerry said. "Just hearing her say it sends a thrill up my leg."

"That's amazing! That's exactly what I feel!" Harry exclaimed.

Marla laughed and said that Cuddihy would join them in a few minutes.

Jim Cuddihy arrived soon after. A burly man with bristly short red-grey hair, whose light-complexioned skin was peeling on his forehead and on the tip of his nose, Cuddihy had the thick arms, torso, and legs of the wrestler that he had once been at Boston College. He shook hands with his two visitors, grabbed a bottle of water, unscrewed its top with several impatient twists, downed a few quick gulps, and dropped himself into one of the chairs.

"Did you take the Red Line to get here?" Cuddihy asked.

"We did," Harry replied. "From Central Square to Park Street, and walked over from there. Why?"

"Did you notice anything strange on the train? Anything at all?"

"I didn't," Harry said. "Jerry, did you?"

"Nope," Jerry said. "Just the usual delighted customers."

"Very funny, Jerry. You're a real wit. No one crying? Or talking to themselves?"

"No," Harry said. "Why? What's going on?"

Cuddihy said, "What I'm about to tell you is sensitive. No blabbing about this with anyone. It will freak people out."

"Of course," Harry said.

Cuddihy said, "We're getting reports that riders on the Red Line are having visions."

"What kind of visions?"

"They're seeing dead people."

Harry and Jerry exchanged glances.

Cuddihy noticed. "What?"

Harry said, "One of our employees came in this morning saying this happened to her."

"On the Red Line?"

"Yes," Jerry said. "Molly told us that her fiancé who was killed last year in Afghanistan was sitting right beside her. She said he was incredibly real. It really broke her up. Harry gave her the rest of the day off to collect herself."

"Good, then you know what I'm talking about. People have been calling the MBTA and collaring our staff on the platforms. They're worried that their fellow passengers who they see acting strangely might be unbalanced and maybe will hurt themselves or others. I instructed our security people to check it out. They confirmed witnessing passengers who were talking to themselves, laughing, or crying."

"That's not so unusual on the Red Line," Harry said.

"They weren't the usual nutcases. When our officers approached these passengers and asked if they could help, they were told no, everything was OK. These were normal folk who didn't want to talk about whatever was upsetting them."

"What about on the other subway lines, or on the buses?" Harry asked.

"Just the Red Line. Every day I get more reports. On Monday a week ago, two reports. On Tuesday, four. Then twelve, sixteen, twenty one. It's getting out of hand. And it's not just people talking or crying or carrying on. We've had some fainters. And at least one heart attack. This is scaring me shitless, Harry. I've put in thirty-two years in the MBTA and have never seen anything like it. What if we've got a virus on the trains that's causing our passengers to lose their minds? If this keeps on, I'll have to post a warning, but I have no idea what the hell I'd warn our passengers about, or what they could do about it. I may have to shut down the Red Line if we can't fix this, and what if it spreads beyond the Red Line? We'll all be truly fucked!"

"What do you want us to do?"

"Find out what's happening on the Red Line, Harry."

"OK."

"Seriously. Will you do it?"

"Yes, Jim, we'll give it our best shot."

"Good. Whatever it takes. This is rush and highest priority. Bill me for time and materials. I'll cover it under your earlier contract so we won't have a lot of paperwork. I assume your rates haven't changed?"

"Still the same affordable rates. I'll send you a brief engagement letter to make everything official. I'll say only that we will assess rider experience on the Red Line. How's that?"

"Fine," Cuddihy said. "Just find out what the fuck is going on and let me know."

He picked up a spiral bound report marked "Confidential – Security Assessment" on its white cover, and handed it to Harry. "This describes all the incidents that we know about. I'm giving it to you in hardcopy because I don't want electronic versions floating around that end up in the *Boston Globe*. Be careful with it."

Four

NEXT MORNING, WHEN Molly Lu returned to the Blair West International office determined to get back to work, Harry told her about their new MBTA project.

"So now maybe you believe me," she said.

"Did you see Robbie again?"

"No, and I looked."

"We'll figure this out," Harry assured her.

Harry called a meeting in the Blair West International conference room involving Jerry and three BWI analysts in their 20s – Maureen Minion, Ashok Chakraborty, and Janice Klein – and he invited Molly to sit in since she'd had the kind of encounter that they would be investigating.

The analysts were smart and they worked well together. Now in her third year at Blair West International, Maureen – whose red hair and pink cheeks made her look younger than her 24 years – had asked Harry for a promotion to become a BWI consultant, the next rung up from analyst, even though she lacked a pre-requisite graduate degree, and Harry told her he would consider it. In case he made the wrong decision, she'd begun to reply to job listings on Craigslist and had updated her LinkedIn profile to attract calls from headhunters. Ashok had been a Blair West International analyst for just over a year and planned to stay one more year while he submitted his applications to business schools. At 5'4", Ashok was the shortest of the three analysts. He had a mustache and a closely cut goatee, and he wore large-frame glasses with thick lenses. A bit on the plump side, he favored the traditional look of a white button-down shirt, always with a tie, and suspenders. Janice, the most accomplished of the three – tall, with an approachable open face, honey blond hair, and grey eyes – worked half-time as an analyst at Blair West International to earn cash for rent and food. During the rest of her days and nights, she toiled as lead production engineer at an e-commerce and social networking start-up. Her site, for which she and her partners had already attracted angel funding, would target professional women who had limited time but a strong sense of fashion, enabling them to customize and purchase clothes, shoes, and accessories.

"We have another project for the MBTA," Harry told them. "It's somewhat unusual."

"It turns out that Molly is not the only rider on the Red Line who's had a strange encounter," Jerry explained.

"What encounter are you talking about?" Maureen asked. She and the other analysts had been out of the office the day before at a training exercise.

"I saw Robbie on the Red Line on my way in to work yesterday morning," Molly said.

"But Robbie…" Maureen did not complete her sentence.

"Yes, I know, he's dead," Molly said. "Harry doesn't believe me, but I saw him real as day."

The room fell silent, with everyone looking at Molly, and then Janice said, "I would have been totally freaked! To see someone who I know is dead! But you sound so calm, Molly. Weren't you scared?"

"I wasn't so calm yesterday when it happened," Molly said. "But I wasn't scared. It wasn't that like I was seeing a monster or anything like that. It was Robbie. I knew him. It was almost normal, like I'd never lost him. All I could think was, Robbie has come back to me! And here he is! I couldn't believe it! The only bad part was that our time together was so short since I found out, after it was too late, that he hadn't followed me off the train at Central."

Harry said, "Other riders on the Red Line also are seeing people who have died, according to our client Jim Cuddihy, and we've been hired to find out why." He handed a copy of the MBTA report to each of the analysts and to Molly. "This describes the incidents reported during the last two weeks. Note the 'Confidential' on the cover. Don't leave it around. It's sensitive."

"Did Jim Cuddihy offer any explanation for these incidents?" Maureen asked.

"He was wondering whether there might be a virus on the Red Line trains."

"Basically he has no idea," Jerry said.

Ashok said, "There's an obvious explanation."

"And what is that?" Harry asked.

"People on the Red Line are seeing ghosts."

"Is that your theory?"

"I don't know, Boss. I'm just guessing. What do people usually think, when they see dead people?"

"Like the kid in the movie, 'I see dead people,'" Maureen intoned, in a spooky monotone.

"Did anyone else see these ghosts apart from the people being visited by them?" Janice asked. "Or maybe take their pictures?"

"According to the MBTA's reports, only the people being visited can see them. And no-one's taken any pictures that we know about."

"Oh, well," Janice said. "I guess we'll just have to use our imaginations."

"MBTA Transit Police were assigned by Cuddihy to interview riders who were acting strangely, for example talking to someone who was invisible to other passengers. Their reports are in the document that I just gave you. As you'll see, the MBTA officers weren't too successful. Most of the riders who were approached said they didn't want to talk about it."

"OK, Chief, what are our marching orders?" Jerry asked.

"I want Maureen, Ashok, and Janice to ride on the Red Line for a couple of days. If you see someone whose behavior fits the profile – emotional, talking out loud to no-one you can see – then ask that person what is going on."

"Why would they tell us any more than they told the MBTA police?" Maureen asked.

"You look less intimidating than uniformed officers. Also this research guide should work better than what they did," Harry said, handing a sheet of paper to each of the analysts, as well as copies to Jerry and Molly.

As they scanned the guide, Harry continued, "First, before you talk to the person, quickly record his or her gender, apparent age and race, whether riding alone or with others; also where your train was when you first witnessed the behavior, noting its location at or between which stations, with your best guess about how many minutes have passed since it left the last station. Then approach the person, introduce yourself as a consultant for Blair West International and offer your business card. Say that we have been engaged by the MBTA to evaluate riders' experiences on the Red Line, and that you'd like to ask a few questions."

"Should we ask the questions on this sheet just as you've written them?" Ashok asked.

"Yes, do that, but feel free to improvise with follow-up questions. We want to learn as much as we can about what the riders on the Red Line are experiencing. If necessary follow your interviewee off the train and continue talking in the station. Tell the person that you noticed he or she seemed to be having an experience that was upsetting. What was happening? Assuming it was some kind of encounter, when did it start and where was the train when it ended? Ask for as detailed a description as you can get. What did he or she see or hear or feel? Was this the first time? If your interviewee describes seeing someone, ask who it was. Wait until the end of the interview for the personal questions, and then say that we'd like contact information in case we need to follow up later, and that it will not be provided to the MBTA or published in any way. Request the person's name, phone number, email address, and town in which he or she lives. If the person refuses, just say thank you and move on."

"Maybe we should try to communicate with the ghost," Janice said.

"How?" Maureen asked. "Harry just told us that no-one can see the ghost except the person being visited."

"We could request that our interviewee relay our questions for us and tell us what the ghost says in response," Janice replied.

"Janice, that's a great idea," Harry said. "You could ask, 'Why are you here?' 'How did you get here?' 'What are your plans?'"

"Thought you didn't believe in ghosts," Jerry said.

"Just in case," Harry replied.

Jerry said, "Then we should also ask, 'What are you?' 'If you're a ghost, what kind of ghost?' And, while you have a line open to the other side, ask, 'What's it like in the afterlife?'"

"Anything you can find out," Harry said.

Maureen asked, "Do you want us to ride the Red Line end-to-end?"

"It's about 50 minutes each way between the Alewife and Braintree stations. There are a lot of trains each day so we can't cover all of them with just three of you. You'll have to sample. You should split up. Draw straws to pick who rides which train. Start at Alewife, beginning with the 8 A.M. train, then the 9 A.M and the 10 A.M.. Ride your train to and from Braintree two or three times before taking a break back here at the office to get caught up on your notes, then three or four more times into the early evening. For now I'm not asking you to ride the late night trains, although we may want to try that later. Let me know how things are going. If there are more people to be interviewed than you can handle, I'll expand our team. If your rides are non-productive, we'll change our approach."

Jerry asked, "What do you want me to do?"

"Learn all that you can about the Red Line," Harry said. "Tunnels, train cars, anything that may be relevant."

"I've already got a head start on that from our work on ClearCell," Jerry said. He laid out a map on the table. "This rough schematic gives us an idea where the Red Line tunnels are." Jerry pointed to the station shown in the map's top left corner, in its northwest quadrant. "From here, at Alewife, the Red Line tunnel runs under a community footpath and park to the T station at Davis Square in Somerville. Then it's routed under Elm Street back into Cambridge and down to the Porter Square station. From Porter Square, the tunnel continues under Mass Ave to the Harvard Square station and then, still under Mass Ave, to our own T station in Central Square. From Central, it runs a bit further down Mass Ave right past us here in the Andleman Building, and then jogs left under Main Street, past MIT, to the Kendall/MIT station. After Kendall/MIT the Red Line rises above ground. It crosses the Charles River on the Longfellow Bridge to the Charles/MGH station on the Boston side of the bridge. Then, it goes back underground under Beacon Hill and Boston Common to the Park Street station. From there, the tunnel runs underneath Winter Street to Downtown Crossing, and then under Summer Street to South Station. After South Station, it continues to the Broadway station in South Boston – via a route that is not shown on this map – and then follows Dorchester Ave to Andrew Square, still in South Boston. From that point on, unfortunately, my map isn't much good; it doesn't show how the Red Line gets from Andrew south to its end-point in Braintree."

"When was the Red Line built?" Harry asked.

"The first section was completed in 1912 connecting Cambridge and Boston, from Harvard down to the Park Street Station. By 1918 other sections had been added continuing from Park Street down to Andrew Station in South Boston. The Blue, Orange and Green Lines were also under construction at about the same time. The most recent Red Line extension was built in the 1980s from Harvard Square northwest to Alewife."

"What have you found out about the trains themselves?"

"According to Wikipedia, the Red Line trains operate in four-car and six-car sets; they run as mated pairs and they're powered from a third rail. They include aluminum-bodied cars each with over sixty seats and a newer series of stainless-steel bodied cars each with about fifty. The standard capacity of each train car is almost 170 seated and standing passengers, although the MBTA estimates that a train car can accommodate as many as 280 riders when they're at what it calls 'crush capacity.'"

"Those are the really fun rides," Ashok said.

Jerry continued, "The seats are covered with vandalism-resistant cloth. They're attached in benches of seven seats that are installed in the middle portion of the train cars, and in shorter benches of three seats that are installed at the ends."

Harry said, "OK, call Jim Cuddihy to arrange meetings with MBTA engineers to get more complete maps of the Red Line tunnels. Also check with the engineers about the Red Line train cars, to verify what you've read about them on Wikipedia. Let's create our own detailed map of the Red Line and mark it up depending on what we learn, for example where passengers appear to be seeing whatever they are seeing. Include the information from the MBTA reports as well as the sightings witnessed by our team. Also search for any records you can find in the archives of the *Boston Globe* and the *Herald* about other similar events that may have occurred in the past."

"What will you be doing, meanwhile?"

"I'm going to think about what we already know, what we learn, and what we still need to find out. And then I'll tell the rest of you what to do."

Janice asked, "Harry, really, what do you think is happening on the Red Line?"

"Well, I don't believe in ghosts," Harry said. "So I'm quite sure that we'll find another explanation. But Molly did see something. And others have as well."

"Not just something," Molly insisted. "Once again, Harry, I did really meet Robbie and it was more than seeing; we talked, and we touched."

"OK Molly, sorry," Harry said.

Ashok said, "I'm still rooting for ghosts."

"Why?"

"Because we'll be world famous! We'll be the elite team that was hired by the MBTA to exorcise ghosts from its subway system! I could cite it in my applications to business schools as one of my notable achievements."

"What you are implying about Robbie?" Molly demanded. "That he's a demon that needs to be exorcised?"

"Calm down," Harry said. "We don't know yet what's happening on the Red Line. And anyway, whatever we find out, we're consultants, not exorcists."

Five

AFTER COMPLETING HER MILITARY service, Alexandra Ben-Tov emigrated from Israel to the US and enrolled at Smith College, the liberal arts school for women in Northampton, a small, culturally busy city nestled in the green forested hills of Western Massachusetts. She excelled at Smith as an honors student in Engineering Science. Her advisor, impressed by Alexandra's quickness and self-discipline, introduced her to contacts at the Massachusetts Institute of Technology.

Alexandra soon joined with MIT faculty and grad students who were exploring new ways to exploit the awesome power of the Internet during the early 1990s run-up to the dot.com boom. She and several MIT colleagues co-founded ABTDigital, Inc., to help enterprises and public organizations deliver online video content on their websites. Over the next fifteen years Alexandra's company grew to employ over four hundred staff based in Boston and in Israel, earning her renown in Boston's high-tech circles. She was interviewed frequently in *Mass High-Tech* and profiled in the business section of the *Boston Globe*; and she served as a Trustee of the Boston Symphony Orchestra and of Polly's House, a shelter for homeless women in Boston's South End.

Because of her fame as a successful tech entrepreneur, Alexandra generated ripples of recognition whenever she entered a room. Also attracting appreciative glances from both men and women were Alexandra's athletic slender build, short brown hair, and olive skin, and her classic strong nose, full lips, and intense brown eyes that were as dark as dark chocolate.

Harry and Alexandra first met shortly after she co-founded ABTDigital, while he was still working at his former consulting company, Roland L. Week, Inc., known as RLW. At the time, Harry spent most week-days on the road and when he was at home, he lived alone in a one-bedroom apartment in Somerville near the Cambridge line, a solitary personal life that he found relaxing and uncomplicated and that he had no desire to change.

They were introduced at a dinner party hosted by Jerry Seligman and his wife Vicki, Alexandra's former classmate at Smith College.

After Jerry and Vicki left them alone, having gone to the kitchen to prepare dessert, Alexandra said, "Jerry tells me you are an up-and-comer in your company." She had a slight Israeli accent that you'd only hear if you were listening for it.

"Jerry's just a kidder," Harry said.

"But you have your own group at RLW." Alexandra gazed at Harry with her dark eyes in a way that made him feel at the absolute center of her attention.

"I was appointed to build our telecoms practice," Harry said. "As a senior member of my group, Jerry shows his respect by calling me a 'boy-wonder.'"

"Well, it's a big deal," Alexandra said.

"Not compared to what you've been doing," Harry said. "Co-founding your own company."

"It has been exciting," Alexandra admitted. "But it's not easy. The VCs that I'm pitching here and in New York and in

Israel love the ABTDigital concept for online video but then they get skittish because most web businesses fail. So we'll see."

"Are you planning to return to Israel?" Harry asked, realizing at that moment that he hoped she wouldn't leave anytime soon.

"It depends. I could go back. We have investors in Israel and I could stay connected with my company from Tel Aviv. But, for now, I like it here."

Earlier, at dinner, Vicki had remarked that Alexandra had served in the Israeli army.

"Like everyone else in Israel," Alexandra said, "except the Orthodox and the Arabs." She said that she had commanded an army patrol on the Golan Heights, "keeping an eye on the Syrians on the other side of the border."

"What were the Syrians doing?" Harry asked.

"They were keeping an eye on us."

Evidently, Alexandra saw something that she liked in Harry. He was good looking in a scholarly kind of way, physically fit but not like a jock, more like someone who took care of himself, quiet spoken but obviously confident, and it also helped that he was unlike Alexandra's father, a former Israeli tank commander who was prone to give orders. She recoiled from men who tried to tell her what to do. Being her father's daughter, she wanted her own hands on the controls and she sensed that Harry did not feel compelled to prove anything, that he was sufficient in his own skin and would accept, even prefer, the role of co-pilot.

Being Israeli, Alexandra took decisive action rather than waiting patiently for Harry to catch on. She called him a few days later. A new movie was playing in Harvard Square that was getting great reviews; would he go with her to see it? She had invited friends from her company to her apartment for dinner; would he like to make it a foursome? She loved canoeing on the Charles River; would he join her?

For their canoeing excursion, Alexandra wore white shorts and a white cotton tank top, both of which she filled out wonderfully, presenting her firm slender body to its best advantage. She took the bow seat in their canoe and Harry placed himself in the stern seat behind her, taking care not to tip them over. A young man who worked for the canoe rental shop let go of a rope holding them at the dock and they eased out onto the water, paddling downriver. Harry watched Alexandra's back move with each stroke, twisting and thrusting from her shoulders down to her white shorts as she shifted on the wood-cane canoe seat, and he drifted into a pleasantly sensual reverie, a daydream that was interrupted abruptly when Alexandra splashed him with her paddle. "You're not pulling your weight," she complained. "Sorry," Harry said, "I was distracted," and he splashed her back, leaving her tank top wet and pasted with a nice transparency to her skin. "Oops, my paddle must have slipped," he explained, when she squawked in protest. "You do that again," she said, "and you're in the river."

It took them half an hour of paddling against a light breeze to reach the John W. Weeks pedestrian bridge that connects Harvard's main campus in Cambridge with the Harvard Business School across the Charles River in Boston. They glided under one of the old bridge's elegant arches, made of red-brick outlined in white stone, and then turned around to return to the rental dock. On their way back, they paddled close to the river's grassy bank on the Cambridge side. People were camped on benches along a path overlooking the river and lying on blankets on the grass. A girl on a bench raised her camera and snapped their picture. "How do we look?" Alexandra called out. "You are a beautiful couple," yelled the girl.

They were a couple. Harry was thinking about Alexandra a lot, and seeing her a lot. He got used to being with her and felt restless when they were apart. One afternoon, while they were walking along Newbury Street in Boston, Alexandra noticed a white linen jacket that she liked in a store window. She purchased the jacket and then proposed that they drop it off at her apartment which was nearby on Commonwealth Avenue so that she would not have to carry it around. The windows of her apartment were open to allow air to flow through the rooms. Harry settled on a sofa while Alexandra was in her bedroom and bathroom getting refreshed. Then she appeared in her bedroom doorway wearing a light silk robe loosely tied at her waist. It left her breasts mostly exposed, their hard nipples pressed against the silk like two perky nubbins. She said, "Harry, I need you to come here to rub my back."

He stayed the night. They alternated their nights together at each of their apartments. They drove to Maine for a weekend at a B&B. As they sat sweating on the slatted wood bench in the B&B's sauna, Harry sponged Alexandra with a cloth dipped in cool water and she did the same for him, each paying special attention to highly sensitive parts of the other's body, and then they retired early after their dinner to have more waking time in bed. At the end of November, Alexandra's lease was coming due for renewal on her apartment, and they decided that since they stayed together so much, it made sense for her to move in with Harry in his apartment in Somerville.

They were married by a magistrate in Cambridge City Hall with Jerry and Vicki in attendance as witnesses. At first, not much changed as they continued living together as they had before.

Then, everything changed. Alexandra became pregnant. They bought a house in Arlington, another suburb next to Cambridge. And they had a baby girl, whom they named Ariel, a name that translates in Hebrew to mean a lion of God, and also refers to an archangel, commonly a boy's name in Israel and a girl's name in the US, a name selected to represent Alexandra's commitment to her adopted country, and also because they liked how it sounded, like the sound of swirling wind.

It wasn't long before Ariel was living up to her name, talking constantly and throwing her small weight around as a dynamic new member of their little family. Occasionally, when music was playing on the radio, she would demand imperiously, "Up, Daddy!" and Harry would lift her up for a hug and then dance with her held in his arms, and swoop her around, and they'd spin as she squealed, "Daddy! Faster! Faster!" until they both got dizzy and he let her down, and then he lay on his back on the floor and she climbed on top of him, and rested her head on his chest.

Each morning Harry would leave for RLW and Alexandra would drop Ariel off at day-care before heading into Boston.

On one of those mornings, a week after Ariel's 3rd birthday that they'd celebrated with cake, ice cream, and a frenzied gaggle of her day care classmates, Harry had just arrived in his office when his phone rang.

"Is this Harry West?"

"Yes, who…"

"I'm Officer Brian Daley of the Arlington Police. Your wife has been in a car accident. She is alright, and gave me your number to call, to let you know."

"Where is she, can I speak to her?"

"She is being taken now to the Mt. Auburn Hospital in Cambridge. Your child was also in the accident and is also being taken to the hospital."

"How is our baby?"

"I don't know. You will need to check on that with the hospital."

Mt. Auburn Hospital was a straight shot up Memorial Drive from Harry's RLW office, about two miles away. Leaning on his horn to weave through the maddening traffic, Harry arrived at the hospital fifteen minutes after his call from Officer Daley. He was informed, when he asked for Alexandra, that she was conscious and being treated for a broken arm and cuts on her face. He also learned from an emergency room doctor that Ariel, his baby girl, had died in the crash.

Alexandra told Harry that she was approaching the day care center when they were hit by a drunk driver running a red light. Alexandra suffered physical injuries but her worst hurt, like Harry's, was emotional, psychological, whatever the right label might be. During the weeks and months that followed, in the evenings after returning from work, she slumped at their dining room table in the dark, motionless for hours at a time. When Harry offered to turn on the lights, she told him, "Leave them off. I don't want to see anything." When he asked, "Is there anything I can do?" she replied, "No, nothing."

"It wasn't your fault."

"I know. It doesn't matter."

Alexandra would not and could not be consoled and Harry gave up trying. In retrospect, he knew that he was wrong to have quit on Alexandra when she was so despairing. Looking back on that terrible time, his only excuse was that he too was unmoored in a fog of grief and rage. Sadness washed over him in waves. He passed by Ariel's empty room and he'd gasp and his knees would buckle. Maybe if he could cry, he might win some relief from the agonizing catch in his throat, but he couldn't.

Eventually, feeling trapped in their house that had so suddenly become too large and too quiet, Alexandra moved out. She disclosed to Harry that she had begun an affair with a woman she'd met in Boston and that she wanted a divorce. Harry was relieved. More than anything, he just wanted to be alone. After he bought Alexandra out of her half of the house, Harry continued to live there, on his own once again, and too numb to move.

William E. Harrington, the drunk driver and repeat DUI offender who killed their child, was sentenced to eight years in the

Concord Reformatory. Two years into his sentence, Harry and Alexandra were invited to attend his first Parole Board hearing as stipulated by the Commonwealth's "victim access" program. They would be allowed, if they wished, to make a statement at the hearing.

To prepare, they met at a Starbucks in Kendall Square near to MIT. Although they'd seen each other at events and parties, this would be their first time together, with just the two of them, since their divorce.

It was awkward at first getting past the stilted small talk: "How've you been?" "Good, and you?" "You're looking well." "So are you." "Work going OK?" "Can't complain."

Alexandra said, "You may have heard that Meredith and I split up."

"Jerry told me. Sorry."

"No, you're not. Anyway, I've decided that I prefer men after all although Meredith was good for me."

"Ah."

Before too long, however, they were able to focus on their common goal, to ensure that Harrington remained incarcerated for the full term of his sentence. Alexandra would review court records on his numerous earlier DUI infractions so that she could explain to the Parole Board why it should not accept his expressions of remorse or his promises to reform. Meanwhile, to illustrate the loss caused by Harrington's heinous crime, Harry would use age progression software to show how Ariel might have looked had she been allowed to live beyond three years of age. He would tell the Parole Board, "This is the young life that Harrington destroyed," and then point to the updated image of their daughter beside one of their last pictures of her as an exuberant three-year-old.

They prevailed at Harrington's first Parole Board hearing. Each year subsequently, they met at the same Starbucks to rehearse and then at the Concord Reformatory to present their arguments to the Parole Board while Harrington, a pale and paunchy figure, listened glumly, and after each hearing they said their goodbyes and went their separate ways. They were successful almost until the end of Harrington's term when he was paroled to serve the final year of his sentence wearing an ankle bracelet that monitored both his location and whether he had been drinking.

After Harrington was released, Harry and Alexandra reverted to seeing each other only by coincidence at social events in Cambridge and Boston. They worked and lived in different orbits. Each had moved on.

Except, however, that Alexandra continued to use Harry's age progression software to help her envision how Ariel's appearance might have changed as time passed. Alexandra's most recent image of Ariel on her PC screen was that of a thirteen-year-old girl, a bright young teenager with Alexandra's dark-eyed intensity and Harry's curly brown hair and determined chin.

That was also the appearance of the teenage girl, precisely in every detail, who sat directly across from Alexandra in her Red Line train car. She wore crisp fitted blue jeans, a pressed blue Oxford shirt of the kind approved for private school uniforms in New England, with a red cloth sash tied around her waist to add flash and style, just the way Alexandra imagined the girl on her laptop screen would have dressed.

Alexandra had boarded the Red Line in Boston at the Downtown Crossing station, heading to a meeting with an ABTDigital customer whose office was located near MIT, an appointment for which she planned to get off at the Kendall/MIT station. She was scanning her notes to prepare for her meeting, and heard in the background the *deng-dong* chime to warn that the doors were closing, and after they were closed and the train was in motion, she heard an announcement on the PA, "Next Stop – Park Street," and at that moment she had looked up.

She saw the girl and when their eyes met, the girl smiled. Alexandra's first sensation was paralyzing, tingling shock in her arms and legs and hands and lips. Her breathing stopped, inhaling and exhaling were placed on hold, and she felt light-headed, and dizzy, like she had vertigo. Her eyes were riveted on the girl. All the other passengers, all sounds and sights, indeed everything else inside the train car, vanished to her. All she could see was the girl, sitting there, smiling at her.

Then, regaining her ability to move, Alexandra leaned forward and said, "I know you."

The girl replied, "I am Ariel."

"It's not possible," Alexandra said, even as she was powerless to deny that she had recognized the girl in the first instant that she saw her.

The girl rose from her seat and stood in front of Alexandra. "I am Ariel," the girl repeated, "I have come back to you."

"We lost you as a baby. You were only three years old. How could you have grown after that, after you died?"

"I appear to you in the way that you think of me," the girl said.

Alexandra's eyes were streaming tears now whether from grief or joy she didn't know, but she couldn't help it, and she told the girl, "I never stop thinking about you," and she stood to hug her, both of them swaying from the motion of the train as it crossed the Longfellow Bridge. The girl was shorter than Alexandra, who was around 5'6", so that her head pressed against Alexandra's chest, and Alexandra could smell her hair.

"I missed you too," the girl said, her words muffled in Alexandra's chest.

For a while they just stood holding each other and Alexandra felt the girl's back and shoulders under her hands, and she thought, "You are my Ariel." Or perhaps she said it aloud, because the girl replied, "I am, and you are my mom."

The Red Line train arrived at Kendall/MIT, which was Alexandra's stop, but Alexandra stayed on. She sat back down again so that she could look at the girl standing before her and also because her legs were trembling, and she held one of the girl's hands. "Why have you come to me now?"

"I don't know," the girl said. "I was no-where. Now I am here with you. I don't know why."

"Will you stay with me?"

"I don't know," the girl repeated. But she was still smiling, a smile of relief and wonderment, like she'd just been returned safely to her home after wandering alone and homesick in the wilderness.

The train entered the Central Square station, its doors slid open, some people got off and others boarded, and the doors closed, and it rumbled forward again. Still Alexandra could see and feel and hear only the girl standing before her. She asked, "Can you tell me anything about yourself after we lost you?"

"You mean, after I died?"

"Yes, after you died."

"I was no-where," the girl repeated. "What matters is that we are together again."

"Yes, that is all that matters."

"All I know is that I am so happy to be with you now," the girl said.

"I wish your father were here so that he could see you."

The Red Line train slowed to enter the Harvard Square station. After the doors opened, a man in an MBTA police uniform loomed in front of Alexandra and asked, "Ma'am, are you alright?"

The girl was gone. The MBTA officer said, "Another passenger was concerned about you. He reported that you seemed distressed. Are you alright?"

"Yes, yes, I'm fine," Alexandra said, but she didn't feel fine because Ariel had disappeared when the stupid transit policeman interrupted them, but it wasn't his fault, he was only doing his job, and he was trying to be sympathetic.

"Would you like to talk about it with me or with a policewoman here in the station?" He offered a small pack of tissues and Alexandra took several which she used to dry her eyes and cheeks. She noticed that the doors were still open, perhaps locked that way until signaled by the MBTA officer that her incident had been resolved.

"No, thank you," Alexandra said, collecting herself, "I'm fine. But I do need to get off the train. I missed my station back there. I was distracted."

After she stepped off the train, the doors slid shut, and the train continued on. The MBTA policeman stayed with her. "Ma'am," he said. "We've been asked to file reports about any unusual events that occur on the Red Line. Can you tell me anything about what you saw? Why it upset you?"

"I prefer not to talk about it," Alexandra replied. "But thank you for your concern. And for the tissues."

Alexandra claimed an unoccupied table on the Au Bon Pain patio across Mass Ave from the Harvard University campus. All around her, people were sitting with their coffees and their sandwiches, chatting and reading books and newspapers, oblivious to her amazing experience. She was still shaking from tremors coursing through her body when she called her assistant. Alexandra said to let their customer know that she would be delayed for their meeting because of an incident on the Red Line. "Apologize profusely on my behalf. I need a few hours. Try to reschedule for later this afternoon. Text me the new time."

"Alexandra, your voice sounds really strange. Are you OK?"

"Sure, I just need some time to get organized."

Her second call was to Harry.

Harry was underground in the Central Square T station, trying to get the feel of the place, not as a commuter rushing through as he did each day on his way to and from the Blair West International office, but as a careful observer, looking for anything that might be related to the strange events on the Red Line. He noticed nothing unusual. Passengers disembarked from each train after it pulled into the station, and others got on. No-one looked unduly distressed. Harry hoped that his three analysts who were now out riding on the Red Line trains were finding more to report. He needed to ping them for quick summaries of they'd seen so far. Cuddihy was demanding to be updated even though they'd only just started but, in fairness, Harry was curious as well, and he didn't want to wait until the analysts returned to the office. He took a mental note to check with Jerry on what more, if anything, he'd learned about the Red Line tunnels and train cars and whether he'd scheduled meetings yet with the MBTA engineers.

He was thinking about the project when he answered his BlackBerry phone, "Harry West here."

"Hi, Harry. It's Alexandra."

Mobile reception inside the station was poor and Harry had trouble hearing Alexandra's greeting over the static. It was amazing that he'd even received the call. "Alexandra, I have bad reception here," Harry said. "I'll have to call you right back."

It had been years since he and Alexandra had talked on the phone, not since their last parole hearing for the killer-drunk Harrington. Was she calling about Harrington? If there were justice in the universe, he'd been found dead, his body bloated and floating face-down in the Charles River. Too much to hope for.

He climbed the station steps up to Mass Ave and returned Alexandra's call as soon as he was above ground. She picked up immediately. "Hi Harry."

"Hi Alexandra, it's been a long time."

"Yes."

"It's good to hear from you."

"Harry…"

"What is it? What's wrong?"

Harry was walking briskly from the T station back to the Andleman Building, holding his BlackBerry to his ear, when Alexandra said, "I saw Ariel."

He had to sit down. Right now, immediately. He found space on a sidewalk bench next to a large woman who was taking in the sun with her eyes closed. "You saw our daughter Ariel?"

"I saw her. We talked. We hugged."

"Were you on the Red Line?"

"How did you know that?"

"Just a guess."

"You don't sound surprised."

"Alexandra, I want to hear what happened. Everything, from start to finish. Are you available now?"

"I am. Meet me at the Au Bon Pain in Harvard Square. I have a table on the patio."

Alexandra stood when she saw Harry coming. She looked strikingly attractive in the patio's dappled sunlight, athletically slim, fiercely dark-eyed, and dressed for business in her tailored light-weight pant-suit, its light putty color setting off her olive skin. Harry approached Alexandra to exchange courteous kisses on each cheek as they had when they'd met on earlier occasions, but she put her arms around him and pulled him towards her in a close hug. Harry reciprocated and they stood together silently by her table at the Au Bon Pain for a few moments, until she released him.

"I'm so glad you came," she said, after they'd both sat down. "You, Harry, more than anyone, must hear what happened."

Almost breathless with eagerness to tell her story, Alexandra recounted how Ariel had appeared to her on the Red Line train, minute-by-minute from the first instant that she saw her, and how she looked exactly like the girl depicted by the age progression software. She showed Harry the image on her laptop screen. "This is Ariel. She is the girl I met on the train."

"She is beautiful," Harry said. He felt the familiar catch return in his throat that had tormented him for months after Ariel was killed. "She looks like you."

"She looks like you, too, Harry."

"Did she tell you anything about herself?"

"She seemed happy to see me. She was smiling."

"I wish I'd been there."

"That would have been perfect."

"How are you doing, Alexandra? Are you OK?"

Alexandra put her hand on top of Harry's on the small patio table. "I was happier during those few minutes on the Red Line train than I've been anytime during the last ten years."

"I'm glad to hear that."

"Harry, when I first told you on the phone about seeing Ariel, how did you know that it was on the Red Line? And don't say again that you guessed."

"All I can tell you, Alexandra, is that you're not the only one who's had this kind of experience on the Red Line."

"How do you know that?"

"Alexandra, I really can't tell you more right now."

"Fine, it's a big mystery," she said, although her darkening expression warned that Harry's reply was anything but fine.

"As soon as I can, I'll tell you…"

"Forget it."

"I've made you angry."

"I'll get over it."

"I know you prefer to be direct."

"Yes, I'm Israeli. So?"

"You've had an incredible experience. I'm sure of that. But I'm finding it hard to accept that you really did meet Ariel."

"Now you're making me regret that I called you."

"I'd love to believe it, Alexandra. I wish it were so. But, let's face it, how could the girl you met on the Red Line have been Ariel? We lost her ten years ago."

"She was Ariel, Harry. Believe me. Or don't, I don't care."

"Perhaps if I saw her and met her like you did, I could get a better handle on it."

"Do you want my suggestion?"

"Yes."

"Keep an image of Ariel in your mind. She told me that she appeared to me in the way that I was thinking of her."

Six

Ashok Chakraborty boarded the 8:00 A.M. Red Line train at Alewife on his first ride down through Cambridge and Boston to Braintree. Then he'd turn around and take the next train back towards Alewife. He'd repeat the cycle until he had completed his morning quota of three round trips.

Ashok's train car was filled with commuters from the western suburbs traveling to their offices in Cambridge and Boston. More passengers got onto the train car than got off at the next two stations, at Davis, in Somerville, and at Porter Square, in Cambridge, and riders who were standing in the aisle in front of Ashok completely blocked his view. However, at their next stop in Harvard Square, enough people left so that Ashok could observe the other passengers who remained.

As his train pulled out from the Harvard Square station, a young girl who was standing a few feet away – dark skinned, studious-looking, wearing glasses, carrying a small backpack – slumped to the floor of the train car. One moment she was standing, bracing herself as the train moved with one of her hands grasping an overhead handhold, and the next moment she was sprawled on her side on the grey linoleum floor with her eyes closed. Passengers called out, "Is she all right?" and "Someone should contact the MBTA!" Several knelt down around the girl, trying to be helpful. A man lifted the girl's head gently off the floor and place it on his jacket which he had folded to serve as a pillow. Someone else collected her backpack and put it at her side. The girl's eyes opened. She looked confused, and dazed, as if she didn't know where she was. Ashok had brought with him a bottled water which he hadn't yet opened and he offered it to the girl. She accepted. Sitting up now, but still on the train car floor, she sipped tentatively from it. He asked whether she was OK. The girl responded in a subdued voice, "I think so," although she still seemed groggy. A woman across from Ashok instructed the girl, "Here, take my seat," and the girl did so, now looking embarrassed at the attention she had attracted. When their train arrived at Central Square, an MBTA officer came on board and said, "We had a call about an emergency." He was directed towards the girl and asked her, "Are you alright? Do you need help?"

"I'm better now," she replied, "Thank you."

"Are you sure," he asked.

"Yes."

"Do you need medical attention?"

"No, thank you."

"Do you want to talk about what happened?"

"No," she replied, again. "Thank you."

She remained in the seat after the MBTA officer left. Ashok asked the girl, "Has this happened to you before?"

"No," she said.

"You should maybe see a doctor."

"I don't need to. I'm not sick."

"But, you…"

"I saw my father right next to me. He's dead, so it was like an apparition, and then he touched my arm, and I could feel his hand, and I could hear him say my name. I think I just must have fainted."

Ashok said, "My name is Ashok Chakraborty. I'm a consultant. My company is working on a project for the MBTA and we're interested in experiences like you just had."

The girl didn't say anything, and Ashok continued, "May I ask you some questions?"

"I really don't want to talk anymore."

"Well, if you change your mind, please give me a call." Ashok handed the girl his business card.

"Thank you, I'll think about it," she said, putting Ashok's card in her backpack. When their train reached Kendall/MIT, she got off.

On his way back from Braintree, just after Ashok's Red Line train left the Downtown Crossing station, a man about ten seats down but on the same side of his train car shouted "WHOA!"

Passengers who were sitting near the man got up and selected other seats. Ashok took one of the just-vacated seats so that he could observe the man without turning his head. He marked in his notebook, "10:12am, middle aged white man, well dressed for business, pin-striped suit, tie, leather briefcase against seat under legs, 10 seconds out of Downtown Crossing heading towards Alewife, shouted in alarm, no Bluetooth." The man jumped to his feet and screamed "Get away from me! Get away! It wasn't my fault!" He waved his right arm back and forth as if to clear a space in front of him. "You can't blame me for what you did!" he shouted. "Leave me alone!"

When the train arrived at Park Street, the man quickly exited. Ashok followed him and caught up with him at the turnstiles.

"Excuse me, sir," Ashok said.

The man ignored him as though he were a panhandler. Ashok followed him through the turnstiles. "I'm sorry; I was on the train with you. I'm a consultant working for the MBTA on a project about the Red Line, and would like to ask you about what just happened on our train."

The man stopped and looked directly at Ashok for the first time. "Who are you? What do you want?" he demanded.

Ashok handed the man his business card. "We've been engaged by the MBTA to observe anything unusual on the Red Line and to ask a few brief questions of riders who seemed to be involved," he said.

The man looked at Ashok's card, turned it over to check the back, but did not say anything, so Ashok continued, "Sir, may I ask you, who were you talking to when you told someone to leave you alone?"

"Well, he's gone now," the man said, more to himself than in response to Ashok's question.

"Who's gone now?"

"My brother-in-law. He didn't follow me off the train."

"You sounded upset."

"Of course I was upset! He put his bloody face right up against mine and accused me. He said, 'I did it because of you,' which was a lie. It wasn't my fault."

"You did sound alarmed," Ashok said, encouragingly.

"It scared the hell out of me. I almost had a heart attack."

"Why did it scare you?"

"Well, he's dead, for one thing."

"What did he do, that he's blaming you for?"

"He killed himself." Here the man pointed at his temple with his right hand, his thumb pointed upwards, and fired an imaginary gun by dropping his thumb.

"And he blames you?"

"Says I gave him bad financial advice."

Ashok said, "It seemed you first saw him when we departed the Downtown Crossing station. Is that right?"

"He was glaring down at me, blood all over his face. I stood to protect myself. His nose almost touched mine, and he smelled rotten, like eggs gone bad, and he said, 'You did this.'"

"That's when you yelled for him to get away."

"Was I yelling?"

"Quite loudly."

"Guess it worked. As soon as I stepped off the train, he was gone." The man looked again at Ashok's business card, which was still in his hand, "Do you have any more questions? I need to get going. I have a meeting."

"Could you let me know your contact information so that we can follow-up if other questions come up?"

"I'm not interested in answering more questions."

"Also so that we can reach you if we discover information that we think you'd like to know?"

"You mean, you'll call me to tell me how it was that I was talking to my dead brother-in-law on the Red Line?"

"Yes, if we can figure it out."

The man thought for a moment and then said, "No, I don't think so. No-one will believe me anyway. So no, I'd prefer not."

The man turned and climbed the stairs leading out of Park Street station. Ashok called out to his retreating back, "Thank you for talking with me," and the man waved his hand above his shoulder to acknowledge that he'd heard. Ashok returned to the platform and boarded the next Red Line train to continue his journey back to Alewife.

Seven

MAUREEN MINION'S FIRST Red Line train of the day departed Alewife at 9:14 A.M. Her train had just left Porter Square station in Cambridge when Maureen saw a fashionably-dressed woman in her late 30s, or perhaps a bit older, lean down and extend her arms towards the open floor in front of her.

"What a beautiful dog," she said, "you look just like my Mirabel!" Then the woman turned towards the man who was sitting beside her. "I love Springer Spaniels," she said. "My Mirabel was a black-and-white, just like yours." The man nodded. He pulled a smartphone from his belt holster and began to read it intently. "Do you mind if I pet her?" the woman asked. Maintaining his focus on his smartphone, the man did not respond.

"Hello, little puppy," the woman cooed, her hands kneading the air in front of her. "You want me to scratch your ears? You like that, don't you? They're so soft, just like my Mirabel's. Look how she's pressing her head against my hand!" When the man ignored the woman's invitation, she returned to the space in front of her knees, "Come give me a kiss," she said. "Oh, give us a kiss, honey face! You love me!" She leaned forward and, closing her eyes, turned her head sideways as if presenting her cheek, and then facing forward again she puckered her lips in a kiss. "I love you too!" she exclaimed. "You've got such a cold nose! What a sweetheart! Yes, that's my hand you're licking, sweetie, it's not your dinner! Someone should feed this doggie. Look at your little tail go! If you wag and wriggle any harder, you're going to fall over!" the woman laughed. "That's my baby!" Again she kissed the space before her and said, "You are so beautiful, just like my lovie Mirabel, you could be her exact twin. Even your collar is the same as hers. What's your name sweetie? Let me look at your collar." She reached forward and it seemed she was holding something in her hand. She looked stunned for a moment and then turned back to the man sitting beside her and demanded angrily, "Is this some kind of stupid joke?"

Finally, the man re-holstered his smartphone and replied to the woman's questions, "Lady, trust me, I haven't a clue what you are talking about. I think you need help."

"This is not your dog?"

"There is no dog here, lady," the man said.

The woman looked back at the floor and her face fell. "She was here just a moment ago," she said. "My Mirabel. My little sweetie."

The train had by now reached Kendall/MIT, and the man rose to leave. "You need help, lady," he said. After he was gone and the train was moving again, the woman stayed in her seat gazing dejectedly at her purse which she held with both hands on her lap. Maureen sat down beside her and said, "Ma'am, I couldn't help seeing what happened back there. Could I talk with you about it? I am working on a project for the MBTA concerning the Red Line; here is my business card; I would like to ask you a few questions."

Eight

MICHAEL WALLACE HUDDLED outside South Station with Ricky and Al, his two bodyguards and all-purpose muscle, and he was cultivating a very bad mood.

He had not ridden on the T for many years; it was too uncomfortable and unclean, with too many people he didn't know who got too close. Wallace's limo driver was supposed to pick him up in Boston but the fucker got waylaid due to a disagreement with Boston police. In other circumstances when he couldn't use his Lincoln Town Car, which had special fittings for security purposes, he would have hired another limo, but the surface-road traffic was bad at this time of day and he was in a hurry. So it would have to be the T.

That it was hot outside was yet another insult, very unlike the well-chilled air-conditioned air to which he was accustomed. He could feel the sweat wetting his doughy closely-shaved cheeks and prickling under his chin and arms. The close heat on the sidewalk outside South Station left him distinctly uncomfortable in his bespoke dark-blue suit and brightly patterned silk tie, with his perfect triangle of matching silk handkerchief poking out of his jacket pocket, and his black laced shoes that were shiny enough to see his own face in them.

Because Wallace dressed well and required his people to follow his sartorial example, for which he provided an ample special allowance, someone casting a cursory glance at Ricky and Al might have mistaken them for beefy investment bankers wearing sharply-tailored business suits. Thus deceived, an ordinary and prudent passer-by would most likely mind his own business and keep walking. However, given their record, Ricky and Al might get a second look from the MBTA transit cops. It would create yet another hassle for Wallace if they were picked up.

And they would be noticed. Al's head was as hairless as a bowling ball and almost as round. He had no eyebrows or eyelashes. His small piggish red-rimmed eyes at the center of the large smooth expanse of his face were closely-set and slightly crossed. He had a tiny bump of a nose and red lips, and a tattoo of a lightning bolt that emerged from his shirt collar and zig-zagged up his thick neck to his jaw-line just in front of his ear. Ricky on the other hand had long hair like Jesus, the way it came down to his shoulders, and his eyes were light grey, so light colored that his pupils stood out like crazed black dots.

When Ricky and Al were in Wallace's presence, only Ricky talked while Al stood by silently, his tongue occasionally darting out to wet his lips while he awaited instructions. Wallace said, "Grab a taxi and meet me at the LiquorMart in Central." He held an ownership interest in the store which he had obtained as a result of the former owner's desire not to have the fingers of his right hand crushed like those of his left hand which had never healed completely. It was good business practice to visit the place occasionally, accompanied by Ricky and Al, to ensure that his interest was being managed properly.

For a big man, Ricky's voice was surprisingly high, like a castrato's, "You want us to wait for you by the front door?"

"No, I'll get there before you. That's why I'm taking the fucking T. I'll be in the back checking the books. Just come straight in and join me there, to let them know we care how well they're doing for us."

Wallace could call upon the services of at least ten guys but Ricky and Al were his favorites. Not just because they were his nephews, since others in his crew also were family, but because they enjoyed their work. Al obeyed orders without question, an attribute that Wallace appreciated, and since Wallace's orders were mostly to inflict pain, that was how Al liked it too. And when Ricky cast a hard stare at someone, that someone's usual reaction of revulsion and fear suited Ricky just fine.

Wallace solicited payments from small enterprises in his territory, mostly in Somerville, and overlapping into Cambridge where he'd been expanding recently. His affiliates, as he called them, included owners and managers of clubs, restaurants, Laundromats, and stores like the LiquorMart, as well as purveyors of frowned-upon substances, the company of women, and other special products. Generally, once a business relationship was established, the payments flowed without interruption. Lapses were remedied quickly by Ricky and Al who would remind Wallace's "affiliate" about his obligations, almost hoping that he would try to resist so that they could proceed to the next stage, of slamming, stomping, pounding, cutting, and chopping. For the most part, it was a well-ordered system.

Wallace's secret to staying out of prison was to inject healthy fear into witnesses so that they would never testify against him. He would eliminate anyone who was dumb enough to talk despite being given fair warnings. Stool pigeons, tattle tales, rats, squealers, snitches, witnesses, ever since he was a small kid in Catholic school, they were all the same, and they made him crazy. He had learned – it was his cardinal rule – to shut up the talkers, no exceptions.

So when assholes who failed to understand the situation would complain to the police, they soon disappeared. Perhaps twelve or thirteen fools were buried in various unlikely places around Somerville, maybe a few more, he had lost count since his first when he was in juvie almost thirty years ago. Most were men, plus a couple of women who couldn't be trusted to keep their mouths shut. Since the talkers would never be seen again, and therefore the condition of their bodies would not serve as lessons to others, they only needed one bullet to the back of the head, or a well-placed cut with a sharp blade, but Ricky and Al were artists who felt compelled to do more. They especially enjoyed collecting souvenirs of body parts while their victims could still suffer pain, fingers, ears, noses, eyes, even testicles when they were really into it. To stay fresh, Wallace himself had dispatched one of the women by strangling her with a leather belt, and a man who'd particularly annoyed him, by clubbing him with a steel hammer, although he preferred to let Ricky and Al take on the witness disposal tasks which for them were treats as good as Christmas bonuses.

It was on one of her return trips to Alewife from Braintree that Janice Klein noticed the fleshy middle-aged man who boarded her Red Line train at South Station and sat about ten seats away from her on the other side of her train car. She noticed him because his hair was slicked back leaving no unoiled stragglers, and because his sharp attire was so atypical for Boston, let alone Cambridge; perhaps it would stand out less in Las Vegas, or New York. Evidently, the man was out of sorts, based on the way his full lips were pursed in a vexed pout.

He had ample reason to feel grumpy. Immediately after their departure from South Station, Wallace discovered that the Red Line passenger standing in front of him was definitely someone he did not want to see. Blood drenched his t-shirt from a deep cut on his neck from which it was still bubbling, his face was bruised all over, and one of his eye sockets was closed. He was top-to-bottom dirty, from the grit in his matted hair, to the dirt smeared on his face and on his clothes and his ragged shoes, like he had been rolling in it, or maybe buried under it.

"Happy to see me, Mikey?" the guy asked.

"What the fuck are you doing here?" Wallace demanded.

"Your boys worked me over. I'm dead. And now I'm back to visit with you, you sick fuck. I'm here to make you sweat. That's what I'm doing here." The man gestured as he spoke with hands that showed bloody stumps where fingers were missing, and dirt fell from him every time he moved.

"Well, fuck off!" Wallace said. "Stay dead."

"Mikey, you had me killed and now you're going to pay," the guy said. "My brothers, my sister, my cousins, my buddies, they all miss me. They think about me a lot. They're still wondering what happened to me, where I went. When they're on the Red Line and I visit with them, I'll tell them. So fuck you, Mikey. They'll be coming after you."

Wallace did not relish seeing the ghost of a fool whose murder he had ordered. This fucking guy bleeding and shedding dirt in front of him on the Red Line had been gotten rid of precisely because he wouldn't stop talking. And now here he was back again boasting that he would talk some more. It was really too much. It was one thing to be generally suspected, that came with the territory, but it was quite another to have the specifics of who, how, where, and when, all laid out in detail by the actual murder victim, a loser who was supposed to be dead and gone and telling no tales.

"Anyone you tell will be fucked," Wallace said. "So, fuck off!"

But the guy had vanished, and standing in front of Michael Wallace instead was a tall blond woman. "Hello, sir," she said, "My name is Janice Klein and I am working on a project for the MBTA concerning riders' experiences on the Red Line. I noticed that you were talking with someone who was not visible to me and I wonder if I could ask you a few questions about it. Here is my business card."

Wallace glanced at the card that the woman was holding out to him. He made no move to accept it. He glared up at her through eyes narrowed into angry slits above his smooth pudgy cheeks. "Fuck off!" he said.

"Sorry to bother you," Janice replied, returning to her seat. In her notes, Janice described the sharply-dressed man, what she heard him saying to the empty space in front of him, and his ill-tempered response to her request for an interview. She noted that he left the train at Central Square.

Wallace berated himself as he climbed the steps from the station out to Mass Ave. He should have taken the woman's card. She could describe him if anyone asked. He'd already forgotten the name she told him, Janice something. It would be better to know who she was and where she worked in case he needed to deal with her. Now he'd have to start tracking the relatives and friends of the dead guy – that asshole – so that he'd be ready if any of them came up from the Red Line babbling about the dead guy's murder.

Later, Janice had better luck interviewing Franklyn Brazeal, a retired Cambridge police officer. Officer Brazeal had been confronted by a man who he had arrested and had died in prison. When the former cop, who was black, tall, thin, and bald, got off at Harvard Square, Janice followed him off and approached him on the platform, her business card in hand.

"Glad to talk," Officer Brazeal said. "You say the MBTA is looking into this, that I am not the only one?"

"You're not the only one," Janice replied.

"Well, his name was Rafael Cruz. He shot his wife and her boyfriend, and took his two kids as hostages. He finally let them go and I was one of two officers who arrested him. He was sentenced to life in prison and I heard he got himself killed by another prisoner in a fight."

"So it was Rafael Cruz who you saw on the train?"

"I couldn't believe it. I don't disturb easily after all my years on the force but I have to admit, seeing Cruz gave me quite a shock, like I was in a spooky movie all of a sudden. Here is a dead guy sitting beside me, who gives me a poke, and says, 'Hey Officer Brazeal, how're they hanging?' I said to him, 'I thought you were dead.' He said, 'I guess I am, but here I am paying you a visit, so you never know how things will turn out.' I said, 'They didn't turn out so well for you, Rafael, too bad you messed up your life.' And he poked me again and said, 'You put me in prison.'"

"I told him, 'You better stop poking me' and he replied, 'What will you do about it? Shoot me?'"

Janice said, "I was watching you and could tell something was going on. So he poked you. Was he threatening you in any way?"

"Not really," Officer Brazeal said. "I was startled, and I can think of others who'd I'd rather have visit me from the hereafter, but it seemed he just wanted to get my attention in order to talk."

"Was he trying to deliver a message to you?"

"Yes, that I should have his death in prison on my conscience since I was the senior arresting officer who put him away. He said the wife and her boyfriend deserved what they got, and that should have been taken into account. It would have been better, he said, if we'd shot him at the scene rather than sending him to prison. I told him I was only doing my job."

"How did this visit from Rafael Cruz end?"

"When I got off the train, he didn't follow. I didn't look back to see what happened to him."

Janice wrote down Officer Brazeal's contact information and asked that he call her if he had any more visits from Rafael Cruz while riding on the Red Line. "Or from anyone else," she added, "since we are trying to find out any patterns in these events."

Officer Brazeal said he would. Janice took the next Red Line train to complete her run to Alewife.

Once Officer Brazeal was on street level outside the Harvard Square station, he called a former colleague on the Cambridge police force.

"Hey James," he said. "You got a minute?"

"Always time for you, Franklyn," Sergeant James Murphy said. "What's going on?"

"Do you believe in ghosts?"

"It's early in the day to be hitting the bottle, Franklyn."

"No, I'm dead sober."

"OK, I'm listening, old buddy."

"You remember Rafael Cruz, that scuzzball we arrested who killed his wife and her boyfriend in their house in East Cambridge, and then hid behind his two little kids?"

"Yep. Heard he was killed in prison. His one good deed, saving the Commonwealth the cost of his room and board. What about him?"

"He – or his ghost – visited with me a few minutes ago when I was on the Red Line on my way here to Harvard Square. He was sitting beside me, kept poking me in the arm. He was real chatty."

"You saw Rafael Cruz. The one who's dead. You're messing with me, Franklyn."

"I'm telling you, James, I'm serious, it was Cruz."

"You're sure?"

"I would have recognized him anyway but he identified himself when we started talking. There's no question who I saw."

"Did anyone else see him?"

"I don't know. I don't think so. It was strange; while I was talking with Cruz, it was if we were the only two people in our train car. It's real focusing, talking with a dead man."

"Franklyn," the Sergeant said, "You're a good friend, but if you'll excuse my bluntness, I'm afraid you've got a few screws loose. Just a sign of age. No offense."

"I'd think so too," Officer Brazeal said, "except that a young lady followed me off the train and wanted to interview me about what I'd just seen."

"No shit. So she also saw Cruz."

"No, she saw me talking to him which she said looked like I was talking to myself. But get this, James, she works for a consulting company that was hired by the MBTA. She told me I was not the only one to have that kind of experience on the Red Line and they've been hired to figure out what's going on."

"What's the name of her company?"

"According to her card, Blair West International. They have an office in the Andleman Building, in Central Square, suite 401. I'll email you her phone number and email address."

Sergeant Murphy said, "I know the building. I'll check them out. I'll ask around about the Red Line. Maybe some of my buddies in the MBTA Transit Police have heard something."

"Keep me posted," Officer Brazeal said.

"Will do, Franklyn," the Sergeant said. "Thanks for calling me."

"I figured the Cambridge police should be informed if ghosts of dead people are materializing under our streets on the Red Line trains. Especially if they are killers who we arrested and sent to prison."

"You've done your civic duty today, Franklyn. You're an upstanding guy."

"Well, about the CPD being the last to know, you've heard what they say about the best way to grow mushrooms."

"Remind me."

"Feed them shit and keep them in the dark."

Nine

AS MORE PEOPLE shared what they had seen, a sensational narrative coalesced out of the jumble of isolated anecdotes: Passengers on the Red Line are seeing spirits of loved ones! Ghosts!

A passenger tweeted to her followers, "On Red Line to Park Street. Woman talking with someone not there."

A Facebook posting from an MIT student, "Heard rumors and today saw for myself. Girl was shouting about her mom rising from the dead right in front of her."

A Central Square resident in a Yahoo discussion group, "Someone should let the MBTA know."

The Police & Fire Log for July 26-August 1 in the *Cambridge Chronicle* reported interactions between Red Line passengers and others who were unseen by fellow riders.

A two-minute video posted on YouTube titled, "Red Line Ghost," showed a well-dressed woman talking animatedly with herself, laughing and then crying, and hugging an invisible person. It was grainy and poorly lit, apparently captured on a cellphone, and already had 112,453 hits.

Marty Roberts' column in the Metro section of the *Boston Globe* was titled, TELL THE TRUTH.

At first you dismiss the stories you hear about the Red Line as too crazy to be believed. Probably just pranks by endlessly inventive students. Or just more evidence that there are all kinds of people in a city including nutters who end up on our beloved Red Line at one time or another.

But you'd think that would be true only for people who are still alive. These stories are about dead people.

According to Cambridge police logs, there have been many reports of people seeing, talking with, and even touching ghosts on the Red Line during the last two weeks. You read that right: Ghosts.

You don't have to look far to see reports about these encounters on Facebook, or on Internet discussion groups. There's even a YouTube video.

I asked MBTA spokeswomen Cheryl Degnan about the stories. She said she would check and get back to me. So far, she hasn't.

I called Lenny Baker, Chief of MBTA Transit Police. His assistant said he would call me back. As of now, no joy there either.

Jim Cuddihy, MBTA's chief of operations is usually a straight-up guy who will tell you what's going on if you ask the right way. I did finally get him on the phone and put it to him directly, "Have you heard the stories about ghosts on the Red Line?"

Here is what he said, "Some questions are so strange that I can't respond to them without sounding strange myself."

So I pushed, "Are you saying Yes or No?"

His answer, "I'm saying No Comment,"

If the undead are riding on the Red Line among those of us who are still-breathing passengers, the MBTA should tell us.

WBZ-TV's Live at Five, Action News headlined, "Ghosts on the T," and put their handsome blond-haired reporter Chad Brown on the scene, setting him up with a TV truck and a cameraman on the plaza in front of the entrance to the Park Street station on the Boston Common. While gawkers bunched behind him, several waving to the camera, Brown began his report:

"I'm standing here at the Park Street station trying to learn more about one of the weirder stories of the day, that there have been repeated sightings of ghosts on the Red Line. Earlier today, I asked the MBTA for its comment, and here is what I was told by Cheryl Degnan, the MBTA spokesperson."

WBZ then cut to interview with Cheryl Degnan, a lanky woman in her 40s, speaking into a WBZ microphone that was being held in front of her, "The MBTA has heard about these stories and we are now investigating them."

"Does the MBTA believe there are ghosts on the Red Line?" she was asked by Chad Brown, who was off-camera.

"Well, Chad, to start with, that would require that we believe in ghosts, wouldn't it? All I can tell you is that until we have results from our investigation, we can't comment on what we believe or don't believe."

"So you are not ruling it out?"

"We're still doing the investigation. We'll announce its results to the public as soon as we have them."

The coverage switched back to the plaza at the Park Street station, where Chad Brown was standing next to a man wearing a camera around his neck and a woman who was holding a map in her hand. He introduced them to WBZ's viewers, "Here with me are Barry and Susan Goodens, from Omaha, Nebraska. They are planning to take the Red Line this evening to Harvard Square. Barry and Susan, have you heard that people have seen ghosts on the Red Line and does it affect your plans in any way?"

Barry Goodens replied, "We're not worried about it if that's what you mean. We were on the Red Line this morning and didn't see anything."

"Except the man who was shouting and yelling about something that was bothering him," Susan Goodens interjected.

"We figured he was one of those entertainers on the subway," Barry Goodens said. "Are you telling us he was seeing a ghost?"

"That's what people are saying," Chad Brown replied. "Thanks Barry and Susan. Now we're going to talk with Marie Langone, another Red Line rider. Marie, you are carrying a picture which I am told is of your sister."

Marie Langone replied, "My sister Ruthie died last year."

"So you are riding the T to find your loved one, hoping to meet her again."

"I'm praying to God that I will," Marie Langone said.

Chad Brown motioned the camera to follow him to the side of the Park Street station. "You will see here that people have left flowers and notes against the wall of the T station here at Park Street to commemorate the passing of their loved ones. I've been informed that there were also candles left here that the Transit police removed."

He directed the camera to pan the crowd behind him and on the plaza. "Many of these folks have come to the Park Street station because of the stories about people meeting their loved ones on the Red Line. Like Marie Langone, some are carrying pictures of their loved ones. I'm sure that we'll be hearing more about these ghosts on the Red Line in the coming days and weeks. This is Chad Brown at the MBTA's Park Street station, reporting for WBZ-TV's Live at Five, Action News team. Back to you, Jessica."

Ten

HARRY'S BLACKBERRY VIBRATED and Harry took the call.

"Holy Shit!" Jim Cuddihy shouted.

"Hello to you, too, Jim," Harry said. "You've called at a good time."

"What's good about it?"

"I'm meeting here with our team. If you'd like to join us, I'll dial you right back on the fixed phone line and put you on speaker."

"Yeah, do it."

Cuddihy picked up on the first ring and continued where he had left off, "I knew this would happen, Harry! Fuck!"

The group in the Blair West International conference room listened politely. When Cuddihy was done and no-one spoke, he asked, "Are you still there?"

"Yes, Jim," Harry said. "We're all still here. You sound a little upset."

"Why wouldn't I be upset? Fucking media!"

"Just to let you know, with me here are Jerry, and our three analysts Ashok, Janice, and Maureen."

"Glad to hear it. I hope you've got news for me."

"We're making progress."

"I hope so. People are losing it, even without the media stoking everyone up. Yesterday, we had a guy, one of our Red Line passengers, who was about to make out with his late girlfriend. He said she appeared to him naked and horny. He took off his shirt, shoes and trousers, and was pulling off his underwear, all hot and bothered and ready to go, when other passengers stopped him. It's insane out there. So tell me, Harry, what have you got?"

"Wait a minute," Jerry said. "What happened with the guy who was taking his clothes off?"

"He berated the other passengers for interrupting him and his girlfriend. Said they should have minded their own goddamned business."

"I agree with him," Jerry said. "They should have let things play out to see what would happen, in the interests of science, I mean."

"Right. Well, anyway, he was turned over to the Cambridge PD who questioned him and let him off with a warning. So, Harry?"

Harry replied, "Our analysts completed forty trips on the Red Line end-to-end between Alewife and Braintree and they witnessed incidents, which we now call 'visitations,' on every trip."

"What do we know about the 'visitors' or 'ghosts' or whatever they are?"

"They are the Red Line passengers' children, parents, brothers, sisters, friends, lovers, enemies, and even their pets. Including, Jim, my own daughter Ariel, who visited with my ex-wife Alexandra."

"Jesus, Harry."

"It was an amazing experience for Alexandra. I wish I'd been with her."

This was news not only to Cuddihy but also to Harry's colleagues, whom he had not told. He sensed that they were looking at him differently than before. He was used to their attention, respect, skepticism, even wariness and on occasion dismay, but their *sympathy* was unfamiliar, and it made him uncomfortable.

Cuddihy said, "Listen, Harry, maybe I should go elsewhere to get this resolved. I'm sorry for your loss but I can't afford to let sentiment stand in the way of solving our problem. I need answers."

"So do I, Jim."

"You can handle it?"

"Can and will."

"No matter where it takes us?"

"Yes, Jim, you have my word."

"Alright, I'll hold you to that. Go ahead."

"OK, Jim, I'll ask our analysts to tell us now what they saw and heard."

Janice spoke first, "In every case, the visitation is experienced only by the person who is directly affected. When other passengers get involved after noticing that the person is behaving strangely, and ask if they can help, the same thing always happens. The visitation immediately comes to an end. The person being visited snaps out of it and says something like, 'now my baby's gone, or my mom is gone, what do you want? Why did you interfere?'"

"Like the guy with his horny girlfriend," Maureen said.

Ashok said, "Except when the visitation is unfriendly and the person wants it to end and is grateful for the interruption."

"About the unfriendlies," Maureen said, "we didn't see anyone who was really terrified. People were shocked and upset. And they might yell, 'get away from me,' but they weren't shrieking like in a ghost horror movie. The visitors always appeared as people known to those being visited on the train. Even if they were bloody or disfigured, no-one described them as being really spooky like death skulls with dripping fangs."

Cuddihy said, "So there's always a personal history, some sort of connection. No visits from Jesus, or favorite saints, or Hitler."

"Right," Maureen said.

"Good. If passengers saw Jesus Christ on the Red Line, I'd have to build chapels in every station."

Jerry said, "If you had Jesus as an attraction, you could charge a lot more for Red Line tickets."

"Yeah, see the Messiah on the Red Line! But if you want to get to work this morning, take a bus! Anyway, good input as always, Jerry, thanks."

"Our team is writing up their observations and mining the data to look for other patterns," Harry said. "Meanwhile, Jerry's been plotting the visitations on a map of the Red Line."

"Alright, Jerry, tell me," Cuddihy said.

"I marked on our map every visitation that we know about. All of them were experienced by passengers on the portion of the Red Line between Davis Square in Somerville and South Station in Boston, which I call the 'zone of visitations.'"

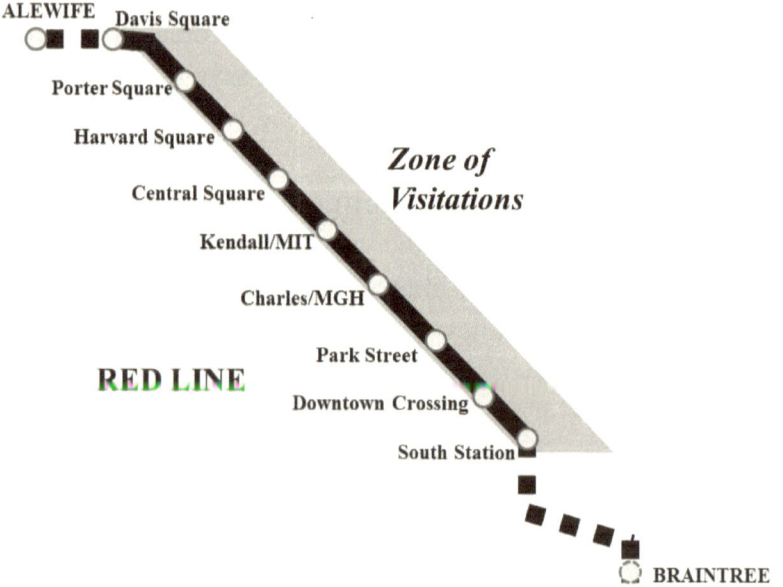

"In every case, on trains heading northwest towards Alewife, the visitors vanished when their trains reached Davis. And the same thing happened heading south towards Braintree; when the trains reached South Station, the visitors disappeared. You can see this on the map."

Harry interrupted, "Sorry, Jim, I realize that you don't have a map in front of you. We have one laid out on our conference table that Jerry's marked up."

"Not a problem," Cuddihy said, "I don't need a map to visualize the Red Line."

Jerry continued, "I marked "Xs" where visitations were reported to have started and "Os" where they ended. Then I plotted these start/finish data using mapping software to reveal where along the tunnel system these events are most concentrated."

"My mapping software juxtaposes every reported incident, its start and stop points, and looks for places along the Red Line tunnel system with the greatest overlaps of these incidents. For example, to keep this simple, if two visitations both start at Harvard Square and both end at Charles/MGH, the software gives a score of '2' to the portion of the Red Line between Harvard and Charles/MGH. If a third visitation starts at Central Square and ends at Kendall/MIT, the software gives a score of '3' to the segment between Central and Kendall/MIT, because it overlaps the longer segment of Harvard-to-Charles/MGH which already had a score of '2'. The software counts the visitation overlaps.

So now, to follow my example, we've now scored three segments of the Red Line system: The score is '2' from Harvard-to-Central, it's a '3' in the overlapping Central-to-Kendall/MIT segment where the third visitation occurred, and it's '2' between Kendall/MIT-to-Charles/MGH."

"Jim, are you following this?" Harry asked.

"Yes," Cuddihy said, "So, what's the answer?"

"The example I just gave you isn't random. The portion of the Red Line tunnel system that scores highest in overlaps of visitations is in Cambridge, between Central Square and Kendall/MIT."

"Right next door to us," Janice said.

"I can narrow it even more. Based on reports of visitations that started or stopped *between* stations rather than at the stations, the data show that the overlaps are greatest as you get closer to Kendall/MIT. So, from our perspective here in Central Square, the zone of hyper-dense visitations starts where the Red Line tunnel branches away from Mass Ave and runs underneath Main Street towards Kendall/MIT."

Cuddihy said, "That tunnel segment is called the Cambridge Tunnel, one of the first portions of the Red Line that was built back in 1912."

Jerry asked, "Might there be something about this tunnel segment that is conducive to the visitations?"

"Hard to say. The Cambridge Tunnel has been in use for almost a century."

Jerry said, "Based on my research to date, there's not much difference between the Red Line tunnels that were built in the early 1900s and the tunnels built around the same time for the Green, Orange and Blue lines. I'm sure you already know all of this, Jim, but for my colleagues here, all of these tunnels were dug with the same equipment and often by the same crews. For all the lines, Red, Green, Orange and Blue, where the tunnels were cut through loose materials like sand or dirt, whether this was done by cut-and-cover or deep boring, they generally have rebar-reinforced concrete walls. Where they were bored through hard rock, the builders just left the bare rock to serve as the tunnel walls. The tunnel ceilings are either reinforced concrete or plain rock, like the walls. In my opinion, based on what we know now, how the tunnels were constructed is a dead end. If the tunnel construction were causing what's happening on the Red Line, we'd also see visitations on the other lines."

Cuddihy said, "You're right about the tunnels all having similar materials and construction."

"But the tunnel construction still could be contributing in some way," Harry said. "Maybe something about the tunnels is interacting with something else that's unique to the Red Line especially in the hot area where it runs under Main Street in Cambridge. We need to find out more about what's on the surface along Main Street. Ashok, Maureen, and Janice, I want you to research all structures on that route. Identify any that could conceivably play a role in the visitations occurring down below in the Red Line tunnel."

Cuddihy said, "You say 'play a role.' What would that look like, Harry? How will you know if a structure on Main Street has opened a wormhole into the spirit world?"

"Jim, we'll stay very alert and hope we know it when we see it," Harry said.

"I guess that's why I'm paying you big bucks, Harry. Call me back when your meeting is over. I need to talk with you privately."

Eleven

'DO YOU KNOW State Representative Walter MacAuliff?"
Cuddihy asked, when Harry called him after returning to his
office.

"He represents South Boston, he hates condoms, and he's
been known to have a few too many before driving," Harry said.
"Not one of my favorites." MacAuliff's most recent DUI arrest
had been captured by a *Boston Globe* free-lance photographer.
The photo showed him being held against a police car,
disheveled and shouting, by two arresting officers. It was
captioned, "Representative Asks: Do You Know Who I Am?"

"That's the guy. MacAuliff is a member of the Joint
Committee on Transportation which oversees the MBTA. He
contacted our General Manager to sniff out whether he should
get involved in our Red Line problem."

"Has he taken a position on it?"

"He's Cardinal O'Rourke's best boy in the State House. The
Church is down on the visitations although they've kept a low
profile so far, so MacAuliff is down on them too. He's asking
what the MBTA is doing to stop them. Says he may request
hearings by the Joint Committee to verify that we're doing
everything possible."

"Should be fun for you, Jim."

"More publicity is the last thing we need. So to head this off, we've offered to confide in MacAuliff on background. He agreed, although he may still push for public hearings later. We're going to meet in his office at the State House."

"You want me to join you?"

"Yes, I'll set up the meeting. You can tell him anything you've already told me. But stick to the facts. No opinions or speculations that he can use against the MBTA. Keep in mind, MacAuliff may come across as a good guy when he's not boozed up or picketing family planning clinics, and he can be a very funny fellow, but fundamentally he's a full-blown shithead."

Cuddihy was waiting at the State House entrance when Harry arrived. They took an elevator to the ground floor, walked down a long narrow corridor to the East Wing, and then down a second virtually identical long corridor to Representative MacAuliff's office three doors from the end.

MacAuliff was seated at his desk facing his door which he had left open, and he beckoned them inside. "You must be Jim Cuddihy and Harry West. Excuse my moving boxes. No point in unpacking. I'm hoping to move again before too long back to a more salubrious neighborhood." Then MacAuliff added, with a roguish giggle, "That's assuming of course that I behave myself and stay out of trouble."

Harry recognized MacAuliff's grin from the photographs of the Representative at the annual Paddy's Day roasts where he famously regaled other Massachusetts politicos with barbed jibes, mocking rhymes, and snatches of Irish songs. MacAuliff stood to reach across his desk to shake hands. He was much shorter than he appeared in his pictures. That, along with his short neatly combed and parted white hair, round face, rosy cheeks, and dimpled chin, gave him the look of a suit-wearing leprechaun, a resemblance also commented upon by his political brethren who customarily introduced MacAuliff at the Paddy's Day roasts as "the Elf from Southie."

Cuddihy said, "We appreciate this opportunity to brief you, Representative MacAuliff. I asked Dr. West to join us since he leads the consultant group that's helping us discover what's causing the visitations on the Red Line."

"How's that going, Harry?" MacAuliff asked.

After Harry told him what they'd found out to date, MacAuliff said, "So bottom line you don't yet know the answer."

"No sir. Not yet. We're focusing now on the portion of the Red Line in Cambridge near the Kendall/MIT station where the visitations seem to be concentrated."

"What you're also telling me is that these visitations are much more numerous than we've heard from media coverage."

"That's true, Representative," Harry said. "Most don't get reported."

"And they were happening for some time before the media found out about them, although the MBTA knew, and you knew as the MBTA's consultant."

"Yes."

"And some people have had bad experiences, which we also don't hear about."

"Yes, not all encounters have been with loved ones."

"Why has the MBTA not warned the public so that passengers can prepare themselves?

"I can answer that, Representative MacAuliff," Cuddihy said. "We feel that it is important to learn the facts before releasing statements that could cause panic."

"So you respond to media questions by saying that you're still investigating."

"Yes."

"What do you think is happening on the Red Line? Do we have ghosts visiting people?"

"We don't know the answer to that, Representative," Harry said.

"But what do you believe? What's your opinion?"

"We're trying to keep an open mind," Harry said, as Cuddihy nodded in agreement.

"What about the moral risk to people who are searching for their loved ones on the Red Line, have you considered that?"

"Not sure what you mean by moral risk."

"Harry, are you Roman Catholic?"

"I'm a non-believer in any religion."

A look of pinched disapproval clouded MacAuliff's round face. "If you were Roman Catholic, like many of the people of Boston who are served by the MBTA, you would know that searching for ghosts is a sin in the eyes of the Church."

Neither Harry nor Cuddihy rose to debate this doctrinal point and MacAuliff continued, "So by continuing to tolerate these visitations and thereby encouraging people to seek out their dear departed, the MBTA is contributing to sinful behavior, in other words, doing the devil's work."

Cuddihy replied, "Representative, we are working as hard as we can to discover the cause of the visitations. When we do, the MBTA will act quickly to bring them to an end."

"Do I have your solemn commitment on that?"

"Yes sir."

"You do know what's at stake for the MBTA if you let me down, do you not?"

"We're doing our best, Representative MacAuliff."

"Excellent!" MacAuliff said, and his wry smile returned. "I assume that MBTA will be properly represented at my Hibernian Brotherhood function next week in the Veterans Hall in Hyannis?"

"We've purchased our usual package of tickets."

"Fine, fine," MacAuliff said. "I'll give serious thought to what you've told me about these visitations and your assurance that you'll end them as soon as you're able. I'll consult with my colleagues whether we need to hold a Joint Committee hearing. I'll let you know. Thank you for coming by."

"What's the Hibernian Brotherhood function?" Harry asked, once he and Cuddihy were back outside the State House.

"That's MacAuliff's name for one of his fund raiser events. It's a political slush fund."

"And yet you buy tickets."

"He can be supportive on MBTA budget issues or he can be contrary, so we prefer to stay on good terms with him."

"Isn't it illegal for him to accept money from public organizations?"

"Do you have something against Hibernian Brotherhood?" Cuddihy asked.

Twelve

HARRY PREPARED FOR his quest to meet Ariel on the Red Line by staring at her age-adjusted image that he'd copied from Alexandra's laptop. He held her image in mind as he maneuvered through a crowd that had gathered on the plaza surrounding the entrance to the T station in Harvard Square, and as he descended the stairs into the station.

Passengers waiting for the next inbound Red Line train were crammed between the yellow corrugated-rubber safety line along the edge of the platform above the tracks, and the red tiled wall at the back. Every few minutes, a warning was broadcast over the station PA system, "Stay behind the yellow line. Leave room for passengers to exit the train." Like those on the plaza above ground, many of the people on the platform displayed photographs suspended on strings around their necks or clutched in both hands, and carried bouquets of flowers.

The first Red Line train was packed too tightly to allow everyone on the platform to get on. Harry waited for the next train. It also was full. Finally, when the third train arrived, Harry was near enough to the front of the crowd to squeeze himself on.

Harry's fellow passengers were mouthing words, some of them silently, others whispering hoarsely, that may have been prayers or perhaps, Harry surmised, the names of their departed.

Harry doubted, but also hoped, that he would see Ariel, and like the others he peered around the Red Line train car just in case she was there. He wondered what it would be like to see and talk with his child whom he knew to be dead, a little person whom he had cherished and still mourned. He yearned for the encounter but, at the same time, he wasn't sure he could handle it. Perhaps it would be too shattering to see Ariel as a ghost, if that's what she was. How would he respond? Would he be able to speak? Would he find release from the awful tightness in his throat? How could he reconcile seeing her with what he knew about the natural world?

Harry stayed on the train until it arrived at South Station. He had seen no sign of Ariel.

At South Station, Harry transferred onto a Red Line train heading back towards Alewife. Although this train also was crowded with passengers bearing photographs and flowers, Harry was able to claim a seat when a man, apparently one of the few riding the Red Line in order to get somewhere, exited at Downtown Crossing.

Slouched on the seat next to him was an elderly man whose morosely lined face reminded Harry of an old beagle. All at once the man straightened in his seat and raised his arms in front of him. "I knew you would come to me," he said. "Sit here beside me." Then he turned towards Harry, his moist blue eyes focused not on Harry but on someone else whom he was seeing in Harry's place. "I have been lonely without you," he complained. "I wish you could have been at the service." And then, chuckling wheezily, he added, "I mean, among us watching it," and he put his arm on Harry's seat-back, and rested his hand on Harry's shoulder.

Harry objected, "Excuse me, sir, you are crowding me here; could you take your hand off my shoulder?" The old man had been looking through Harry but now, startled, was looking directly at him and evidently taking an intense dislike to what he was seeing. "Why did you bother me?" he asked. "Do you realize what you've done?"

"Sorry," Harry said. "Your hand was on my shoulder."

"My Ellie was my partner for forty-five years. We did everything together. She took care of me. Every morning, she made my breakfast and she watched that I took my pills. Now I live by myself. I eat alone. I watch TV alone. There is no-one to talk to in my apartment. Ellie was here with me and you made her disappear."

"I'm sorry," Harry repeated.

"You should be," the man said.

He stood and shuffled slowly towards the train car door, leaning heavily on his cane. He glared angrily back at Harry one last time just before he exited the train at the Kendall/MIT station.

Harry hated crowds. Even the cheerful crowds on New Year's or on July 4th gave him claustrophobia. Once he was in their midst, it wasn't long before he longed desperately to escape. Apparently his search for Ariel, which had been an ordeal since he'd entered the Harvard Square station, was all for naught. He would not meet Ariel today. Perhaps he'd try again later. For now, he'd had enough.

The people jostling on the platform at Central only reluctantly provided room for Harry and several others to disembark, before they pushed their way on.

While he was still on the platform, Harry felt, or sensed, that he was being observed, and he looked back.

A girl was staring at him through the glass window of the train car door. He saw her only briefly before the train began to move forward. During those few seconds, she was all that he saw. Everything else, the train, the station, the other people around him, they all faded into background. He recognized her, convinced down to his very core that the girl standing behind the train car door was Ariel.

Thirteen

"DR. FRANCES GOURMELON is waiting for you in the conference room," Molly Lu told Harry. "She says she's been sent by our client, Jim Cuddihy."

Dr. Gourmelon sat at the head of the table like she owned the room. Her large square-shaped head was crowned by unruly curly grey hair. Her grey eyes behind her gold-rimmed glasses beamed with kindness, intelligence, and empathy. She had full pink cheeks, wide lips, and a strong chin. Her amply proportioned shoulders, arms, and chest were covered bohemian style by a deep purple cotton muumuu emblazoned with slashes of brilliant red and yellow streamers.

"You must be Harry West," she said, greeting him with a big cheery smile and extended her plump hand, a ring on each finger, to be shaken. "I am so very pleased to meet you."

"Welcome to Blair West International, Dr. Gourmelon. I understand that you were sent to us by Jim Cuddihy?"

"He didn't exactly send me."

"Oh?"

"Perhaps I gave the wrong impression to your receptionist. I didn't want to bother her with the details."

"You can bother me. I like details," Harry said, as he took a chair at the table.

"Excellent," Dr. Gourmelon said. "As you should. When I learned that you are working for the MBTA on finding the ghosts, I informed Mr. Cuddihy that I could help. He said that he didn't care one way or another if I contacted you, so here I am."

"So actually he didn't send you but he didn't tell you not to come either."

"Exactly."

"How did you find out that we are working for the MBTA?"

"After one of my clients experienced an encounter on the Red Line, she was approached by one of your staff. She immediately came to me for a consultation and I promised to check with the MBTA." Dr. Gourmelon laid her be-ringed hand gently on Harry's arm, and said, "When we know each other better, Harry, you will discover that I always do what I promise. I called the MBTA and I told the girl who answered why I was calling. They forwarded me to Mr. Cuddihy, who confirmed your assignment, sort of."

"Sort of?"

"He didn't deny it."

"Dr. Gourmelon, do you have a business card?"

"Absolutely!" She started digging in her large cloth bag from which she extracted a silver card case on which were engraved, in italics, the letters FEG. Dr. Gourmelon said, "A gift from a grateful client," and handed Harry one of her cards. It read, "Dr. Frances E. Gourmelon, Ph.D., President, Institute for Psychical and Paranormal Research," and it listed an Essex street address in downtown Boston along with email and phone contact information.

"So, you're a psychic," Harry said.

"I prefer to think of myself as a psychical researcher and as a consultant, just like you, Harry," she replied. "I serve my clients by providing a channel to the spiritual domain."

"Ah," Harry said. He nodded as if this clarified everything. He glanced at his watch. "Dr. Gourmelon, I don't mean to be rude, but I am not getting why you are here. Do you have information that you want to share with me?"

"I'll get right to it because I know that you are busy. I possess a gift that enables me to communicate with the spirit world. Hire me as your team's spiritual consultant and I'll find out why the spirits are appearing on the Red Line."

"How will you do that?"

"I'll make contact with them while I ride on the train."

"That's it?"

"I'll need quiet around me so that our sessions will not be disturbed."

"The Red Line has been quite crowded lately," Harry said. "I was just on it and I can assure you that there are no quiet train cars."

"That's no problem. Just set aside a train car for my personal use."

"I doubt that will be possible."

"Why-ever not?" Dr. Gourmelon asked, sounding honestly surprised.

"I can't imagine the MBTA would close off a car for you to ride alone."

"There are plenty of train cars on the Red Line."

"And they're all full. It would be embarrassing for the MBTA to have pictures posted on the Internet of you sitting in the middle of an almost-empty car, communicating with invisible spirits, while all the other Red Line train cars are standing-room-only. So, no, it won't happen."

Dr. Gourmelon abruptly changed the subject. Revealing what seemed a marvelous ability to read Harry's mind, she asked briskly, "Have you been visited by a loved one on the Red Line, Harry?"

"Not while I was on the train," Harry said. He could have stopped there but he felt a license, even a compulsion, to confide in this empathetic woman. "I did see someone when I looked back just after I got off, when I was still on the platform. She was standing behind the door and staring at me through the glass."

"Who was she, Harry?"

"I believe… she was my daughter, Ariel."

"It's terrible to lose a child," Dr. Gourmelon said in a choked voice. "Believe me, Harry, I know." She touched his arm again, this time in deepest fellowship. "Your daughter Ariel, when did she pass?"

"She was only a toddler. It was a drunk driver."

"Such a shame," Dr. Gourmelon said. She did not ask how a toddler's ghost would be tall enough to be seen standing inside the doorway of a Red Line train car. Instead, she said, "Think about my offer, Harry. How wonderful it would be to learn why the spirits are visiting with us now on the Red Line, including your daughter."

"Dr. Gourmelon, I'll talk with our client at the MBTA and then we'll see."

"That's all I ask."

She rose from her chair and approached Harry with her arms extended wide to envelope him in a solid, comforting hug which to Harry felt like he was being squeezed against two warm pillows. Dr. Gourmelon smelled sweet, like newly-baked chocolate chip cookies. "Perhaps your Ariel will get in touch with me," she said. "I'll let you know."

"I'd appreciate that," Harry said. "Thank you."

As soon as she was gone, Harry called Jim Cuddihy.

"Cuddihy here."

"Jim, this is Harry. I just had a visit from a psychic named Dr. Frances Gourmelon who says that you sort of sent her to us, to see if she could help us do our jobs."

"No, I told her she could contact you if she wanted to. I couldn't tell her not to; it's a free country. Anyway maybe you could use the help."

"From a psychic?"

"Look, Harry, my regular Red Line customers are being squeezed off the trains by people in search of their loved ones. We've got TV cameras and microphones pushed into my passengers' faces while media types ask them how they feel after seeing their dear departed. MacAuliff is breathing down our necks as you well know. I realize that you are making progress but when someone offers to help, I'm not in a mood right now to tell them to go away."

"She told me that she would contact the ghosts directly for us to find out why they are visiting your Red Line passengers."

"Good for her. Maybe we'll learn something."

"But she'll need her own Red Line train car so that she won't be bothered by other passengers while she's communicating with the spirits."

"Fuck that!"

"Jim, every hour that I spend on our project, including my time entertaining psychics who are offering to help us do our job, is another hour billed to the MBTA."

"You made your point, Harry. I won't send you any more psychics."

Fourteen

"THESE ALL SEEM innocuous," Harry said, as his three analysts showed him their pictures of the buildings and open spaces along Main Street.

Starting at the top of Main Street where it splits from Mass Ave, and heading towards the Kendall/MIT station, pictures that they projected on the screen in the BWI conference room depicted a three-story office building, a warehouse, an open parking lot, another office building, a Mexican restaurant, a Thai restaurant, another office building, another parking lot, and MIT's Technology Square, a business park with seven large office buildings.

"How about laboratories that might be doing experiments that could interact with the environment in some way?"

"Further down Main Street we do have MIT lab buildings," Janice said. "The Brain and Cognitive Sciences Complex, a new building with lots of glass as we show here, hosts numerous facilities for neuroscience experiments including a magnetic bay in the basement. Then there's the Parsons Laboratory, which studies chemical and biological systems in water and in the environment, the Whitehead Institute which does biomedical research, the Broad Institute with its genomics research labs."

"What are these?" Harry asked, as Janice projected images of two plain one-story brick buildings with barred windows.

"They're known only by their numbers, E51 and NE22. Maybe they're warehouses. There's no other information about them on the MIT website."

"We need to learn what's going on in these buildings."

"There's also the Center for Life Systems," Maureen said, depicting on the screen a modern three-story glass structure, square-shaped, with green shrubs and small trees visible on the roof. "Labs in this building do all kinds of experiments in biology, energy systems, chemistry, nuclear science, and some interdisciplinary labs as well, such as one that is focusing on bio-nuclear systems."

"Could be of interest," Harry said. "Anything else we should look at?"

"Not that we saw," Ashok said, as he clicked additional photos onto the screen, "Along the remainder of Main Street between Kendall/MIT and the Charles River, are several office buildings, the MIT COOP, the Kendall Hotel, a Marriott hotel, a student residence building, and about a block of open space where a new complex is going to be built."

Harry said, "So we want more information about the lab projects, in addition to whatever's happening in those two nameless buildings, E51 and NE22."

Fifteen

A FIRM HANDSHAKE was one of the first things that Harry noticed about Julia Braun, Vice President for External Affairs at MIT, when she welcomed him and Jerry to her office. She was almost six feet tall and wore little apparent make-up. Her long dark brown hair cascaded onto her shoulders and she had bangs down to her eyebrows, a hairstyle that was favored by 1960s folksingers who played at Club Passim in Harvard Square and that had never gone out of fashion in Cambridge.

Ms. Braun's manner was professionally courteous and businesslike. She apologized to Harry and Jerry for making them wait. She said that she had been running late all morning. She told them that she had another meeting for which she would have to excuse herself in about thirty minutes. "Your administrative assistant told us that you're here about a project you are doing for the MBTA," she said. "Can you tell me more about it, and how I can help you?"

"We are a consulting firm with offices in Central Square and in Hong Kong," Harry replied.

"Yes, I know. I checked your website."

"We've been engaged by the MBTA to determine the causes of strange events you may have heard about on the Red Line."

"You mean the ghosts? It's really sad, seeing all those people carrying their photographs, hoping to catch a glimpse."

"Some do, catch a glimpse I mean," Harry said.

"Are you saying that there really are ghosts on the Red Line?"

"We don't know what they are. All we know is that when an encounter happens, it's a powerful experience."

"And you're looking for help from the University to identify what's causing these phenomena."

"Yes, we are looking for MIT's help," Harry replied.

Jerry said, "Our data show that a high proportion of these… visitations… occur here in Cambridge."

"Of course they would," Julia Braun said, "where else would the spirits want to visit?"

Jerry continued, "…and in particular they occur along a stretch of the Red Line tunnel system where it runs under Main Street down to the Kendall/MIT station, where there are a lot of MIT buildings nearby."

"I see," Ms. Braun said, more warily now. One of the urban legends that flourished among residents of Cambridge who lived in the vicinity of MIT, was that when their lights dimmed, or cable service sputtered, or cats disappeared, or pet rabbits died in their cages, or tap water turned cloudy, or hair turned prematurely grey, they were suffering collateral damage from out-of-control experiments by the mad geniuses at MIT.

Harry said, "We believe that something in the vicinity of Main Street may be causing the events on the Red Line."

"And since MIT labs are located on Main Street, you believe that we're involved," Ms. Braun said.

"That's what we need to find out."

"You know, I've heard this before," Ms. Braun said. "People are quick to blame MIT when things go wrong. We're a big target."

Jerry said, "We'll be glad to show you our analysis, Ms. Braun. We didn't start our investigation with MIT in mind. Our data led us in this direction. Now we need either to rule MIT out as a probable cause, or dig deeper." She thought that Jerry, with his big bouncing eyebrows and grey-haired pony-tail, would blend in easily in the MIT labs, while Harry seemed more of an executive type, like MIT's growing cadre of entrepreneur-profs.

"What are you looking for, exactly?" she asked.

Jerry said, "We need more information about experiments being conducted near Main Street. The first reports about the visitations on the Red Line were received about three weeks ago, So we're interested especially in research projects that started up within the last month."

Harry added, "In particular, we want to know about projects that involve technologies or substances that might impinge upon the Red Line tunnels such as radiation, or gases, or chemicals, or biological elements, or energy pulses, anything that could disrupt the environment in some way."

Julia Braun's assistant knocked on her door and said her next meeting was waiting.

"Please tell them I'll be a little while longer."

She took a moment to add to notes that she was writing on a yellow pad on her desk. "I understand what you're asking for," she said. "My staff is small and already overloaded so I'd need to hire someone to pull this material together, which will carry a cost. Also information about some of our lab projects is privileged, including classified projects for the Department of Defense. I'll need to check with MIT's General Counsel on what we can release."

Harry said, "Our client is the Chief Operating Officer at the MBTA. You and he can talk about cost and any other arrangements."

"Good."

"As you may be aware, the Red Line visitations have seriously disrupted the T's service."

"I'm well aware. I use the Red Line every day."

"The MBTA is hearing from political and business leaders and public interest groups. Which is why, if an MIT lab is responsible, your General Counsel should want to get this resolved quickly."

"I'll talk with him and get back to you soon. Meanwhile please do have your MBTA client call me. What's his or her name so that I'll know to take the call?"

"Jim Cuddihy."

After the meeting with Julia Braun, Harry called Cuddihy. Marla answered, "I'll let him know you're on the line. Poor man. He must have stayed over last night. I found him asleep with his head on his desk when I got in this morning."

"What do you have for me, Harry?" Cuddihy asked. His voice was raspy.

"Marla says you slept at your desk last night."

"You have no idea. I'm exhausted. Can't wait until this is over."

"We're getting there, Jim. We just met with the MIT VP for External Affairs. Her name is Julia Braun. We asked Ms. Braun for her help to identify what is going on in MIT labs located near Main Street that could affect the Red Line. She says that MIT will cooperate."

"That's heart-warming considering that they may be fucking up our transportation system."

"But she also told us that she'll need to hire staff, which will carry a cost. I told her that you will call her to work out any arrangements."

"OK, I'll call her. Give me her number."

"I'll send you her contact info in an email as soon as we hang up. Also, there may be legal issues. Ms. Braun is checking with

MIT's General Counsel about how much information they can share about ongoing research projects, including classified projects funded by the DOD."

Cuddihy grunted, "I'll get our lawyer involved as well."

As promised, Harry emailed Julia Braun's contact information to Jim Cuddihy and also emailed Ms. Braun to expect Cuddihy's call.

In a second email to Ms. Braun, on which Cuddihy was copied, he proposed a research plan that would be structured in three steps similar to a consulting engagement: Step 1, List all projects in MIT labs along Main Street; Step 2, Select for further review the projects that could conceivably have affected the Red Line; and Step 3, Follow-up with the leaders of these higher-interest projects to learn more about what they are doing and when they started doing it.

Sixteen

HALFWAY ACROSS LONGFELLOW BRIDGE on a Red Line train that was heading into Boston, as the train was slowing on its approach to Charles/MGH, a passenger shouted, "Leave me alone!" He bolted to the end of his train car where, under a sign, "Emergency Instructions -- To Stop Train In Emergency and Unlock Door, Pull Ring Then Lever," he yanked a red metal ring to remove a small glass cover, reached inside, grabbed the lever, and pulled it towards him.

The train's brakes screeched like giant fingernails scraping a blackboard. Passengers shouted and fell, tumbling one on top of the other. Packages careened along the floor. A baby stroller tipped over emitting panicked shrieks from its occupant. A rider sitting near where the man had pulled the lever, yelled, "What the hell are you doing? What's wrong?" The man ignored him. "Get away!" he screamed, crazed, frantic, waving his arms and ducking his head as if he were dodging swirling hornets. When the train doors opened, he clambered over passengers who were on the floor, and jumped out. He scrambled over the four-foot-high steel fence that separates the Red Line tracks from the Longfellow Bridge roadway. Then, according to witnesses, he tripped, and stumbled onto the road. Within seconds, he was struck by a car and his body was thrown into the lane of another car, where it was run over by the second car's front and rear wheels.

The *Boston Globe* identified the victim as Rodney Williamson, married with two school-age children. His home was a renovated brownstone in a gentrified part of Boston's South End. He had been employed as a senior analyst at First Boston Investments. Williamson's wife said that he had complained of being harassed while riding on the Red Line by visions of his brother-in-law who had committed suicide. The *Globe* reporter noted that in recent weeks numerous Red Line passengers had described seeing visions of people they had known who had passed away and that the MBTA was investigating. While such visions were welcomed by many passengers, including those who carried and displayed pictures of loved ones, some encounters were unpleasant, as apparently was the case for Mr. Williamson.

Red Line passengers in Williamson's train car described him as highly agitated and confirmed that he acted alone to stop the train and that he jumped out on his own. One of the riders told the *Globe*, "I thought maybe our train had hit something on the tracks or there was a terrorist attack. Maybe if we'd known that the guy planned to jump, someone could have stopped him. He was out of his mind. Crazy."

The MBTA Transit Police collaborated with the Cambridge and Boston police departments to investigate the incident. No charges were laid against the two drivers whose cars hit Williamson. According to police, they were not speeding and had no opportunity to avoid Williamson when he fell onto the road in front of them.

The victim's headshot in the *Globe* was of a middle-aged man with thin light brown hair. "I know him," Ashok said, when Jerry showed him the story. "I saw him during one of my rides on the Red Line. He was very upset. I tried to interview him after he got off the train. He told me that he was confronted by his dead brother-in-law who had shot himself. He said that the brother-in-law blamed him for giving bad financial advice. He wouldn't tell me his name but I'm sure this is the guy."

Marvin Jones, a silver-haired trial lawyer famous for his high-profile criminal and civil cases, appeared on the front doorstep of the Williamson family's home before the TV cameras to announce that he would represent the family in seeking justice from the MBTA. Attorney Jones asserted that the MBTA was morally and legally responsible for the safety of its riders.

"In this tragic incident," he declared, "the MBTA failed egregiously to maintain a safe environment on Mr. Williamson's Red Line train. No-one can feel safe when ghosts are allowed to invade the Red Line and harass and torment innocent passengers literally to drive them to their deaths. On behalf of the Williamson family, Mary-Ellen and her two small daughters Sarah and Michelle, I will soon be discussing with the MBTA how it must accept full responsibility for this tragedy. Of course if the MBTA is not forthcoming, we will pursue a lawsuit for very substantial damages which we expect to win."

A reporter asked, "How can you blame the MBTA for visits by ghosts? Surely that is beyond the MBTA's control."

Jones replied, "If we have to, we will make our case in Court. I don't believe in trying my cases in the public media." Several reporters could be heard laughing at this. Jones customarily did promote his cases in the media in order to establish a favorable climate for jury selection and, if necessary, to lay groundwork for an appeal. A dogged, pugnacious, and frequently successful advocate, Jones never hesitated to confide in selected reporters, regardless of judges' gag orders. When judges levied fines for his misbehavior, Jones dismissed them as "a cost of doing business." When sentenced to jail for contempt of Court, he claimed that jail-time provided an opportunity for business development with future clients.

Jones gave no sign that he heard the reporters' snickering. "That's all for now," he said. "The Williamson family requests that everyone respect their privacy as they mourn their tragic loss."

A pastor of a Baptist church in Wisconsin preached to his small congregation, mostly members of his extended family and of a local freedom-first militia, that it wasn't just any ghost that chased Rodney Williamson off the train. Rather, it was one of the Lord's "avenging spirits." Squinty-eyed as though he were taking aim through the sights of the rifle mounted on the back window of his pickup truck, with his close-cropped grey hair and voluminous mutton-chop mustache, the screwball pastor's rants provided irresistible copy for cable news channels and supermarket tabloids.

"Williamson will be only the first among many," he declared "His fate and the other encounters with spirits that have transpired on the Red Line subway are providing final warnings about the fast-approaching end of days. God's holy warriors are gathering on the Red Line in order to wreak the Lord's justice. For the sinner Williamson it is too late. But for other people in Boston, you have been duly admonished to renounce sexual perversion, racial mixing, relativism, and socialism, or face God's terrible wrath." The pastor's sermon might have gone unnoticed except that it was covered by a local TV station affiliated with one of the Christian cable networks, and a viewer posted it on YouTube where it went viral.

Asked for his reaction on a Boston morning radio news show, the Mayor of Boston responded, "Look, get a grip. Take a deep breath," adding, in his trademark mumble, "Boston is a great city. Trust me. We have nothing to fear." He said that Williamson's fatal accident on the Red Line, however tragic, was a "one-time" event. "Even so," the Mayor said, "it's time for

MBTA to regain control over the Red Line. I expect that they will. They don't need any reminding from me."

The Office of the Governor of Massachusetts issued a statement: "The Governor has discussed the matter with the MBTA General Manager and with the Secretary of Transportation, who serves as chairman of the Board of Directors that governs the MBTA, and he is following the situation closely. The Governor has full confidence in the MBTA to resolve the issue in a way that protects everyone's interests. Nevertheless, if it becomes necessary, he is prepared to intervene."

Jim Cuddihy was quoted directly by the *Boston Globe* reporter, "The MBTA is investigating these occurrences on the Red Line that have been reported to us. We regret the loss of life of one of our passengers. Let me assure you that we are making good progress in our efforts to determine the cause of these unusual events. As soon we do, we will shut them down immediately and permanently. We will return the Red Line to normalcy."

When asked how MBTA was responding to the lawsuit threatened by Attorney Jones, he replied, "No comment."

Seventeen

DR. GOURMELON REASONED that spirits must inhabit successive human beings. After all, they survive the death of their physical hosts and then stay in contact with the living through the medium of sensitive persons like herself, or through openings between the physical and the spiritual worlds, such as on the Red Line. If spirits were not, in a sense, *re-used*, their realm would become impossibly overcrowded as more people died, and also a new spirit would need to be created every time a new person was born which would violate conservation of energy, a fundamental rule of physics. However, on whether the spirits might occasionally inhabit creatures other than human beings, like fish or cockroaches, Dr. Gourmelon, not being a Buddhist, had not yet formed an opinion.

Assuming that she herself had been reincarnated, Dr. Gourmelon believed that one of her former human manifestations must have been British. She loved almost everything about the British. If asked why, she would praise their civility, their stoicism, their weakness for silly bits on TV, their mastery of the Mother Tongue in all their social strata from cockney to posh, their odd names for villages, streets, and cottages; their beer, and tea, and fried food; their damp climate and wooly sheep and best-of-Britain pigs; their much beloved dogs and cats; their monarchy and its reliably entertaining royal theatrics; their ancient ruins, old stone churches, and graveyards, and hedges, and haunted country houses. Dr. Gourmelon even identified with their loutish football hooligans, since she sensed that in her earlier life she must have been a barmaid, most likely of the lusty, full-figured variety. She could recall the scene so vividly that it had to have been real; she was standing behind the bar on a sawdust-covered wooden floor, exchanging raucous insults with her friends and customers, smelling the ale slopped over the rims of stoneware china mugs, reaching for coins slapped noisily on the bar, breathing smoke from the fireplace. It was a scene that she sought to re-live, the sights, smells, and sounds of her far distant past, when she vacationed each year in Great Britain and made sure to visit the local pubs.

During her day-to-day life in Boston, Dr. Gourmelon indulged her fondness for things British through her steadfast loyalty to products that were proudly Made-in-England. In her condo above her Institute's offices on Essex Street in Boston, you could find bath and kitchen soaps from Crabtree & Evelyn Ltd., By Appointment to Her Majesty Queen Elizabeth II; emollient skin cream, also royally endorsed, from Murray Deeside Marketing Ltd.; a hairbrush of fine wood and selected bristle from G. B. Kent and Sons, PLC.; English Breakfast and Earl Grey teas packed loose in cans from R. Twining and Company Ltd.; plain biscuits from Carr's of Carlisle Ltd.; Orange Fine Cut Marmalade and Black Cherry Jam from Wilkin and Sons, Ltd.; and the Cadbury PLC chocolate chips that she stirred into cookie dough for her home-made chocolate chip cookies.

Dr. Gourmelon lived alone. But being highly social by nature, a pre-requisite for communicating with the dead as well as with the living, and possibly also a remnant of her former life as an English barmaid, she preferred to breakfast in the company of other people. For this daily morning ritual she had found the perfect place, the Horse & Plow Café, a British-themed restaurant inside the lobby of the Millennium Hotel, located only two blocks from her condo.

As on most other mornings, Dr. Gourmelon was waiting at the entrance to the Horse & Plow Café when it opened at 7:00 A.M. As usual, she claimed her favorite table, a four-seater that offered a view of the hotel lobby, and she ordered her standard Special English Breakfast, two fried eggs with sausages, slices of baked tomato, brown beans, slices of white bread served toasted and dry with butter and strawberry jam on the side, a blueberry scone, and a pot of strong black tea. While enjoying her morning sustenance, Dr. Gourmelon caught up on news and current events in the *Boston Globe* that she had purchased in the hotel lobby.

The story on page one of the *Globe* jumped out at her, "Death on Red Line Said to Be Caused by Ghost." She read about the unfortunate Rodney Williamson. Poor man, he should have talked with someone about his problem, she thought. A professional like her could have advised him on ways to deal with an angry spirit. Now, apparently, a different kind of professional was on the scene, Attorney Marvin Jones, Esq., following the sweet scent of money.

Then Dr. Gourmelon read the quote attributed to the MBTA's Jim Cuddihy, that when the MBTA discovered how visits by the spirits were happening on the Red Line, it would "shut them down immediately and permanently."

Why would the MBTA seek to prevent people from communicating with their departed? That was just wrong. Poor Rodney Williamson's encounter was an anomaly. Most visitors on the Red Line were loved ones, not angry spirits. Surely the minor inconveniences suffered by regular Red Line commuters did not justify such a drastic and perverse response by the MBTA.

Dr. Gourmelon reached to turn the page on the *Globe* article. When her fingers touched the paper, the back of her hand suffered a sharp painful *whack* like the snap from an elastic band. Perhaps a small nerve in her hand was acting up, or a muscle, or maybe a vein, or arthritis. She'd call her doctor about it. She reached again to turn the page. Again, a smarting blow on the back of her hand made her draw back. She flexed her hand and shook it slightly. She decided to give her left hand a rest. But when the fingers of her other hand touched the paper, the back of that hand also suffered a stinging blow. Wary of further punishment, Dr. Gourmelon decided for the moment to leave the *Globe* open on the Williamson story, and sat back in her chair, trying to puzzle out what was happening. She concluded, based on her long experience communicating with the spirit world, that the other side was signaling her to pay more attention to that story in the *Globe*, in particular the part about the MBTA's plan to stop the visitations.

Jeremy Stanger, manager at the Horse and Plow Café, noticed that his good customer had reached several times towards her newspaper and each time had suddenly withdrawn her hand, apparently in pain as if she'd touched something hot. Now she was sitting very still and just staring at the paper, looking perplexed. Wishing to help in case Dr. Gourmelon was in distress, but at the same time reluctant to intrude, Jeremy, an affable Brit from the village of Wythop in England's Lake District, fell back on a familiar remedy. He would bring her more tea. He strode to Dr. Gourmelon's table bearing a teapot on a small tray.

"Can I interest you in fresh tea?" he asked.

Dr. Gourmelon was unsure how to respond because when she saw Jeremy's lips move, she heard a deep, hollow voice, definitely not his, that intoned, "Do not let them close the door."

Standing in front of her table, and becoming quite uncomfortable about the strange way that Dr. Gourmelon was staring at him – she seemed not to recognize him, not just as Jeremy the restaurant manager but perhaps not even as a fellow human – he repeated, "I've brought more tea if you'd like me to freshen your cup."

This time Dr. Gourmelon heard him correctly. "Yes, please," she said.

"Is everything alright?" he asked.

"Yes," Dr. Gourmelon replied, "Thank you for asking."

After refilling her teacup, Jeremy left the new pot on her table along with her bill for breakfast. Each morning it imparted the same information, "English Breakfast Special, $8.85" and "Thank you, Jeremy." But on this bill Dr. Gourmelon read different words that shimmered in shiny black lettering, "Do Not Let Them Close the Door," and "It's Up To You."

Harry sniffed a familiar aroma when he arrived later that morning at the BWI office. Molly Lu was away from her desk and no-one else seemed to be around, so he called out, "Has someone been baking chocolate chip cookies?"

Janice Klein's head poked up above the sidewall of her cubicle. "Haven't seen them, Harry, but they do smell delicious. When you find out where they are, please let me know."

Harry found Dr. Frances E. Gourmelon in the conference room ensconced as before at the head of the room's large table. Laid out open in front of her was the *Boston Globe*. "Hello, Harry," she said. "I just set myself up here. I hope you don't mind."

Harry replied, "I do mind, Dr. Gourmelon; you really should have called before coming."

"Normally I would have, but I'm here on a very urgent matter."

"Also, you should not have entered our office uninvited."

"Your receptionist was away from her desk."

"If she was away you could have left your card and we'd have gotten back to you."

"No you wouldn't, Harry. Don't lie to me." Suddenly her voice had gone cold, like that of a kindly aunt who has been gravely disappointed in her formerly-coddled nephew and wishes to make her disapproval abundantly clear.

"Why are you here, Dr. Gourmelon?"

"Did you see this article in the *Globe* about this poor man, Rodney Williamson, who was killed when he jumped from the Red Line train on the Longfellow Bridge?"

"Yes."

"Well, in this same article, your client Jim Cuddihy says that when the MBTA discovers how spirits are able to visit passengers on the Red Line, he plans to block them, or in his words, to shut them down."

"Yes, I saw that too."

"And you, Harry, are helping Mr. Cuddihy to accomplish his objective."

"Is that a surprise to you? You knew that we were engaged by the MBTA."

"You are making a mistake, Harry."

"Well, I don't know what I can do..." Harry began, but Dr. Gourmelon interrupted him, "When we first met, I believed that you were trying sincerely to find out more about the spirits, that you wanted to learn why they were visiting on the Red Line. I never dreamed that you were conspiring with your client to block the visitations."

"That's his choice. Mr. Cuddihy is responsible for operating the T."

"For just one moment, Harry, listen to what you are saying," Dr. Gourmelon demanded. "Spirits of loved ones are returning from the void of death and they are bringing joy, such great joy to people! How could you not understand that after seeing your own daughter Ariel? Now you and your Mr. Cuddihy plan to stop them! How outrageous! How arrogant!"

"It's not my call," Harry replied. Even if she were right that because of his project for Cuddihy, that he and Alexandra would never see Ariel again, a fact that Alexandra wouldn't receive at all well when she found out, he didn't enjoy hearing this muumuu-clad psychic lecturing him about it.

"Yes it is your call, Harry," Dr. Gourmelon replied. "You don't have to help the MBTA achieve their monstrous plan. If you do, you will be just as guilty as they are."

It seemed to Harry that Dr. Gourmelon's stout body had expanded like the swelling of an outraged bullfrog. She looked bigger, and heavier, filled to over-flowing with righteous wrath.

"Dr. Gourmelon, you must leave now."

"The spirits are disturbed," she declared. "They demanded my help. No-one has the right to shut the door to the spirit world."

"Well, you can take that up with the MBTA," Harry said. "But now you must go." Harry stood to guide Dr. Gourmelon out.

This was one visit that would not end with a good-bye hug.

Her last words to Harry before she sailed down the hallway outside the BWI office were, "You will regret this."

Eighteen

JULIA BRAUN ASSURED Harry that MIT would act decisively if any of its lab experiments were found to be causing the disruptions on the Red Line. "The death of that poor man on the Longfellow Bridge has certainly captured our attention," she said.

Harry said, "Attorney Marvin Jones is demanding a big settlement for the man's family."

"On what grounds?"

"The MBTA was negligent in allowing the visitations that terrified Williamson so that he panicked and jumped out of the train."

"That's the trial lawyer's playbook, 'if you have the law, pound the law, if you have the facts, pound the facts, if you have neither, pound the table.'"

"Jim Cuddihy says that if MIT is responsible for the visitations, he'll expect you to join the MBTA in defending against the lawsuit."

"I'm shocked," Julia Braun said.

A storage room down the hall from Julia Braun's office in the MIT Admin Building was cleared to accommodate Ashok Chakraborty and Hannah Tsang, an MIT grad student who was hired by Ms. Braun to work with Ashok as a part-time research assistant. As agreed by the MIT and MBTA lawyers, they could collect information from public sources about MIT projects. Any classified projects that they might discover would be off-limits for further investigation unless they received written permission from MIT's General Counsel. They could take notes on information provided by the university but no documents could be copied or removed from the building.

To gather information on projects in MIT labs located near Main Street, Hannah scoured laboratory websites, MIT newsletters and newspapers, lab reports that had been submitted to the MIT Corporation, and articles and professional papers that surfaced in Internet searches.

Ashok reviewed Hannah's information to select for further investigation the projects that might possibly have affected the Red Line.

Most of the MIT research projects that Hannah identified were easily dismissed because they were too localized. Typically these involved examination of tiny samples under microscopes entirely inside lab premises, including such lab-bound projects as the research to study "optogenetic perturbation of single neurons and entire networks in vitro and in vivo," "single unit recordings in monkey IT cortex to investigate the neural encoding of facial identity," and "molecular mechanisms of bidirectional synaptic plasticity and meta-plasticity and the contributions of these mechanisms to naturally occurring synaptic modifications in the brain."

However, several labs and projects warranted a second look. Hannah discovered that MIT's Building E51 on Main Street was not a warehouse as it appeared from outside. Instead it housed a laboratory sponsored by the US Department of Homeland Security to test methodologies for counteracting psychotropic drugs that might be released into the air or water, including hallucinogens, hypnotics and opioid analgesics. The lab's existence and mission inside Building E51 were not a secret. On the other hand, neither were they being advertised for fear of attracting break-ins by thieves hunting for free samples. The lab had been in operation for almost a decade, starting long before the first reports of the Red Line visitations, which apparently would disqualify it as a cause. However, Ashok decided to check further. Perhaps the lab had more recently begun to work on a new drug or changed its procedures.

Following the agreed protocol, when Ashok emailed his questions to the director of the lab in Building E51, he did so as a representative of the "MIT Project Survey" over the signatures of Julia Braun, VP for External Affairs at MIT, and of Dr. Harry West, Managing Partner at Blair West International. The lab director responded that, indeed, only a few months earlier the lab had begun experiments on a potent hallucinogen. She confirmed that if this hallucinogen were released as an inhalant in Red Line train cars, it could cause passengers to experience visions. However, she added that there was no way that this substance could be responsible for the Red Line visitations. Like all the psychotropic drugs being tested in the lab, the test hallucinogen was doled out by Homeland Security in extremely small quantities according to a rigidly managed supply schedule. Even if this psychotropic substance had found its way onto Red Line train cars despite all the precautions to prevent any leakage outside of the lab, the quantities were so minute that the dosage-per-exposed-person in the large Red Line train cars would have almost no effect. Also, the potency of the air-borne drug would dissipate within less than a minute.

Also of interest was the MIT Nuclear Reactor Laboratory which provided facilities for both in-core and ex-core irradiation experiments. Although the MITR was located a long block away from Main Street, Ashok speculated that radiation from its experiments might have found a route into the Red Line tunnels, perhaps through fissures in the rock underneath MIT or through ventilation shafts. If so, could that have produced the visitations as experienced by Red Line passengers? In response to Ashok's question about radiation leakage, the MITR director claimed that no radiation was escaping any of the experiments, a fact that had been confirmed and re-confirmed through continual testing by MIT under strict guidelines and monitoring by the U.S. Nuclear Regulatory Commission. Ashok's reaction to the MITR director's assurance was, "Yeah, sure." He instinctively distrusted official statements that all was well, especially such statements related to nuclear energy. However, the MITR director's response to Ashok's second question, about potential effects of radiation poisoning, did seem to eliminate the MITR as a likely cause, given that the symptoms would present as nausea, vomiting, and diarrhea, rather than as visitations, whether real or imagined.

Hannah identified an intriguing news item on an MIT website that had been posted by MIT's Bio-Nuclear Systems Laboratory. The article described tests that had started recently in the lab to explore the formation of life, for which the BNSL was employing wireless transmission of high energy electric pulses.

In Ashok's email to the BNSL directors, Drs. Wec Bluestein and Suzanne Hersch, he asked, "When did the BNSL begin its tests?" "What do these tests involve?" "What are 'high energy electric pulses' and how are they transmitted wirelessly?" That same afternoon, the BSNL directors replied, "We suggest meeting to discuss."

Nineteen

DEEP IN THE BASEMENT of MIT's Center for Life Systems, the Bio-Nuclear Systems Laboratory explored how *being* differed from *not-being*.

The BNSL Director, Professor Wec Bluestein, was an MIT lifer – undergraduate, graduate, and professor. Now in his 60s, he had the thin rangy frame of a long distance runner, having competed in every Boston Marathon since 1991. For Dr. Bluestein, the BNSL culminated his lifelong quest to define the existential mystery of "life" using all the tools of science and technology.

For Professor Suzanne Hersch, the lab's Associate Director, whose brilliance as a grad student had so impressed MIT that she was recruited to join the faculty even before she had completed her doctoral thesis, BNSL's path-breaking work would confirm her great promise. Working with Wec, her former professor and mentor, was a bonus. Who knew? If things went as they expected, she and Wec might someday win Nobel prizes as discoverers of the secret of life.

Despite its campus nickname as the Frankenstein Lab, the BNSL was not reviving corpses borrowed after nightfall from cemeteries or morgues. Not yet anyway, the professors assured their students. Its actual goal was audacious enough, to transform inanimate chemicals and materials into living organisms, initially single cells and then, if all went well, into much more complex life forms such as algae.

The Bio-Nuclear Systems Lab's initial $10 million from affiliates – two pharmaceutical companies, one based in New Jersey and the other in Zurich, and a biological research arm of the US Department of Defense – was sufficient to assemble the technologies that were needed for proof-of-concept tests. After these tests demonstrated the validity of the lab directors' vision, the affiliates would provide a second round of funding.

Drs. Bluestein and Hersch were accustomed to entertaining emissaries from companies and government agencies who might, if sufficiently impressed, sign up to contribute funds. Today their four guests – Harry, Jerry, and Ashok from Blair West International, and Julia Braun representing the MIT Corporation – came loaded not with money but with questions.

"Before we tell you about our work at BNSL," Dr. Wec Bluestein said, "perhaps you could enlighten us about your MBTA engagement."

Harry replied, "Are you aware of the news reports about Red Line?"

"If you mean the ghosts," Dr. Bluestein said, "the answer is Yes, and not just from the news reports. I have seen my fellow Red Line passengers talking to the open air. But what does that have to do with us?"

"The MBTA engaged us to discover the cause of these incidents."

Jerry added, "Our analysis shows the greatest concentration of visitations in the portion of the Red Line tunnel that runs under Main Street to the Kendall/MIT station."

Dr. Bluestein demanded, professorially, "Define 'greatest concentration.'"

"Red Line passengers have experienced more encounters while the Red Line trains are passing under Main Street, as compared to any other segments of the Red Line system."

"And you think we may have something to do with this?"

Harry replied, "Your lab is on Main Street. Your experiments are reported to involve high energy pulses. They're also reported to have started at about the same time as the incidents began on the Red Line."

"Fair enough," Dr. Bluestein said. "How would you like to proceed?"

Harry said, "You could show us your lab and describe what you are doing here."

The lab directors led the group down to the building's sub-basement. Dr. Bluestein tapped a small blank screen located on the wall beside a heavy metal door. A keypad appeared on the screen, and he entered a password and then pressed his thumb against the screen so that it could read his thumbprint.

Ashok asked, "Why all this security?"

"It's mandated in our agreements with affiliates," Dr. Bluestein said. "Also our wireless energy transmitter can be dangerous if it's operated by people who lack proper training."

On the other side of the metal door was a viewing room that looked into the lab space through thick glass. The actual lab was surprisingly small, perhaps no more than twenty feet on each wall, or four hundred square feet in area. Two people wearing yellow hazmat suits that covered them from helmets to booties paced around the lab, checking equipment, and tapping with styluses on handheld devices. At the far end of the lab stood a glass tower about five feet in height including a white rounded cap on top, and about three feet wide on each side. Two openings on one of the sides allowed a lab technician to insert his or her hands into permanently-attached rubber gloves, in order to manipulate materials and objects inside the structure. A bank of flat monitor screens hung on the wall of the lab to the right of the viewing room. Just below these screens was a table covered with open laptop PCs, several microscopes, and other assorted equipment. Arrayed along the wall on the other side, to the left of the viewing room, were stainless-steel barrels that resembled beer barrels except for the instrumentation on their covers. Near the top of the far end wall, close to the ceiling, a large exhaust fan rotated slowly.

Dr. Hersch said, "We operate the lab as a sterile clean room in order to avoid introducing microbes or any other any type of living organism into the test space. The atmosphere in the room is continually emptied by the exhaust system so there's actually a slight vacuum in there. We want to make sure that nothing can grow in the lab except for the materials inside the glass tower, which we call our incubator. The only oxygen in the lab is inside the incubator, plus of course the oxygen carried in small backpack tanks by each lab technician for his or her personal use. Inside the incubator, in addition to the oxygen-rich environment, the test materials include ammonia, phosphorus, carbon, hydrogen, nitrogen, and sulfur, plus amino acids and sugar molecules. The exact mix of these inanimate substances is our lab's secret sauce, like the flavoring of Coca-Cola's syrup."

"For our proof-of-concept tests, micrograms of each test material are sucked into the incubator by a vacuum picker from sterilized storage cabinets underneath. The gases and oxygen are injected in precisely measured quantities via pre-installed tubes. Then we bombard the incubator with energy pulses. This causes a molecular-level reaction to occur in the test materials. Afterwards the test materials are inspected using our Low Voltage Electron Microscope, or LVEM. You can see the LVEM viewing column that is inside the incubator, extending down from its top. It has a focal adjustment that allows viewing without disturbing the test materials. Using LVEM, we can observe very small objects down to the structure of individual cells. We look for evidence that cells are dividing, thereby reproducing themselves, which means that they are living cells."

"To deliver the energy pulses, we adopted a technology that transmits electric power wirelessly by coupling magnetically resonant objects, one at the transmitter and the other at the reception site. In our case, the glass walls of the incubator are banded by very thin and very precisely measured strips of copper to create a coil that is magnetically resonant with the transmitter. The wireless transfer of power from the transmitter to the resonant receiver produces an electric energy pulse that bombards the materials inside the incubator."

"We're very proud of this wireless electricity technology which, by the way, was invented at MIT," Julia Braun said. "We call it WiTricity."

"Where's the electric pulse transmitter?" Jerry asked Dr. Hersch.

"It's underneath us. You'll notice that the floor of our viewing room is roughly two feet higher than the floor of the lab. This provides a convenient space for the transmitter. Also it gives us a better view. Don't worry, it's completely safe," she said, pausing for a chuckle from the group. Dr. Hersch had given this tour, and delivered this witticism, many times before.

"And everything works as expected?" Harry asked.

"Initially we had set-backs in calibrating the energy pulses," Dr. Hersch said. "We didn't tune the electromagnetic frequency of the reception site accurately and the test vessel failed to energize. Then, after we fixed the tuning, our transmitter generated an excessive electrical jolt that destroyed the materials inside the vessel and de-stabilized the monitoring equipment in our lab, which took time to repair. Finally, however, our clever technicians were able to bring the energy pulse technology under control. "

"Fortunately we got it fixed after only a few days of tearing out our hair," Dr. Bluestein said. "Which is a good thing because, as you can see, I don't have a lot to spare."

Dr. Hersch continued, "Once everything was up and working, energy pulses were transmitted and received properly by the test vessel. Since then, we've been amazed and excited about the evidence we've found of life formation."

"So you've demonstrated that life can be created from inanimate materials when hit by a strong pulse of energy," Harry said. "That's an important discovery, it seems to me."

"We agree, and so do our partners. They are committing now to provide our next round of funding so that we can move from proof-of-concept to the production phase of our testing."

"What will that mean?" Jerry asked.

"We'll ramp up the energy pulse. Right now the effectively delivered power or EDP is about the same as that delivered by a car battery. We will increase it in stages to an EDP that will be about fifty times greater."

"When did your experiments start, exactly?" Harry asked.

"On July 6th, almost four weeks ago," Dr. Bluestein said. "When were the first sightings reported on the Red Line?"

"On July 8th the MBTA received its first report," Jerry replied. "We were called in on July 20th when the MBTA realized it was dealing with more than just a few isolated events."

"Have you continued your experiments consistently since July 6th?" Harry asked.

"Every four hours, six per day, seven days a week," Dr. Hersch said. "The test itself takes less than a minute, but there's set-up time for each one, and then time to record the results."

Harry asked, "Is there any way that anything you are doing here could affect the Red Line trains?"

Dr. Bluestein replied, "I doubt it very much. We've been extremely careful to contain our lab activities within this lab space."

"What about exhaust from the lab?"

"The exhaust system runs through an ionizing air purifier and it's vented through a chimney on the roof of our building."

"What about the test materials?"

"They are exposed to the electric energy pulse in minute quantities, as Dr. Hersch told you, and they're kept inside the glass incubator until disposed of though MIT's hazmat procedures which the university employs for all biological and radioactive materials. We employ very rigorous procedures."

"What about the energy pulse? Could that escape the lab somehow?"

Dr. Hersch replied, "That's also quite unlikely. The transmitter, and the copper coil surrounding the incubator which acts as the receiver, have been precisely tuned to the same resonant frequency, as I've described to you earlier. For any other object to receive the energy pulse would require that it also be tuned to that frequency."

"How could we test for that?"

"We can ask Steve Cheng that question. He's a post-grad tech who works in our lab and also worked on MIT's WiTricity project, so he understands the magnetic coupling technology. Steve has been our secret weapon in getting our system to work. I'll invite him to join us when we get back to our conference room."

Steve Cheng knocked on the conference room door five minutes after Dr. Hersch called him. He had long straight black hair that he brushed back with his hand when it flopped over his forehead and covered his round granny glasses. He looked much too young to be an authority on advanced technologies for wireless transmission of electric power, let alone for creating life from inanimate materials. Nevertheless, as someone apparently accustomed to being the smartest guy in the room, which meant something in a room at MIT, he displayed serene self-confidence and gave no sign of being intimidated by his elders and nominal superiors. Dr. Hersch introduced Steve as BNSL's technical guru and told him that Harry and Jerry were consultants who had questions about the WiTricity system. "Glad to help," Steve said.

Harry said, "Before you joined us, we were asking whether objects outside the lab could resonate with the lab's electric energy transmitter."

Steve replied, "Sure, why not?"

"So the energy pulses could escape the lab?"

"Sure."

Dr. Hersch said, "Steve, I told our guests that the other object outside the lab would have to be precisely tuned to the same frequency."

"Yes. That's true," Steve said.

Dr. Bluestein intervened, "I must object. This line of questioning is unfair to Steve. He might respond differently if he knew the context for Harry's question."

"How so?" Harry asked.

"Steve gave you a theoretical answer to your question about energy pulses escaping our lab. But your question has real world consequences. Perhaps if Steve knew the significance of saying yes or no, he would couch his response differently."

Steve Cheng said, "I guess I do need to know what this is about."

Harry asked whether Steve was familiar with the situation on the Red Line, and Steve said that he was. Harry then explained that the MBTA had engaged Blair West International to determine the cause of the visitations on the Red Line. He said Jerry's analysis suggested that they might be attributable to work going on in an MIT lab located near Main Street.

"So you want to know if the BNSL energy pulses could affect the Red Line trains in some way."

"Yes, that's what we're trying to find out."

"Well, my answer is still 'Yes, a WiTricity energy pulse could escape the lab,'" Steve said. "It's not likely," he added, with a nod in the direction of Dr. Wec Bluestein whose eyes had locked onto him like a tractor beam, "but it's theoretically possible."

"How far might the energy pulse be transmitted?" Harry asked.

"In theory, the distance is quite limited, usually less than fifty feet. But sometimes you get surprised. A highly sensitive receiver would increase the receptive distance."

"How would you test whether another object was resonating?"

"We'd bring instruments to test whether the receiving object was energized and if so, we'd check whether it was magnetically resonant with the transmitter."

"OK, here's another question for you, Steve, and for others here on the MIT side," Harry said. "Do you know how far away the Red Line tunnel is from the outer walls of your lab?"

Dr. Suzanne Hersch replied, "I don't think we have that information."

Steve said, "It's not far."

"Now, Steve, how would you know that?" Dr. Bluestein asked. He sounded irritated with his talkative technology guru.

"When we're inside the lab, we can clearly hear the rumble of the Red Line train when it goes by. In fact, we can feel the vibration."

Twenty

STEVE CHENG AND Jerry Seligman were cleared by Jim Cuddihy to enter the Red Line tunnel to test for magnetic coupling with the BNSL's electric power transmitter, but they still needed additional approval from the U.S. Department of Homeland Security. Post 9/11, non-MBTA-employees had to be vetted by the FBI before they could enter the subway tunnels.

After FBI agents interviewed Steve at MIT, and Jerry at BWI, the agency concluded that neither had connections with terrorist groups. Boston's local FBI office completed its review within two days of Cuddihy's request. The review had been fast-tracked by the FBI's Special Agent-in-Charge who knew Cuddihy from their joint membership on a task force to protect essential infrastructure in Massachusetts from terrorist attack. Also the Special Agent rode the Red Line every day into Boston and he missed his quiet commute, before the visitations, when he could always find a seat to catch a quick nap.

Steve, Jerry, and two MBTA engineers entered the tunnel via a technician's door at the end of the Kendall/MIT platform. The tunnel was lit dimly by fluorescent lights long at the top edge of the walls. To improve visibility, the MBTA engineer leading the way carried a large flashlight, and the other walking at the rear also had a flashlight in hand.

They walked single file along a narrow path that hugged the tunnel wall. There was a three-foot-high metal rail along the outer edge of the path to prevent technicians from slipping off. "Stay right behind me," the first engineer said, "and don't lean over the rail." Just then, as if to reinforce the engineer's warning, a train roared by them on its way to Kendall/MIT from Central, buffeting Steve and Jerry with its blast of air and noise. Every fifty feet or so there were gaps in the protector rail to allow access to several concrete steps down to the tracks. Steve and Jerry pressed against the tunnel wall when they walked by these openings.

Distance from the Kendall/MIT station was marked by numbers painted in white on the tunnel wall. The MBTA engineer at the front of their line stopped in front of the marker for 730 yards. "We figure the closest point to your MIT lab is between the markers for 730 and 780 yards," he said. "Where do you want to start your testing?"

"Let's go to the mid-point of your estimate, at about 755 yards, and set up there," Steve Cheng said. "By the way, how are these tunnels constructed?" he asked the lead engineer.

The MBTA engineer's answer confirmed Jerry's prior understanding that he had reported to the Blair West International team. "Construction varied depending on the depth of the tunnels, the nature of the ground, primarily whether it was soft ground or hard rock, and proximity to water. This portion of the Red Line was built using rebar-reinforced concrete in the walls and roof arch. If you could see through the concrete, you would think, with the rebar mesh all around us, that we were inside a steel cage."

"That kind of structure also might resemble a gigantic antenna," Steve said.

At the midpoint between the markers for 750 and 760 yards, Steve extracted a device from his backpack which he said was a magnetic coupling tester invented and built by the MIT

WiTricity group. It looked like a tablet computer, about half an inch thick, with a touchscreen in front. Steve removed two metal cylinders, each about four inches long and less than an inch in diameter, from the tablet's outer edges. He placed the cylinders on the ground, leaning against the tunnel wall, about one yard apart from each other. He said the cylinders would pick up the magnetic resonance frequency of the tunnel walls and would thereby determine whether the tunnel was receiving electric energy transmitted at that frequency. The cylinders would communicate their measurements back to his tablet device using wireless Bluetooth technology.

"I'll collect electric energy level data now to set a baseline," Steve said. "Then I'll compare my baseline data against the measures that I'll take during the next test in the lab, which will occur in five minutes." As Steve was checking his screen and recording the data on the device's flash memory, another Red Line train churned by.

"OK, here we go," Steve said. "The next lab transmission of an electric energy pulse should occur just about now." The rest of the group watched Steve closely to discern his reaction, if any, while he monitored the screen. The tunnel was dead quiet, no trains nearby. "Wow, is this awesome or what!?" he exclaimed.

"What do you see there?" Jerry asked.

"I just got a resonance reading that matches our transmitter frequency. And there was a big electric power surge in the tunnel."

"I didn't feel anything," one of the MBTA engineers said, watching curiously as Steve monitored the data on his tablet device.

"You wouldn't. You can't feel it. But it happened. I'll correlate the time-stamps when I get back to the lab. This is really cool!"

Twenty One

IT WAS TIME finally to report the results of the Blair West International project to the MBTA. Harry suggested that BWI's findings should be presented jointly to the MBTA and MIT so that they could decide together what to do next. Cuddihy agreed.

The meeting was hosted at MIT by Julia Braun. Attending in addition to Harry, Cuddihy, and Ms. Braun were Jerry, Steve Cheng, Drs. Hersch and Bluestein, and Barry Levin, MIT's General Counsel who sat at the side of the room instead of at the table because, he said, his role was only to observe.

Harry spoke without notes, "Blair West International was hired by the MBTA to discover the cause of the dramatic incidents that are occurring on the Red Line. Through excellent detective work by our team, in particular Jerry Seligman as well as our three analysts, we determined that these incidents, which we call visitations, are concentrated in the portion of the Red Line system that passes close by MIT. Based on Steve Cheng's data and on his analysis, we believe that the visitations are caused by an electromagnetic charge in the Red Line tunnel which energizes the tunnel and the trains passing through the tunnel. We've identified the source of the electromagnetic charge as the energy pulse transmitter in the Bio-Nuclear Systems Laboratory. It is very significant that the visitations on the Red

Line began just after the BSNL started its tests using the energy pulse transmitter. Now, Steve will provide details about his data and answer your questions. Steve, you have the floor."

Steve began, "So, my data show that electrical energy pulses from the BNSL are energizing Red Line trains."

"Hold on a minute, Steve," Dr. Wec Bluestein said. "When we installed the WiTricity system, we were assured by the WiTricity project leaders and by you personally that the energy pulses would be confined to our lab. So are you sure? And if you are, how can this be?"

"It's not what we expected," Steve admitted. "But the data are clear. The Red Line tunnel is magnetically resonant with our energy pulse transmitter. The tunnel receives an energy pulse at the same time as when we bombard the glass incubator in our lab. The received energy is amplified by the tunnel's large size and by its construction with rebar mesh in the concrete walls. Being a reverberant chamber, the tunnel holds the charge and even propagates it in each direction. When Red Line trains pass through the tunnel, it is like they are driving through the center of a resonant magnetic coil and they also become energized."

"Let me get this straight," Cuddihy said, "my Red Line trains are being lit up by your energy pulses."

"Yes. That's one way to say it."

"And that's why riders are seeing ghosts on the trains?"

"I don't know the answer to that question."

"What do you mean, you don't know?"

Harry said, "Jim, we don't know whether the Red Line passengers are seeing ghosts."

Cuddihy responded, "Let him answer. He seems to understand the technologies that are creating this fiasco."

Steve said, "I can tell you about the magnetic coupling of our WiTricity system with the Red Line tunnels and the effect this is having on the Red Line trains, which causes some passengers to believe that they are seeing people who have died. But my data don't tell us that what they are seeing are ghosts. It could be something else."

"Like hallucinations," Dr. Bluestein said.

"Right. Maybe."

Jerry asked, "Steve, you're sure there's an electrical charge inside the train cars, and not only in the tunnel?"

"Yes, I also took measurements on the trains."

Jerry persisted, "And just to be clear, the electrical charge in the trains derives from the charge in the tunnel, which in turn is caused by the energy pulse transmitter in the BNSL."

"That's how it looks to me. It's on the same resonant magnetic frequency as inside the lab."

Cuddihy said, "Then, all you need to do to stop messing up my Red Line passengers is stop blasting the tunnels and trains with your damned energy pulses."

"In principal, yes."

"But in practice it's not so simple," Dr. Bluestein said. "Our lab is obligated contractually to our affiliates to continue running our proof-of-concept tests in order to trigger our next round of funding. It's not our fault that the MBTA's Red Line tunnel is magnetically resonant with our transmitter."

"It may not be your fault," Cuddihy said, his face reddening. "But it is your problem. The Red Line is in chaos and, you may have heard, because of your energy pulses we've already had one passenger fatality on the Longfellow Bridge."

Julia Braun intervened, "Jim, we take responsibility for MIT's role."

"Not just responsibility, Julia. Also a share of the cost. Our lawyers will be in touch about the lawsuit from the victim's family."

Barry Levin, MIT General Counsel, interjected, "Jim, tell them to call me directly."

Julia Braun said, "Steve, this may be a dumb question. Could you adjust the transmitter's resonant frequency so that the tunnel is no longer affected?"

"We could do that. We'll also need to re-calibrate the copper coil on the incubator so that it will couple with the transmitter at the new frequency in order to continue running the BNSL experiments."

"How long would that take?" Dr. Hersch asked.

"Maybe a week or two. The incubator would have to be taken apart, and then re-assembled, and then we'd need to troubleshoot. It depends on whether we hit any problems. This can be a complicated process, as you recall."

"I do indeed," Dr. Hersch said.

Harry said, "Wec, you told us that in the next phase of your tests, you planned to increase the power transmitted by your energy pulses. Could you remind us by how much?"

"In the production phase, we will employ a power level fifty times greater than during our current proof-of-concept tests. Not getting up there immediately, of course, but in progressive stages."

"Jesus, Mary, and Joseph!" Cuddihy groaned.

Barry Levin spoke up again from his seat at the side of the room, "Wec, if you agree, I'll negotiate a mod to the contracts with the BNSL affiliates to allow a short hiatus in your proof-of-concept testing while you transition to a different energy transmission frequency."

Julia Braun asked, "Wec and Suzanne, does that work for you?"

Dr. Hersch replied, "We'll get back to you on that. We have to consider the effects on our experiments of changing the resonant frequencies of the energy pulses. We don't know whether we'll get the same positive results at a different frequency. If not, we'll be stuck, because I doubt that we'd be allowed to revert back to what we are using now."

"I have another question for Steve," Harry said. "Are you confident that the Red Line tunnel would not couple magnetically with the transmitter at a different resonant frequency?"

Steve said, "I'm not sure. We'd have to run tests. The tunnel is so large it may be poly-resonant. By that I mean, that it might couple magnetically at different frequencies."

Cuddihy leaned forward and placed his hands, both clenched into fists, on the table. Grinding out his words between gritted teeth, he said, "This chit-chat is giving me brain bubbles. First I hear cooperation, then I hear doubt and delay. I just want to know, putting aside all the *bullshit*, when will you fix that energy pulse transmitter so that I can tell our General Manager, and the public, that the Red Line is safe again for our regular live passengers?"

Dr. Bluestein said, "I'm sorry that you're frustrated Jim but we're doing nothing wrong in our lab. At every step, we've obtained necessary approvals to proceed further. Why should we put at risk our amazing and important BNSL project after we all have worked so hard to get to this point?"

"Because you have no choice. You're destroying the city's public transit system."

"Well, instead of putting the onus on us, maybe the MBTA could modify the Red Line tunnel so that it doesn't resonate with our transmitter."

Julia Braun said, "We need to work out our position internally at MIT before we can give the MBTA a clear answer."

"You'd better work it out fast," Cuddihy said. "This is not just the MBTA's problem anymore. We have to fix this. Delay will cost you as much as it costs us, or more."

"We understand," Julia said.

As Harry and Jim Cuddihy paused on the sidewalk on Mass Ave in front of Julia Braun's building, Harry said, "Jim, we should talk about what comes next."

"Yes, we should," Cuddihy replied, "Harry, I'm not big on lavishing praise, but thank you. You did what I asked."

"You're welcome."

"You discovered the source of the visitations. We can finally see the end to this thing. You guys are terrific."

"I'm glad we were able to help."

"So your project for me is done. We'll take it from here."

"Are you sure, Jim? You still have to find a solution with MIT, as well as dealing with the other stakeholders, like Attorney Marvin Jones, Red Line passengers, politicians."

"MBTA can handle it. We'll sort out MIT, no matter what they're saying now, and the others. You can turn off your meter."

"Well, alright then, Jim, as of this moment we are no longer working for you," Harry said.

"So noted."

"Now, I have a question for you."

"Shoot."

"Have you considered not ending the Red Line visitations, at least, not entirely?"

"What do you mean?"

"Perhaps you could work something out with MIT to continue energizing the Red Line tunnel after normal operating hours, so that people will not be completely cut off from encounters with their loved ones."

"Like for you and your daughter."

"Yes, but not only for us, obviously."

"No way in hell, Harry."

"That's an understandable first response. We can build on that. Think about it, OK?"

Twenty Two

HARRY BRACED HIMSELF against a pole as his Red Line train car swayed, rattled and creaked its way into Boston where he was to meet Alexandra for coffee.

He'd asked Cuddihy for permission to reveal to Alexandra what he had been doing for the MBTA. "Sure, tell your ex-wife," Cuddihy said. "Just her, though, no-one else. And make sure that she knows that everything you tell her is confidential."

A teen-age girl who was standing next to Harry, where previously he recalled the presence of a cadaverously thin, gangly man with troubled skin, looked up at him and said, "Hi, Daddy."

She was the girl he had seen behind the door of the Red Line train as it left Central Square, the girl whose image was displayed on Alexandra's laptop and copied onto Harry's BlackBerry.

"Ariel," he said. Momentarily he lost the power of speech to say any more than her name. Here after all, finally, was his only child who was lost to him so long ago, lost forever and completely based on everything he knew about the world, standing beside him as if they were in an alternate universe in which she had not died but had grown into a teenager from whom it was commonplace to hear, "Hi, Daddy."

When Alexandra described her joy to be able to see and hold their daughter, Harry had imagined how wonderful his own encounter with Ariel would be. He had been her Daddy. Her tiny hand had grasped his fingers when she was learning to walk. He had read to her at bedtime, comforted her in his arms when she was upset. He had dreamt of this moment. They would hug. She would say how she loved him and he would tell her the same. There would be tears in his eyes and in hers as well.

Unaccountably, however, joy was now in short supply. The girl clearly was peeved. She scowled at him. Her dark eyebrows were drawn together in resentment. "You hate me," she said.

Harry replied, "Are you Ariel?" Perhaps there had been a mistake. Where was the love?

"So you don't recognize me. Mom did. Why don't you?"

"Of course I do. It's so incredible to see you," Harry said.

"I don't want to talk with you anymore," the girl said. "Go away." The glare in the girl's intensely dark eyes reminded him of Alexandra's when she had been crossed. "You don't care about me."

"Ariel…"

"What?"

"What have I done?"

"You want to get rid of me so that I can't visit Mom, or you, anymore."

"That's not true."

"Yes it is. Don't deny it."

"Ariel, do you know how you are able to visit us?"

"No, I am just here."

"Then why do you believe…?"

"I don't want to talk about it. You know what you've done. Stop asking me questions."

"Ariel, I've missed you terribly," Harry said.

Ariel rolled her eyes in exasperation. "Sure you have," she said.

"We may not be able to meet again. It would mean a lot to me for us to hug while we still can."

"While we still can. If that was so important, if you missed me so much, you would not be trying now to get rid of me."

"Ariel, I am not trying to get rid of you."

"You know it's true. Stop denying it."

Ariel's baleful expression warned Harry against further attempts to deny his wrongdoing. She added, "Why won't you help me and Mom, even if you don't care about seeing me yourself?" and then maintained a glum silence as their train pulled out from his planned stop at Downtown Crossing. They arrived next at South Station. Some riders got off and others boarded, and the doors slid closed. Ariel made a reluctant move towards Harry that suggested she might relent and be willing to be hugged, albeit sullenly with her arms down at her sides, but as the train left South Station she disappeared, and Harry found himself gesturing towards the very thin man who was attempting to ignore him.

Harry was already fifteen minutes late for his coffee with Alexandra by the time he made it back to the Downtown Crossing station. He climbed the stairs two-at-a-time out of the station and then half quick-walked and half jogged to the Starbucks on Winter Street where they had arranged to meet.

"You're late," Alexandra said, not sounding particularly friendly. She never did like to be kept waiting. "Another five minutes and I'd have been gone."

"I have a good excuse."

"Yes, well, you said you could reveal your big secret now. Is it about the visits on the Red Line?"

"It is. But first, my excuse for being late; I met Ariel on my way here. We were together on the train until we reached South Station, then she vanished."

"That's wonderful, Harry!" Alexandra exclaimed, forgiving him for the moment.

"Have you seen Ariel again?"

"No, and I've devoted hours on the Red Line looking for her. How was she?"

"She's angry with me."

"Why?"

"She said that because of me, she would be unable to meet us again. She said that I don't care.

"Is that true, Harry?"

"I do care, Alexandra."

"You didn't answer my question."

"She does have a point about the work I've been doing."

"She does?"

"That's why I wanted to talk with you." Harry described the Blair West International project for the MBTA, and their discovery of MIT's probable role in causing the visitations.

"So, Ariel is right," Alexandra said, scowling as she took on what Harry had just told her. "Because of you, we'll be cut off from Ariel again just when she's come back to us. You've shown the MBTA how to do it. You gave them the tools."

"That was our assignment, Alexandra."

"Harry, what were you thinking?"

"I don't know what else I could have done. I took the case. I made a commitment to our client."

He'd done his job. And now he was catching hell, chastised by his daughter who wasn't even alive, by his ex-wife, and by an irate psychic. Chastising he could take. Worse was the nagging hollow sensation inside that however unlikely the chance that people were in fact communicating with their loved ones on the Red Line, that he might have contributed to destroying that once-in-forever chance, not only for himself but also for others including, in particular, Alexandra, who sat glowering at him, grasping her coffee like she might at any moment douse him with it.

"You could have resigned from your precious project," Alexandra said. "You could have told me earlier; I might have thought of something before it was too late."

"I did propose to our client that he allow visitations to continue."

"You did?"

"I asked whether he'd consider it if they were late at night when they would not inconvenience regular Red Line passengers."

"And, how did he respond?"

"No interest. He's determined to return the Red Line back to the way it was before."

"Why is it up to the MBTA to decide whether we meet our loved ones who we miss so terribly?"

"Alexandra, what is the MBTA supposed to do? Turn the Red Line over to people searching for spirits of deceased family members?"

"If you mean, like me, searching for our Ariel, yes, I do mean that. Why the hell not?"

A silence settled heavily between them as they sat across from each other at their small Starbucks table. It was not a companionable silence. Finally Alexandra, who had been looking everywhere around the Starbucks store except at Harry, turned to face him. "I can't handle what you've done, Harry. I don't think we should see each other anymore."

"Meeting for coffee twice in three years is not exactly seeing each other."

"You know what I mean."

"If that's what you want," Harry said. He stood up from their table and left to return to his office, without looking back.

PART TWO

THE VISITATION ROOM

Twenty Three

HARRY ANSWERED HIS PHONE, unsure whether he was dreaming. The clock radio by his bed reported the time as 2:44 A.M. "Hello?"

"Harry! Are you awake?"

"I am now."

"This is Alexandra!"

"I recognize your voice."

"Are you busy this morning when you get into work? We need to talk."

"I'll try to fit you in," Harry said.

"Good. I'll be at your office first thing. Now, get some sleep. I want you well rested when we meet tomorrow."

When Harry arrived at his office, Molly told him, "Alexandra is waiting for you in the conference room. She insists that you join her there now before you do anything else."

"So I wasn't dreaming," Harry said when he stepped into the conference room and saw Alexandra at the head of the table in Dr. Gourmelon's favorite seat.

"I have a brilliant idea," Alexandra replied.

"I thought we wouldn't be seeing each other."

"I changed my mind."

"Did you really call me this morning at 2:44 A.M.?"

"I did. So what? You'll thank me. Take a seat." Alexandra could hardly have been more different than yesterday's morose, angry ex-wife. Smiling, her lithe body almost dancing in her seat, her hands in constant motion, her dark eyes lit with enthusiasm, she was a new woman.

Harry sat.

"Here's my idea," she said. "Let's create a special place where we can meet Ariel, like on the Red Line."

"A special place? How?"

"Don't be slow, Harry. We already know the technologies that will be needed. Didn't you say yesterday it had something to do with electric energy pulses?"

"Did someone spike your orange juice this morning?"

"Answer my question."

Harry answered it, "We discovered that the Red Line tunnel is magnetically resonant with an electric power transmitter being used by the lab at MIT, and that this resonance is amplified somehow to energize the trains that run through the tunnel."

"So we'll use the lab's energy pulse technology to create the same conditions in our special place."

"But we don't actually know how everything works to enable the visitations."

"What do you mean, you don't know how it works?" Alexandra demanded.

"For example, do the visitations result solely from the energy pulses or are they produced by an interaction between the energy transmissions and something on the Red Line trains? Do attributes of specific passengers play a role? Also…," Harry paused.

"Yes…What?"

"Alexandra, you must understand, there is still a basic question about what's been happening on the Red Line trains, about whether the visitations are actually occurring or are just imagined by those of us who've experienced them."

"Are you saying we only imagined that we met Ariel? That she wasn't there?"

"We can't be sure."

"You told me she was angry with you. How could you have imagined that?"

"Maybe I felt guilty about helping the MBTA and I projected that onto Ariel's resentment of me."

Alexandra said, "Harry, you know that I'm not a gullible, fanciful person. I'm hard-headed."

"Hard as granite," Harry agreed.

"I believe with my hard head that Ariel came to me, that I saw her, that we talked, and we hugged."

"So it doesn't matter to you that maybe it was all in your mind?"

"I don't believe that it was all in my mind, but anyway it doesn't matter, Harry. The experience was so real."

"You'd need a lot of money to build the special place for visitations."

"I've thought of that. I'll fund it myself. I'll sell my shares in ABTDigital."

"Alexandra, identifying the relevant features of Red Line trains, and then re-creating them in your own special place, could cost millions, assuming that it's possible to do it."

"I can afford it."

"It's your money…"

"Yes, it is."

"And you can spend it any way you want…"

"What I want is to see Ariel again."

"There's a better way."

"What way is that?" Although she bristled at being challenged, Alexandra had learned from her experience as an entrepreneur that it was in her interest to listen to suggestions that might help her to achieve her objectives. "I'm not giving up on meeting Ariel," she said.

"You don't have to."

"So tell me, what's the better way, Harry?"

"You can fund the special place by creating a new business around it."

"This is personal, Harry. I'm not looking to build another business."

"You'll need cooperation from MIT and the MBTA. They may offer sympathy about Ariel but they'll be much more supportive as stakeholders in a new business."

"I can understand that," Alexandra agreed. "They're not sentimental."

Harry continued, "This is not just about us and Ariel. You've seen the crowds at the Red Line stations and on the trains. We can build the special place so that others can meet their loved ones as well. We'll share it with them. They'll be happy for the opportunity. We'll have no shortage of customers. And because of the revenues that they'll produce, you'll have access to the capital that you need to execute your plan."

"Wrong pronoun. That *we* need."

"OK, that *we* need," Harry said.

"You've convinced me, Harry!" Alexandra said, brightening considerably. "Let's make it a business. Then there's just one other thing…"

"What's that?"

"Someone has to take charge."

"You're the boss, Alexandra."

"No, Harry, I nominate you to serve as CEO of our new venture."

"Why me? This is your idea. You run with it and I'll support you."

"I would, except that ABTDigital still requires too much of my attention."

"So does Blair West International, in my case."

"Jerry Seligman can take over for you at Blair West International. He's been there with you since the first day when you founded the firm. You know he can do it. And you'll still have Blair, of course, running things in Hong Kong."

"I'll have to think about it."

"Look, Harry, you're perfect for our CEO. You're obsessively well organized; you have a track record assembling and managing teams; and you know as much about the visitations as anyone. With Ariel out there, you have a big personal stake in making this work, just like I do. And you owe it to me, and to her, after what you did for the MBTA. Anyway, you should try something new after only doing consulting for your whole life."

"Consulting is what I do, Alexandra. I'm good at it."

"Don't worry. I won't abandon you. I'll be very much involved at every step, just not the person in charge."

"But you'd still try to exercise control, only you'd do it through me."

"Of that, you can be sure," Alexandra replied with a big smile. "This is too important for me to sit idly by and let you screw it up."

"I'm inspired by your confidence."

"Don't fight it, Harry. Say 'Yes.' You know you want to."

If Alexandra's scheme actually worked, they could see Ariel again, whatever that meant, and he'd have more time with Alexandra, an alluring prospect when she wasn't angry or depressed. "OK, I'll do it," Harry said.

"I knew you'd agree. We're going to make this work, Harry.

"Yes."

"We'll be with our daughter again."

"Yes."

"Nothing will stop us. Nothing!"

Twenty Four

"NOW, HARRY, AS our new CEO, tell me, what shall we do next?" Alexandra asked.

Taking the reins that she had thrust into his hands, Harry said, "We need to collect measurements on the Red Line while the visitations are still happening so our first priority is to get to Jim Cuddihy before he blocks the visitations. I want to recruit Steve Cheng to join us since he understands the technologies, and to get MIT on our side since we'll need access to its energy pulse system. And we'll need to raise working capital."

"OK, let's get started," Alexandra said.

"Isn't that my line, as your CEO and leader?"

"I'm right behind you," Alexandra said. "Now, let's call Jim Cuddihy."

When Harry introduced Alexandra, Cuddihy remarked jovially that she was much more attractive than Harry had led him to believe. Alexandra acknowledged the compliment with a slight smile and nod. Cuddihy said, "So, Harry, what are you selling?"

"Not selling, Jim. We're here to let you in on an opportunity."

"Aha."

"I heard that your engineers are working on a system to block the lab's energy pulses so that they won't affect the Red Line."

"Where did you hear that?" Cuddihy asked, somewhat less cheerfully. "It's supposed to be confidential."

"I have my sources, Jim."

"Alright, but keep it to yourself. What we've designed will jam the electromagnetic signal coming into the tunnel from the MIT transmitter. It's like putting up a magnetic shield. As soon as we finish testing, I'll get it installed in the Red Line tunnel under Main Street."

"When do you expect that will be?"

"Five weeks, plus or minus. I'm cracking the whip to make our engineers work faster. They're whining about the pressure but I can probably get them down to three weeks. If they had their way, they'd test forever. Why do you want to know?"

Alexandra said, "We want to create our own space for visitations of loved ones like those now occurring on the Red Line."

"Uh huh, Alexandra. That makes good sense given all the fun we're having now on the Red Line."

Harry said, "So we need time to take measurements on the Red Line while the visitations are still happening."

"Yeah, so?"

"It will help us if your magnetic shield were not installed too soon."

"Not installed too soon!" Cuddihy blurted. "Jesus F. Christ! I'm killing myself trying to get it installed yesterday! We've finally found a way to put things right on the Red Line, and after all the shit I've been taking, are you out of your minds?"

Alexandra said, "We understand, Jim. The visitations are disrupting your Red Line service."

"And exposing us to legal extortion from Attorney Marvin Jones any time that a passenger has a bad experience."

"But there's another way to look at it," Alexandra said.

"What might that be? I know what I'm looking at and I don't like it."

"Take a step back. Think about what's really important."

"I have. And I know the answer. Fixing the Red Line."

"Another step farther back, Jim. Think about how we're all mortal, how we all suffer loss. All of us, you, Harry, me, everyone. Every person confronts death, the loss of people who are close to them, and then their own. It's horrible, and we have absolutely no choice in the matter."

"We're born, we die. That's what churches are for."

"For some, that's true. But churches carry a lot of baggage and they're not for everyone. The visitations on the Red Line have provided wonderful moments for many people, including religious people. I know that first-hand, as does Harry."

"You're referring to your daughter."

"Yes, our daughter Ariel, whom we lost years ago when she was just a baby, has visited both Harry and me on the Red Line, and we hope to meet her again."

"Is that what this is all about? As I told Harry earlier, I'm sorry about your daughter but I have a public transit system to run," Cuddihy said.

Alexandra said, "We believe that our special place could make a big difference to people's lives like the Red Line encounters have. We also believe that we can pay our way because it could be a really great business."

"Alexandra, with all respect, you can't be objective."

"So listen to why we think so," Alexandra said, with some asperity. "As you may know, Jim, this wouldn't be my first start-up."

"I know. I've heard of ABTDigital."

"Actually, the MBTA is one of our good customers."

"I know that as well."

"Being in contact with VCs all the time, I see lots of business proposals. I know what to look for. I can tell you that this new business will have everything, unlimited customer demand, a feasible execution strategy, and no serious competition. People will be glad to pay for visitations like Harry and I had on the Red Line with our Ariel."

"That may be," Cuddihy replied. "But our plan to stop these so-called visitations on the Red Line was approved by all the top MBTA execs, me included, and required a lot of handholding of the politicians and everyone else. What you're asking for would mean a big step backwards."

Harry said, "Not permanently, Jim, just for a short while."

"How short?"

"Just until we've collected measurements of relevant conditions on the Red Line so that we can replicate them."

"Sorry, Harry. I can't delay the development of the magnetic shield. If I did, and if another Red Line passenger were hurt while visitations were still going on, the lawyers would be all over us like white on rice. I might as well hand Marvin Jones, Esq., the keys to our transit system."

"So don't delay the development of the magnetic shield," Alexandra said. "Just stop cracking your whip to speed it up."

"I'd like to help. I owe Harry for finding the source of the Red Line visitations as quickly as he did.. But they're costing us money and they're riling the powers-that-be."

Harry said, "Jim, we'll pay the MBTA substantial compensation for not accelerating your deployment of the magnetic shield."

"Substantial money would definitely make a difference," Cuddihy acknowledged.

"We're not asking you to delay it. Just don't push it as hard."

"How much time would you need?"

"We don't know yet," Harry said. "Steve Cheng can give us an estimate. I'd guess five or six weeks, about the same time as you estimated it would take the engineers to complete their testing if you weren't hectoring them to work faster. That's all we ask."

"Fuck, Harry," Cuddihy said. "OK, send me something describing your business plan and how the MBTA will be compensated and I'll review it with our General Manager. Keep me posted. If you leave me hanging, I'll whip the engineers twice as hard."

The Elevator Pitch Café just up Massachusetts Avenue from MIT, where the MIT campus verges into Central Square, offers more than caffeine re-fueling. Popularly known as the LP, it provides a venue for advancement of Commerce. Its tables are put to productive use by recruiters and job applicants, prospective business partners, investors and entrepreneurs, writers and agents, students and tutors, researchers and grant-givers, fundraisers and philanthropists, and real estate brokers and homeowners ready to make a change, in short, by people who are buying and people who are selling.

When Steve Cheng entered the LP, Harry caught his eye and Steve came over to be introduced to Alexandra. After they shook hands, Steve excused himself briefly to pick up a coffee, and then returned to join them at the table.

"I've been looking forward to meeting you, Ms. Ben-Tov," he said.

"Call me Alexandra," she said. "Harry's told me many good things about you."

"I attended your presentation at Sloan on entrepreneurship," Steve said. "Very inspiring."

"Thank you, Steve. I'm glad the Sloanies keep inviting me back. I believe that Harry has told you about our idea?"

"To open up locations where people can experience visitations like those on the Red Line."

"What do you think of it?"

"I can see the appeal. It's a cool idea."

Harry said, "In our locations, we'll need to replicate the conditions on the Red Line that enable the visitations, the active ingredients. Do you think the technology will be available for us to do that?"

"Well, we know that the BNSL's WiTricity system is energizing the Red Line trains so you'd need to re-produce that same energizing effect. Maybe there are other factors as well. You can take measurements on the trains, isolate what seems to be important, and then test to see what works."

"So, technically, it's possible." Alexandra said.

"It should be. You'd have to try, in order to find out."

"Glad to hear it," Alexandra said. "Steve, we didn't ask you to meet with us just to pick your brain. We want you to join us."

Steve looked surprised. "I love what I'm doing now at MIT."

Harry said, "To be clear about our motives, Steve, we have a personal stake in this because we want to see our daughter again."

"I heard about that from Jerry," Steve said.

"But we also believe that this is a great business opportunity on its own merits. Otherwise, Alexandra wouldn't put her reputation behind it."

"What would you want me to do?"

"We want you to replicate the enabling factors for visitations on the Red Line. As you just told us, this means taking measurements, running tests, designing the test room. When our technology is working, we want you to build our Visitation centers. And then when we're operational, if all goes well, you'll become our Chief Technology Officer."

"Would I have technicians and engineers to help me?"

"Yes, of course."

Alexandra said, "Steve, we need you. We'll pay you at a level competitive with anything you could get at another start-up, which certainly will exceed what you're getting now at MIT. You will be employee number three in our start-up with all that

that implies for your equity stake in the venture. But even more than that, you'll be part of something that could change the world, and you'll help to steer it from the beginning."

"Will you join us?" Harry asked.

"Do you need more time to think about it?" Alexandra asked.

"No," Steve said, "Count me in."

As they convened in Julia Braun's conference room at MIT, Harry introduced Alexandra to Julia, to Drs. Bluestein and Hersch, and to MIT General Counsel Barry Levin. Also at the table was Steve Cheng.

Alexandra spoke first.

"Harry and I are here to describe a new venture that is very important to us personally," she said. "It will also be a fantastic new business. We requested this meeting with MIT stakeholders because this is the most efficient way for us to get started." She described how the venture's customers would communicate with their departed, just like on the Red Line, in what she and Harry were now calling "Visitation Rooms."

Suzanne Hersch asked, "Steve, do you believe that Harry and Alexandra can build a room that is enough like Red Line trains in terms of what they call relevant attributes, to enable visitations to occur?"

"Yes, in principle," Steve replied.

"In principle?"

"It should be possible. But no-one has done this before, so getting it right would involve experimentation, and testing."

"We're certainly familiar with that scenario," Dr. Hersch said.

"Where do we come in?" Julia asked.

Harry replied, "We'll want to purchase a license to use MIT's wireless energy transmission system, like the system now deployed in the BSNL. We'll request space at MIT for our test room. We'll grant equity points to MIT as one of the founding partners of our new venture. We'll leave it up to you how to share these equity points among the MIT Corporation and MIT's most direct participants in the venture such as Wec and Suzanne."

"Harry, what roles will you and Alexandra play?" Dr. Bluestein asked.

Harry said, "We'll work together to get our venture started. Alexandra will raise money from VCs and will Chair our Board of Directors. At her request, I've agreed to serve as CEO."

Julia turned to the MIT General Counsel and asked, "Barry, do you have an opinion about this?"

"I do," Levin said. "This all sounds very exciting and I don't want to be the skunk at the picnic…"

"No need to stretch for metaphors, Barry," Dr. Bluestein said. "It's enough that you're a lawyer."

"It's my job to protect the Institute," Levin replied, not amused.

"Sorry. Go ahead."

Levin continued, "Here's the thing. Will MIT be associated with a venture that sells spiritualism, telling people that they will be able to communicate with ghosts, exploiting their credulity and their grief? Alternatively, what if our technologies produce a form of mind altering, like dispensing an hallucinogen? In either case, it will not reflect well on MIT. Also, lawsuits will rain down on us if side-effects emerge later from exposure to our licensed technology, or if a customer harms himself after a bad encounter."

Alexandra replied, "Barry, we have the same concerns. Customers will sign releases acknowledging that no visits from loved ones are guaranteed and that they are proceeding at their own risk. During our testing phase, we'll monitor effects on our test partners' physical and mental health to ensure a very low probability of medical issues."

"I'll want to see the results of those tests," Levin said. "And also the language in the waivers that will be signed by the customers."

"We'll share all of that with you," Alexandra promised.

"I may have some suggestions."

"Absolutely, glad to hear them," Alexandra said.

Julia asked, "Any other thoughts from around the table?"

Dr. Bluestein said, "I've worked out a theory that may explain the visitations on the Red Line, if you're interested."

"Yes, Wec, we're all ears," Harry said.

"It goes back to the fact that animals are sensitive to electromagnetic signals that emanate both from manmade technologies and from natural phenomena. For example, two hundred years ago, Galvani, the famous Italian scientist, inserted a copper hook into the spine of a dead frog and then noted that the frog's legs twitched during a passing thunderstorm."

"One reason that spinal copper hooks never caught on as a fashion accessory," Alexandra said, supportively.

"Yes, Alexandra, twitching legs were a big turn off," Dr. Bluestein said. "More recently, scientists have found that atmospheric electromagnetism produces an increase in negative ions. So, for example, the density of negative ions is greater in the vicinity of lightning, or waterfalls, or ocean waves, or breezes through forests. Why do we care about this? First, because negative ions are atomic particles in the atmosphere that have extra electrons, they cancel out positive ions, which have fewer electrons and tend make people depressed. And, second, and this is a key point, negative ions are believed to increase the level of serotonin in the brain, a chemical that improves your mood. You see where I'm going with this?"

"Negative ions make you happier," Harry said.

"To put it very simply, my hypothesis is that our energy pulses are increasing the density of negative ions in the Red Line trains, and one way or another these negative ions are altering the minds of Red Line passengers. Some of the more susceptible passengers believe that they are seeing their loved ones."

Alexandra said, "Hang on, Wec, I have to stop you there. It seems to me that you're saying that when Harry and I encountered our daughter Ariel on the Red Line, we were just hallucinating as if we were on some kind of negative-ion-induced LSD trips."

"I wouldn't put it that way, Alexandra."

"How would you put it, then?"

"I'm not talking about LSD trips. I'm providing an explanation doesn't require believing in ghosts which, for me, is a big plus."

"When I met Ariel, I was just as lucid as you are here, today. She was not imaginary. She was not a figment. Maybe your negative ions didn't make me, and Harry, and all the others hallucinate. Maybe instead the negative ions had a different effect, making us much more sensitive, or creating an opening for her to come through."

Dr. Bluestein was about to reply when Harry raised his hand to stop him. "Wec, it doesn't matter who's right," he said.

"I want to respond to Alexandra."

"No, not now, Wec," Harry replied. "Your theory is intriguing. It's worth exploring further. For now, however, the most important thing is that the visitation experience is very intense and realistic, as both Alexandra and I found out. The Visitation Rooms will provide an opportunity for people to continue having this kind of experience, whether or not it results from enhanced serotonin in our brains."

"Suit yourself," Dr. Bluestein said. "But you don't need paranormal fairy tales involving openings, and so on, when science can do the job."

Julia asked, "Suzanne, what's your take on all this?"

Suzanne Hersch replied, "Science is amazing in the way that it leads you down unexpected paths. What Wec and I are doing at the BNSL is already wonderfully exciting. Now we have an opportunity also to contribute to a venture that explores life after death. I'm all for it."

Dr. Bluestein said, "I'm for it too, mainly because I can't wait to see what happens when the Visitation Rooms are built."

Julia said, "Unless Barry objects violently, I agree that we should support Alexandra's and Harry's plan."

Levin said he had expressed his concerns but if Julia and others at MIT wished to proceed anyway, he would not oppose it.

Harry said, "We haven't mentioned Steve's role. Steve understands the technologies better than any of us. So during our test phase, we've asked him to take the lead in developing and building our Visitation Rooms. When we go live, we'll also expect him to serve as our Chief Technology Officer."

"Now I do object," Suzanne Hersch said. "We need Steve in our lab. You're trying to poach him from us."

"And he has knowledge of our work that we must protect," Dr. Bluestein said.

"We will not compete in any way with BNSL," Harry replied. "And we'll pay to license the technology that you're using."

Steve said, "Dr. Bluestein, I'll continue to protect BNSL's confidentiality."

"So, I assume you've already decided to join them," Dr. Bluestein said.

"I have. It's something I want to do. I'll still be available to support the lab if you need my help."

Suzanne Hersch said, "Well, it's wrong that you're leaving us now, Steve, but it's your decision. We won't hold you up."

"Anytime you need me, Dr. Hersch, 24/7. You have my cell number."

"If necessary, I'll take you up on that, you can be sure."

Julia said, "I think we're all in agreement. Harry and Alexandra, please send us the paperwork on the financial deal that you are proposing for MIT."

When Harry returned to the Blair West International office, he asked Jerry Seligman to join him in his office.

He told Jerry, "I need to focus on our new venture. I want you to take over for me managing Blair West International in the US."

"Is Blair on board with that?"

"I'll confirm it with him as soon as you agree."

"Obviously I'll do it," Jerry said. "I've basically been running the place anyway."

Harry called Stephen Blair, his business partner in Hong Kong. Blair was a life-long expatriate Brit, born in Singapore, and brought up by nannies there and in India where his father served as a military attaché to Her Majesty's embassies. Blair and Harry had collaborated on projects in Hong Kong and Malaysia while both worked at Roland L. Week, Inc.

Just before RLW slid into its final death spiral, they resigned to form Blair West International, comprising Blair and his assistant Elizabeth Lee in Hong Kong, and Harry and Jerry in Cambridge.

Their new company's first project, for Mr. Shih, head of the Hong Kong Government's Communications Department, confronted them with money laundering and murder. The murder victim was Erin Haig, a business reporter in Hong Kong who was collaborating with Harry and Blair, and with whom Harry had become personally involved. Harry's role in solving Erin's murder had generated fifteen minutes of fame for him as "Hero Consultant" and brought international recognition to their new firm.

Harry and Blair talked by phone at least once every week and maintained a project management system that was accessible online in both offices, so Blair was fully aware of Blair West International's recently-concluded engagement for the MBTA. He knew about the other-worldly events on the Red Line. However, Harry's plan to leave BWI in order to lead a venture to open Visitation Rooms was a surprise.

"I wish you'd asked me first," Blair said.

"I didn't want to bring this up with you until we had agreement from the MBTA and MIT."

"Well, Jerry will make an excellent managing director for us in the US but I should have been told earlier. How will you handle your client relationships?"

"I'll contact each of them directly. They already know Jerry since we work together on most of our assignments. I'll still be associated with Blair West International as a partner, unless you object, and I'll be readily accessible to Jerry if he needs help."

"Yes, do stay on as a partner. I have no interest in buying out your share in the company. You said something about a kicker for Blair West International. Have you hired a football player?"

"Blair West International will have a financial stake in success of our Visitation Rooms. I'm setting up a BWI venture fund that will receive equity in recognition of our work to determine the cause of the Red Line visitations."

"Alright, Harry, you have my blessing. Tell Jerry to contact me so that we can make appropriate arrangements. Do call me occasionally and also keep me posted by email when you feel the urge. By the way, what are you calling your new venture?"

"Our code name is 2V, for 'second-visit.'"

At the top of Alexandra's list of prospective investors was Edward Hutchins, managing partner of Light House Capital, a venture capital firm that put to work funds residing in a Hutchins family trust. Light House Capital occupied the entire top floor of a three-story brick building that it owned on Merchants Wharf, a renovated wharf that jutted into Boston's harbor on wood pilings that dated from the early 1800s. The firm's office décor spoke softly of Old Money, featuring exposed wooden beams, model sailing ships, and brass fittings. Edward could trace his family tree back to the Mayflower. Subsequent Hutchins ancestors had helped to found the Commonwealth of Massachusetts; had served under George Washington when the General was headquartered in Cambridge during the Revolutionary War; and, several generations later, had led units of New England soldiers during the Civil War. In the 1880s, Edward's great-great-grandfather Hiram Hutchins founded a bank in Boston that prospered nicely in family hands until 1983 when it was merged into the First Bank of Boston. Following a family tradition, Edward attended Harvard University and then, after he graduated, took time off to explore the world. A passionate mountain climber, Edward persuaded the Boston Museum of Science, where one of his uncles was a Trustee, to sponsor his climbs of five peaks, each on a different continent, and each exceeding 18,000 feet, including Everest in the Himalayas, McKinley in Alaska, Aconcagua in the Andes, Elbrus in the Caucasus, and Kilimanjaro in Africa. Edward's photographs from his climbs were on permanent display in the Museum's Explorers' Gallery and had been published in the *National Geographic*.

Edward looked older than his fifty-four years because of his white hair, his ascetically thin, even gaunt frame, and his posture that was slightly stooped due to a back injury sustained on one of his climbs, but he still chopped all of his own firewood for a wood-burning stove that heated his home, a converted horse barn in the Town of Lincoln, west of Boston.

Light House Capital had done well from its investment in ABTDigital and since then Edward frequently solicited

Alexandra's opinions on other investment opportunities. When she had called him about 2V, he said he wanted to know more.

Edward greeted Alexandra, European style, with a kiss on each cheek, and shook Harry's hand warmly when Alexandra introduced them. "Ah, the mysterious Harry West," he said. "The blast from Alexandra's past."

"And present," Alexandra said. "We're partners in our new venture."

After one of Edward's assistants delivered tea to their conference room, he said, "Tell me about 2V."

Alexandra described their concept for Visitation Rooms. "And the financials aren't bad either," she said. "We expect to reach positive cash flow by our second year, when we'll have multiple Visitation Rooms open, and should be able to self-finance growth after that."

Edward said, "I'm always interested in financials, Alexandra, but first I need to process the part about meeting spirits. You believe that you can actually enable visits from spirits of the departed, in your Visitation Rooms?"

Harry replied, "Like on the Red Line, people will see, talk with, and touch their loved ones. But whether the visitors are actual spirits or some other kind of manifestation, we don't know."

"I don't believe in ghosts."

"Nor do I," Harry said. "But I have to admit that I'm unsettled by what I've seen on the Red Line."

Alexandra jumped in, "Edward, both Harry and I met our daughter Ariel while we were on Red Line trains."

"What was it like for you, seeing her?"

"Intense," Alexandra said.

"My mother passed eight years ago," Edward said. "I wonder if I would meet her again in your Visitation Room."

"As we'll tell our customers, we can't guarantee a visit from a loved one," Harry said. "On the other hand, we won't open our first Visitation Room until we know that our technology works. To ensure that it does, we're planning first to construct a test room at MIT."

"So there's a risk that your technology won't work."

"There is. We won't know until we try."

"If it does work," Edward said, "I'll be one of your first customers. I miss her."

"We'll be there as well for our Ariel," Alexandra said.

Edward asked, "Will you have any competitors?"

"Possibly," Harry said, "but we'll have a significant head-start with the technology we're licensing from MIT and our testing on the Red Line."

"This is all very strange," Edward said.

"Is that a problem for you?" Alexandra asked.

"No, I like it." Edward said. "2V would be Light House Capital's first portfolio investment that offers access to the spirits. The religions have done quite well with this space. So if 2V works as you expect, and you capture some of their market share, I can see how you could get huge."

"Edward, you get it, and that's why we brought this to you," Alexandra said. "I've always said you are one of the smartest VCs I know."

Edward laughed and said, "I'll assume that's a compliment, Alexandra. How much are you looking for?"

Harry replied, "Two million to get us through our development phase and into our second year of operation."

Edward signed a standard Non-Disclosure Agreement, and Harry handed him a binder with 2V's projected financials.

Alexandra asked, "Can you get back to us quickly, Edward? We're on a tight schedule to collect data in the Red Line train cars so that we can build our 2V test room."

"How much time can you give me?"

"We're telling each of our prospective investors that they have two days to decide."

Twenty Five

JIM, CUDDIHY ASSIGNED two MBTA engineers to help Steve Cheng calibrate energy levels and the chemical composition of the air in Red Line train cars before, during, and after electric energy pulses from the BNSL.

Steve hired an MIT grad student to write a software program to replicate the features of Red Line train cars in the 2V test room, including an algorithm to specify the effectively delivered power needed for the test room given its smaller size.

The 2V test room was constructed in the basement of MIT's Center for Life Systems, the same building that housed the BNSL. Following Steve's detailed plans based on his computer model, carpenters attached a magnetically-resonant steel mesh on three of the test room's walls and on its ceiling. Energy-reflective two-way glass was installed in the fourth wall separating the test room from the viewing area, which was formerly an adjoining closet. The viewing area provided space for monitoring equipment and for up to three people if they didn't mind standing close to each other. As in the BNSL, the floor of the viewing area was raised in order to accommodate a WiTricity transmitter that would beam energy pulses into the test room.

Harry speculated that objects inside the Red Line trains – for example the cloth-covered seats – might have interacted in some manner with the electric charges, so Cuddihy lent 2V a bench of three Red Line seats that Steve placed along one of the test room walls.

It took four weeks for Steve and his crew to build the 2V test room in which they could reproduce the energy level measured on the Red Line trains. The first 2V test partners were two white rabbits, a hamster, and Steve's cat. Whether they were visited by fellow animal spirits was hard to determine. Apart from occasional twitches of their paws and tails when the room was energized, they did not display any alarm, or joy, or any other type of excitement while they napped in their respective cages. Most significantly, the furry volunteers' vital signs remained within normal ranges and at the end of their sessions they emerged still alive.

Harry engaged Dr. Dhwani Patel, a physician-researcher at Massachusetts General Hospital, to assess potential health effects on humans from exposure in the energized test room. For this purpose, Dr. Patel developed a multi-part health-monitoring regime. A record of test partners' vital signs would be monitored using gear attached to various parts of their bodies. They would be interviewed about what they saw and felt, digital cameras would collect a searchable video record of events in the room, and subsequent follow-up interviews would be conducted to reveal any delayed effects.

In week five, Steve declared the test room ready for 2V's first human test partner. Molly Lu volunteered. She told Harry that she wanted another chance to meet Robbie. After signing consent forms which absolved both 2V and MIT of any liability for any physical or mental injuries, Molly was outfitted with sensors connected by small suction cups on her wrists and chest, and with a beanie sensor-cap to wear on her head that had been developed in an MIT neurosciences lab to measure brain waves.

Each sensor was connected by a hair-thin wire to a DataPak device that Molly put in a side pocket of a cotton jacket provided by 2V for the test. The DataPak had the dimensions and weight of a pack of cards and a USB port for insertion of a flash memory drive.

"Here's what's going to happen," Steve told Molly, while Harry and Alexandra stood beside her, "You'll sit in the easy chair in the center of the room. You don't have to, but I'd prefer that you stay seated while you are in the room. There is a remote controller on the arm of the easy chair that you can use to select background music and wallpaper video on the flat screen that's hanging on the wall facing the chair. You can dim the lights but you can't turn them off entirely since we need some light for our video recording. OK?"

"Yes."

"You'll probably be thinking about Robbie. It's OK for you to look at a photograph of him if you've brought one."

"I don't need a photo of Robbie to remember him," Molly said.

"If you want anything, anything at all, just say so out loud. We'll hear you and you'll hear us when we talk to you. We'll be watching through the glass. This glass is two-way so you'll be able to see us as well. If you want to break off the session for any reason just let us know, and we'll end it immediately."

"How long will I be in there?"

"Fifteen minutes, about the same time as it takes to ride the Red Line between Davis Square and South Station."

Once Molly was settled in the easy chair, Steve tapped a touch-screen hand-held device to energize the room. A monitor in the viewing area tracked the results of measurements taken every tenth of a second. A dotted line on the screen rose quickly towards another line that represented the target energy level. In another window on the same monitor, a digital counter tracked the increase in density of the room atmosphere's negative ions, a measurement suggested by Dr. Wec Bluestein.

At first, Molly remained quietly in the chair with her eyes closed. After ten minutes, she opened her eyes and used the remote to select an image for the video screen, ocean waves crashing against a rocky shore. When fifteen minutes had elapsed, Steve pressed a button on a console which turned on a speaker in the room and he asked, "Molly, are you alright?"

"I'm fine. How long has it been?"

"You've had fifteen minutes. We're de-energizing the room now and will take you out."

"Can I stay longer? Nothing happened."

"We need to download the data from your flash drive. We can try again."

Molly was unhappy when she came out of the room. "I really don't want to quit now," she said. "I feel like I am deserting Robbie. I need to be in there for him."

Alexandra asked Steve, "Can we give Molly another try after we download her vital signs and brainwaves data?"

"We should check first with Dr. Patel," Steve said. He texted Dr. Patel, who was seeing patients at Mass General, to ask her about the safety of taking successive turns in the 2V test room. Within a minute or so, Dr. Patel responded by calling Steve's cellphone. She requested to see the data on Molly's vital signs. Steve inserted Molly's flash drive into a laptop and uploaded the data file to Dr. Patel. Steve's cellphone buzzed again. Dr. Patel wanted to talk with Molly directly. Molly told Dr. Patel that she felt fine and had no dizziness or headaches or any other symptoms, and that she wanted to go back in. Then she handed the cellphone back to Steve who listened to Dr. Patel's instructions.

When his call with Dr. Patel was concluded, Steve told Molly, "Dr. Patel agrees that you can have another session."

This time Molly started with the ocean scene on the flat screen. She also placed a wallet-size photograph of Robbie on her lap. At the twelve minute mark, she said, "Nothing's happening." When her second fifteen minutes ended, she came out of the test room, dejected and disappointed. "Maybe it's just too much to ask," she said. "At least we met on the Red Line. I'll always treasure that."

After Molly left, Alexandra said, "Let me try."

Alexandra, like Molly, stayed in the test room for two consecutive fifteen-minute sessions. Also like Molly, Alexandra experienced nothing except frustration.

The next week of testing with other test partner volunteers produced the same result. As each day passed, Harry's and Alexandra's initial frisson of mild concern morphed increasingly into moderate alarm, and from there gave way to waves of panic. "No need to worry," Steve said. "We have the situation under control. We just need to tweak what we are doing until our technology works."

Cuddihy alerted Harry that the MBTA magnetic shield was fully tested and ready now for deployment in the Red Line tunnel. He had to order its installation. "I can't put it off, Harry. So I hope your venture has everything it needs."

"I understand, Jim," Harry said. "We appreciate the time you've given us."

Crossing his fingers, and knocking softly on his wood desk, he added, "Steve says that we've finished collecting data in the Red Line train cars so we should be in good shape. Good luck on returning the Red Line to normalcy."

Twenty Six

DR. FRANCES GOURMELON DROPPED her cellphone into her capacious cloth bag and returned thoughtfully to her cup of strong black tea at the Horse and Plow Café. Her nephew Teddie Bulger, an engineer at the MBTA, had just shared *very* interesting information, confirming her suspicion that the MBTA was blocking visitations on the Red Line.

Teddie said that the MBTA had installed some sort of electromagnetic barrier in the tunnel but was keeping it quiet to avoid attracting attention. Apparently the MBTA barrier was working because Dr. Gourmelon's clients were telling her that neither they, nor anyone else they knew, were seeing loved ones anymore on the Red Line. People were getting discouraged.

Jeremy, the Horse and Plow manager, came by frequently to Dr. Gourmelon's table to offer more tea and to check that she was enjoying her breakfast. Dr. Gourmelon tried to put him at ease by accepting the tea with a big smile. "Thank you so much, Jeremy, I'd love some more," she said, adding, "Breakfast this morning was splendid. Much appreciated!"

"You're most welcome," Jeremy said. "Just give me a wave if you need anything."

If only she had been visited by her own darlings on the Red Line! But she was too famous as a psychic and spiritualist to be seen in Red Line train cars looking for them. She'd have wanted the privacy and quiet of her own train car, which she didn't need the MBTA's consultant, Harry West, Ph.D., to tell her would be difficult to arrange.

In an interview with the *Boston Globe,* she had warned the MBTA against blocking the visitations, while also raising public awareness about the MBTA's plan to do so. In that piece, the *Globe* had quoted her directly without its customary tone of snide condescension, finally recognizing that this topic was, after all, her area of expertise. And she'd tried to persuade Harry West to stop helping the MBTA.

Dr. Gourmelon resolved to do more even though she had not received additional reminders from the spirits, those painful slaps on the backs of her hands, since her earlier episode in the Horse and Plow Café.

Thus Teddie's other news was even more intriguing. He was one of the two engineers assigned by the MBTA to help a young MIT hot-shot named Steve Cheng to collect measurements in the Red Line tunnels and on the train cars. They recorded electrical energy levels and the chemical elements in the air and, he told his aunt, he believed that Cheng wanted these data for reasons that went beyond mere scientific curiosity. When Teddie asked Cheng about it, he received a vague answer, like "we're trying to work out what is going on." Then Teddie was tasked to deliver a bench of Red Line car seats to a special new room being built at MIT. He hung around for a while until someone noticed him and he was asked to leave. He asked why, and they would tell him only that what they were doing was confidential. But the guy directing the project was the same Steve Cheng, and Teddie overheard him talking to someone about energy pulses and a 'Visitation Room.'

"What are they up to, Teddie?" Dr. Gourmelon asked.

"I'd guess they are trying to copy the Red Line train car environment in their special room."

"Can you get your hands on their technical plans?"

"I don't know, Aunt Frances. Cheng keeps his plans in one of his netbook computers but he is a suspicious sort. He never lets it out of his sight."

"Well, if you get a chance, go for it. You'll make your Aunt Frances very grateful."

"I will, Aunt."

"You're a good boy."

Dr. Gourmelon mused, why would MIT want all those measurements of electrical energy levels on the Red Line trains and then build a special secret room in which, as Teddie overheard, they were planning something to do with energy pulses? Apparently there was a connection between the energy pulses and the visitations, since the MBTA was now blocking them on the Red Line and the visitations had stopped. Might they be attempting to enable visits from the spirits in the secret room as had occurred on the Red Line? If so, she would cheer them on. But more than that, this time she *would* be involved, not only to fulfill her mandate from the spirits but also, when visitations resumed, to be sure that she would see her darlings once again.

Harry West might know what they were planning. He was willing to talk when they first met and had even confided in her about a visit from his daughter Ariel. But their second meeting had gone badly; in fact it had been a disaster. After she condemned the MBTA's plans to shut down the Red Line visits, and reprimanded Harry for his role in those plans, it was clear that he just wanted to be rid of her, which was understandable and entirely her fault. She had been too upset by her experience at the Horse and Plow Café to think clearly. Now it was time to mend fences.

Dr. Gourmelon waited obediently in a visitor's chair in the reception area across from Molly Lu's desk. When Harry arrived later that morning at Blair West International, where he was still using his office which Jerry said he was welcome to do as long as he needed it. she greeted him with a big smile, "Good morning, Harry!"

Molly said, "Dr. Gourmelon was standing at our door when I arrived and I asked her to take a seat here."

"Thanks, Molly," Harry said. "Dr. Gourmelon, to what do we owe the pleasure of your visit?"

"I've come to apologize," she said, rising to her feet much more nimbly than one would expect from someone of her size and shape. "I was rude to you in our last meeting. I have no excuse. I'm sorry."

"Your apology is accepted, Dr. Gourmelon."

"Here, I've brought you a peace offering." She dug down in her cloth bag and pulled out a cookie tin from which, even though it was sealed, emanated a rich aroma of chocolate chip cookies. "Freshly baked," Dr. Gourmelon said.

"Look Dr. Gourmelon, I'm grateful for the gesture. But we really can't accept these from you, and we have a lot of work to do today, so…"

"Then I'll tell you quickly another reason that I've come here this morning," she said. "I've become aware that the MBTA is blocking further visits from the spirits."

"I couldn't comment on that," Harry said. "We've concluded our engagement for the MBTA."

"I am not blaming you, Harry. I realize there's nothing you can do about it. I am here because the spirits have demanded that I take a certain action and I feel I have no choice but to comply."

Harry played along. "What certain action have they demanded?"

"I must create a space for them in which they can once again meet with those they left behind."

"That's a very worthy objective, Dr. Gourmelon."

"I'm so very glad that you feel that way, as I do."

"How will you go about it?"

156

"I will build a special room that has the exact same features as a Red Line train car. I'll call it a 'visitation room.'"

As she spoke, Dr. Gourmelon stared at Harry with searching, unwavering concentration. He willed himself to look blandly into Dr. Gourmelon's large grey eyes and not to glance at Molly, hoping that his face revealed nothing more than mild interest in what she was saying.

"What will that involve, Dr. Gourmelon?" Harry asked, casually.

To Dr. Gourmelon, who had a keen eye for even the smallest of signs, Harry's studied nonchalance proved beyond any doubt that he was hiding something. And Molly, the receptionist, looked positively stricken. Dr. Gourmelon knew that she had touched a nerve.

"Well, Harry, that's why I'm here. I want your help. No, let me restate that, *we* want your help. A door was opened for the spirits on the Red Line. To find out why or how, we need measurements to be taken in the Red Line tunnels and in the train cars, and then we'll know precisely how to construct our special room."

Again she paused to observe Harry carefully, while also flicking her eyes towards Molly. And again, Dr. Gourmelon was not disappointed. Each was poker faced, revealing everything in their struggle to give nothing away.

"I'm sorry but I can't help you," Harry said.

"But you told me that you were no longer working for the MBTA."

"That's right, we're not."

"So there would be no conflict."

"I'm not worried about conflict, Dr. Gourmelon. The measurements you need would have to come from the MBTA," Harry said. "We don't have the tools…"

"But you do have the contacts, Mr. Cuddihy for example. You can make an agreement with the MBTA to take these measurements for us."

"Dr. Gourmelon, frankly I am not prepared to join with you in your project."

"But, you agreed that our objective is worthy. And if we succeed, you will be able to visit with your Ariel again."

"I mean no disrespect, Dr. Gourmelon, but I do not perceive you as a client, nor as a partner. And I'm sorry," Harry added, conjuring up a little white lie so that he could bring this uncomfortable interaction to an end, "I need to prepare now for a conference call."

"Harry, of course, I understand completely," Dr. Gourmelon said. "I'll leave you to it." She shook Harry's hand and bustled out of the BWI office. Left behind on the reception area coffee table was her offering of chocolate chip cookies.

"Molly," Harry said, "I don't intend to eat Dr. Gourmelon's cookies nor should anyone else here. Let's get rid of them."

Molly said she would wrap the tin in plastic and toss it in the dumpster behind the Andleman building.

"Did you stay with Dr. Gourmelon the whole time that she was here?"

"Every minute. Even though I've been desperate to use the restroom. After last time, I wasn't about to let her wander."

"Well, she's evidently picked up some information about 2V and she was probing us to confirm what she'd heard."

"Do you think she succeeded?"

"Despite our best efforts, I do."

"Harry, how could she possibly build a visitation room that works? You can't do it, and you have help from MIT and the MBTA."

"I doubt that she can. Anyway, Molly, don't give up on our team just yet. I know you were disappointed in your test session but you'll have other chances. We're just getting started."

So was Dr. Gourmelon. When she called Teddie, she told him, "You were right. They're trying to re-create the Red Line environment in their special room at MIT. The only reason to do that is to invite visits from the spirits. You're an engineer so you can figure out what they are doing and let me know. I want to you become friendly with Steve Cheng. Tell him you're thinking about the next stage in your career after the MBTA, and that you were impressed with the work he was doing in the Red Line tunnels and train cars, and ask for his advice."

"That's quite a stretch, Aunt Frances. He's just a young guy. I've been around a lot longer than him. Why would he believe that I want his advice?"

"Flatter him. You'll be surprised how well that works."

Twenty Seven

"WHAT ARE WE MISSING?" Harry asked. "We've matched the Red Line train cars in energy level, and atmosphere, and even the seats."

"Steve, could there be trace elements in the Red Line air that you overlooked?" Alexandra asked.

"We tracked every element we could measure, including the CO^2 exhaled by passengers. Everything's included in the aerosol that we've been injecting into the room," Steve said.

"How about visually, what riders see inside the train cars?" Harry asked.

"According to our data," Steve replied, "the visitations on the Red Line occurred at different times during the day and evenings, when trains were at or between stations, when they were almost empty or full, when they were inside the tunnels or in the open crossing the Longfellow Bridge. Such a wide range of visual environments makes it unlikely that visual cues are a causal factor."

"Touch?"

"Passengers in the train cars were sitting by themselves or with others next to them, on their feet holding one of the hangers, or leaning against an aluminum pole by a door, bumping into each other or not touching anyone. Plenty of variety there as well."

"Smell?"

"As Dr. Bluestein predicted, when the Red Line train car was energized we found a high concentration of negative ions, which may carry a smell and taste. But the density of negative ions also increases when we energize the 2V test room, so that would be covered. Other smells in the Red Line train cars would be included in our atmospheric aerosol. For example, riders on the Red Line produce all kinds of smells, some that we don't need to discuss in detail, and they are all mixed in."

"How about motion?" Alexandra asked. "The Red Line trains are moving, whereas our 2V test room stays still."

"Not all visitations occurred when the trains were in motion. Some began when the Red Line train was still at a station. Let's hope this is not a factor. It wouldn't be easy to reproduce motion in a Visitation Room. Even if we could manage it, the cost would be horrendous."

"So, Steve," Harry said, "You're our technology guru. What do you suggest?"

"Let's just keep doing what I've been doing. I've been trying different energy levels with a variety of injected atmosphere aerosols. There are many more combinations we can test."

"The problem is, we're going to run out of time, money, and test partners," Harry said. "We need another idea."

Alexandra asked, "How about sound? A Red Line train car is noisy. Maybe the sound waves inside the train interact in some way with the energy level, or with the properties of the atmosphere."

After a pause, Steve said, "I'm so embarrassed. We missed sound. It could definitely be a factor. Sound waves are like pressure waves, pushing things around. They might re-distribute the electromagnetic energy and the negative ions in such a way that they trigger the visitations.'

Harry said, "So instead of background music, let's pipe into the room the sounds people hear in a Red Line train car."

"I'll make the recordings," Steve said. "Maybe we'll get lucky."

"Before we leave here," Harry said, "let me tell both of you about Dr. Frances Gourmelon."

"The psychic," Alexandra said.

"She was waiting for me at the Blair West International office, in our reception area, where she had stayed under Molly's supervision until I arrived. She told me that she wanted to apologize for our earlier meeting."

"Apologize for what?" Steve asked.

"For being rude when she blamed me for helping the MBTA to shut the door on the spirits."

"Blame that you deserved," Alexandra said. "Although you've redeemed yourself, lately."

"She also told me that she had been commanded by spirits to create a new space, a special room that will have the attributes of Red Line train cars so encounters with spirits can continue. She says that she will call it a 'visitation room.'"

"That witch! She's stolen our idea!" Alexandra exclaimed.

"Clearly she's heard what we're doing in our 2V test room and probably figures that I'm involved. I think she was checking her information by watching very intently for our reactions to everything she said."

"Did she get what she wanted?" Alexandra asked.

"She doesn't miss much. She was like a large dog keeping an extremely close eye on a toddler eating a hamburger."

"What's that like?" Alexandra asked. "I've never had a dog."

"Total concentration, ready to snatch it at the first opportunity."

"Poor toddler! So defenseless!" Alexandra said, her tone not entirely sympathetic.

"Mock all you want. You had to be there."

"The toddler can get another hamburger. We've got only one shot with 2V." Turning to Steve, Alexandra said, "We need better security. You know the most about our technical data and our approach so you are the most likely target. Be careful of strangers sniffing around."

"I'm already paranoid," Steve said. "I keep our hard-copy documents in locked files. I pay for a laptop theft and loss security service. I've installed multi-level password gates on our PCs."

"Well, despite all that, we have a leak somewhere, so ramp up the paranoia."

"What does this psychic Dr. Gourmelon look like?" Steve asked.

Harry said, "Late fifties, stout, curly grey hair, grey eyes, glasses. She wears colorful tent-like muumuus and wherever she's been, she trails a scent of chocolate chip cookies."

"Hard to miss," Steve said.

Steve needed help from an MBTA engineer to capture sounds inside Red Line train cars during their fifteen-minute runs between South Station and Davis Square. When the assignment for an engineer to work with Steve was approved by Jim Cuddihy and posted in the MBTA tech center, Teddie Bulger approached his manager and requested the job.

Steve's recording equipment picked up all the Red Line noises, the rattles, creaks, swooshes, squeaks, and rumbles in the train cars; the blurts emanating from the PA system; and passengers' conversations. Since Steve didn't know which of these sounds might be important, he left them all in.

Teddie helped. He recommended locations in the train cars to attach the microphones and he made sure no one touched them. He checked and re-checked the equipment. Showing interest, he asked Steve why he was making these recordings. Steve replied, "For a research project."

Teddie asked, "Is this the same research project as before, when we took the measurements on energy levels in the tunnels and train cars?"

"We have a lot of projects going on," Steve said, discouraging more conversation.

Later, Teddie told his Aunt Frances that it was a safe bet that the Red Line sound recordings were destined for use in MIT's special room.

Twenty Eight

WE'RE ALL SET," Steve said.

With sensors attached to her head, arms, and chest to monitor her vital signs, Alexandra took her place in the 2V test room's easy chair.

Within seconds after Steve tapped the touchscreen on his handheld device to energize the room, inject the aerosol, and play his new Red Line soundtrack, Alexandra bolted upright in the chair.

"What are *you* doing here?" she demanded.

After a pause, Alexandra continued, her voice ringing with defiance, "Yes, yes, I know. But it's my decision, isn't it?" She fell silent again, apparently listening, and then she said, "You can stop now. You don't know anything about me. You never did. I don't want any more of your advice." And, after another pause of a minute or two, more softly, "Yes, alright, I will send her your love. I am glad you visited me. I love you too."

She sat back in the chair, her eyes closed. After another five minutes had elapsed, she said, "I am ready to come out."

"What happened?" Harry asked, when Alexandra had rejoined them.

"A visitation happened."

"But you didn't seem to be enjoying it."

"You could tell that I was not talking with Ariel?"

"We figured that out."

"It was my father, Ofer Ben-Tov, known to everyone in Israel as Beni. He died while I was still a student at Smith."

"I don't recall you talking about him very much, except to say he got on your nerves."

"We didn't get along. That was one of the reasons that I left Israel. Even when he was at home, he couldn't leave behind his job as a tank commander in the Negev. He seemed to think that I was like one of his soldiers and therefore obliged to obey his orders."

"Can you tell us about the visit?"

"As soon as I sat down, I saw him standing in front of me like he used to before he got sick. He was short, and stocky, and he'd stand with his hands on his hips and his chin in the air, like General Patton, who was one of his heroes. He was looking down at me with a big grin on his face, and he said, 'so, here I am again, not so easy to kill off.' I was hoping to see Ariel so I did not greet him very warmly."

"We got that impression out here, as well."

"He complained that I wasn't very welcoming, and then he launched into one of his tirades about why I should return to Israel, have more children, take care of my mother, that sort of thing. I never enjoyed his lectures. Now that he's dead, I have even less time for them, and I told him that. He backed down and just asked me to send my mother his love, and said he loved me, which I didn't hear all that often before. And then he vanished."

"While he was there, did you notice anything different about the room?"

"The room… I didn't even see the room when Beni Ben-Tov was standing in front of me. I only saw him, and all I could hear was his voice, until he was gone."

Steve said, "Let's check the data on your vital signs." He inserted Alexandra's flash drive into a laptop PC and pointed out how the lines representing different measures shifted on the screen. Within seconds after the 2V test room was energized, Alexandra's heart rate had increased, as did the frequency of her brainwaves, especially in portions of her brain associated with emotion, vision, hearing and speech, and she showed a strong galvanic skin response. "Definitely something going on there," he said. "How do you feel?"

"I feel tired, but contented, like I've just had a real work-out," Alexandra said.

"Like after you've been running?" Harry asked.

"More like after having sex, all relaxed, and warm, and cuddly."

"Way too much information," Steve said.

"If our customers feel the same way," Harry said, "we'll have to beat them off with sticks."

Steve and Alexandra laughed, and Harry added, "I mean that in a good way."

"I'll email Alexandra's data to Dr. Patel," Steve said. "We'll want to hear from her that Alexandra's vital signs stayed within acceptable ranges."

Harry said, "Assuming Dr. Patel doesn't raise any alarms, it's time for us to start testing for real. Steve, let's give Molly another run. Get more volunteers. Once we've had a series of successful encounters, make changes in the test room to find out whether they make a difference, for example remove the Red Line seats, maybe adjust the atmosphere, and play with the sound to see if you can make it less obtrusive."

"OK."

"Also, now that we've got our technology working," Harry said. "I want a session in the test room."

Harry settled in the 2V test room easy chair, listening to the soundtrack of the Red Line doors sliding shut, the metallic clatter of the steel wheels turning on the steel rails, the squeaks and rattles as the train followed turns in the tunnel, the muffled announcement on the PA that the train was approaching Downtown Crossing which sounded like, "Dunton nging" "Dunton nging" "Mind the doors."

The teenage girl sitting cross-legged on one of the room's Red Line seats said, "Hello Daddy."

"Ariel! I'm so glad to see you again." Harry noticed that Ariel was not scowling balefully at him like last time. "Are you feeling better about me now?"

"Now that I can visit with you and Mom again, I'll forgive you," she said. "But who's that woman with you? That's not Mom."

"What woman?"

"She means me, Harry." Harry had been so focused on Ariel that he had not noticed the woman standing beside his chair. She moved in front of him without, however, blocking his line of sight to Ariel. She looked to be in her late 30s, had short reddish-brown hair, emerald green eyes, and a slim build. "Do you remember me, Harry?"

"Erin, of course I do! This is a wonderful surprise!"

"So who is she, Dad?" Ariel demanded.

"Ariel, please say hello to Erin Haig. Erin, Ariel."

"Is Ariel your daughter, who you told me about?"

"Yes, although now quite a bit older than when she was taken from us."

"Daddy, were you talking about me with this stranger? Telling our business? Does Mom know?"

"Ariel, Mom does know about Erin. And Erin was not a stranger. She was a journalist in Hong Kong who was my very good friend when I was there, who was murdered while doing research for a story."

"Whoa," Ariel said. "Gross!"

Harry asked, "Erin, do you know what happened after…?"

"No, tell me, Harry."

"We caught the bastards who did it. One of them is still in prison in Hong Kong and the other died after being assaulted by another inmate."

"That's good to hear, Harry. Although it doesn't do much for me, actually."

"I understand, Erin. What happened to you… it just shouldn't have."

"Do you ever think of me?"

"Of course. All the time."

"Do you think about our time together in the shower?"

"Daddy! What is she talking about?"

"Ariel, sweetheart," the red-head said, "We were just having fun. It's nothing to be ashamed of."

"I'm not your sweetheart. And I don't like hearing your stories about you and my father."

"Ariel," Harry said, "Your mom and I weren't married at the time. I think you and Erin would have gotten along very well. She was a wonderful woman, and an excellent journalist."

"Maybe," Ariel said, settling a frank gaze on Erin that was hostile, but also curious.

"Harry," Erin said. "You did your best in Hong Kong. What happened to me was not your fault."

"I'm sorry," Harry said. "I could have done more. I shouldn't have let you go to that meeting by yourself. But, thank you for saying that."

On the Red Line audio being piped into the room, the voice of an MBTA conductor cut in, "Dvss Sqzz" "Mind the doors." And Erin and Ariel were gone.

Alexandra said, "You were having quite a conversation. What was that about how we weren't married at the time?"

"You know how you were surprised to see your Father?" Harry asked.

"Yes."

"For my surprise, I had two visitors. One was Ariel, who no longer seems angry at me. And the other was Erin Haig, my friend in Hong Kong who I told you about, who was murdered there."

"And they were talking with each other? They could see each other?" Steve asked.

"Yes. Apparently."

"That's nice," Alexandra said, coolly. "A new friend for Ariel."

Steve received over seven hundred applications in response to a brief notice published online and in the Boston, Cambridge, and MIT newspapers which read, "MIT Lab Looking for Test Partners Who Have Experienced Bereavement. Test Relates to Memories of Those Who Passed Away. Will pay $100 for thirty minutes." The volunteers were interviewed by Steve and Harry in order to exclude those with evident emotional or mental problems, and also to determine who, if any, had already encountered loved ones on the Red Line. They selected 130 to serve as 2V test partners.

One hundred and two of the test partners experienced a visitation, a 78% success rate. Ninety-eight of them met a person they had known, and four encountered former pets.

Dr. Dhwani Patel determined that their vital signs remained well within normal ranges and therefore did not indicate health risks. Based on her series of interviews with the test partners, Dr. Patel found no effects on mental stability.

During the tests, 2V instruments tracked the changes in the room's energy level, atmosphere, and background sound. Based on these measures, Steve identified two causal factors for visitations, the energizing produced by magnetic resonance with 2V's WiTricity transmitter, and Red Line sounds that were played in the room. Test partners reported being distracted by the Red Line railway noises, so Steve shifted the sound mix to a higher frequency above human hearing while retaining its distinctive wave pattern. This change had no effect on likelihood of visitations. Lacking evidence that ingredients of the air on the Red Line trains were a causal factor, Steve stopped injecting the atmosphere aerosol into the 2V test room. The Red Line seats in the test room also had no discernible effect one way or another but the 2V team decided to keep them anyway since they were occasionally convenient.

Now that the technology was working, 2V's Board of Directors – Dr. Wec Bluestein; Edward Hutchins, 2V's lead investor; Gary Pollack, who also served as 2V's interim counsel; Alexandra, and Harry – voted to launch the new venture.

Henceforth, 2V would be known as LifePlus, Inc.

Twenty Nine

TEDDIE BULGER APPLIED for a job at LifePlus as an engineer technician. Harry called Jim Cuddihy to double-check the vaguely couched reference from Teddie's manager at the MBTA, "Teddie Bulger has met my expectations as an engineer on my team." Cuddihy said that he barely knew Teddie but had not heard anything negative about him. Background research revealed that Teddie was carrying several thousand dollars of credit card debt although he had been making his minimum required payments on time each month. He had no criminal record apart from a prank vandalism incident when he was a freshman at Boston College.

Steve was not looking for engineering geniuses, just technically competent assistants who would follow orders cheerfully and wouldn't demand a high salary. Having met those criteria, Teddie was hired.

Teddie's day-job was to help Steve build the first LifePlus Visitation Room in the basement of the Boston Marriott Hotel on the Waterfront. His second job was to keep his aunt Frances Gourmelon fully informed. She wanted to know everything, down to the smallest details: How did they energize the Visitation Room? What was the significance of Red Line sounds? What would the Visitation Room look like? Size? Color of walls? Furnishings? How were they structuring the company? Who were the execs, in addition to the LifePlus CEO Harry West? How would they allocate time slots for customers in the Visitation Room? What would they charge?

It took three months to dismantle the 2V test room at MIT and to construct the new LifePlus Visitation Room at the Marriott. Now, with Opening Day approaching, the pre-operational Visitation Room was functioning even better than expected. Somehow word seeped out about test partners' astonishing encounters, despite everyone's pledges of confidentiality. The Marriott received more inquiries every day, "Is the Visitation Room open yet?" "How do I Sign Up?" "Please accept this deposit for my reservation." All inquiries were forwarded to Cecilia Bridges, LifePlus's first head of Marketing, Strategic Partnering, and Customer Support, who replied on behalf of the new company, "We will let you know when we open. Thank you for your interest. Stay Tuned."

Alexandra had recruited Cecilia directly from the MIT Sloan School of Management where she was famous, according to Steve, for "taking on a hundred projects at once and getting them all done." Her dark hair and eyes and intense manner reminded Alexandra of Ariel, as well as of herself when she had just graduated from Smith College. As a newly-minted Sloan MBA, Cecilia was being pursued by several other start-ups and had received offers from Google and from Zynga, a hot online gaming company, so it took some effort to entice her to join LifePlus but, as usual, Alexandra was very persuasive.

LifePlus employees used the company website at www.visitationroom.com as a shared communication platform to keep track of progress on their respective tasks. The website would become accessible to the public on the day of the LifePlus press release. At that time, the LifePlus online reservation system would go live, offering 15-minute time slots, 24 hours a day, 7 days a week, at a cost of $50 per time slot. Opening Day would follow three weeks after the press release. The first time slot would be available at 9:00 A.M. on Opening Day.

Technicians and customer support staff were trained in their respective roles. Steve hired an online LiveChat service based in Nebraska to respond in real-time to customers' questions.

Harry rented office space for LifePlus in a building on Memorial Drive. It was within walking distance of the Red Line's Kendall/MIT station, and was suitably modest for a start-up, a single room with four desks that could be used by anyone working in the office, plus a round table for meetings.

"Seven days until our press release, and counting," Harry said to his LifePlus colleagues – Alexandra, Steve and Cecilia – who were seated with him around their meeting table in their new office. He handed each of them a plastic covered binder. "This is today's printout of tasks to be completed before Opening Day," he said. "Cecilia and I have identified the person who is primarily responsible for each task and others who are supporting him or her. This checklist should be updated on our website as soon as a task is completed, along with any explanatory notes you feel will be useful. Cecilia and I will check this file frequently."

A chirp from Harry's BlackBerry alerted him to an incoming text from Dr. Gourmelon, "I know all about LifePlus and your press release next week. Can we discuss?"

Harry handed his BlackBerry to Alexandra. "Just what we need, our favorite psychic," she said.

Steve asked, "What's going on?"

Harry said, "Dr. Gourmelon claims she knows all about LifePlus and she wants a meeting."

"Damn!" Steve said. "I've been insanely careful about security."

"I'll meet with her," Harry said.

"I'll go with you," Alexandra said. "You're too polite to handle her all by yourself. Last time, you were a toddler's hamburger."

"Is that an Israeli expression?" Cecilia asked.

"Apparently Dr. Gourmelon has that effect on Harry," Steve said.

"No point in putting it off," Harry said, as he keyed Dr. Gourmelon's number on his BlackBerry.

"I received your text. What do you have in mind?" he asked, when Dr. Gourmelon picked up.

"Let's discuss that when we meet," Dr. Gourmelon said.

"How about this afternoon at 2:00 P.M. at Blair West International? I'll bring my colleague, Alexandra Ben-Tov."

"That time is fine. I look forward to meeting Alexandra," Dr. Gourmelon said.

Thirty

WHEN DR. GOURMELON was ushered by Molly Lu into the Blair West International conference room, she gave Harry a cheerful wave and said to Alexandra, "You must be Alexandra Ben-Tov. I'm Frances Gourmelon and I'm very pleased to meet you."

Alexandra ignored Dr. Gourmelon's outstretched hand. "You claim to know a lot about us," she said.

Dr. Gourmelon plumped herself down in a chair opposite Alexandra's. "I know everything, my dear. I know the technologies you are using for your Visitation Room in the waterfront Marriott based on measurements that your young MIT engineer made earlier on the Red Line. I know that you will announce your Visitation Room in a press release next week; that you will rent out the Visitation Room in fifteen-minute time slots; and that Opening Day is scheduled for three weeks after your press release."

"So, you've been a good spy. What do you want?"

"I want you to succeed. I want your Visitation Room to open as you have planned," Dr. Gourmelon said, with a kindly smile.

"We're doing our best to achieve that," Harry said.

"Of course you are," Dr. Gourmelon said, laying her hand on his arm which Harry – noticing Alexandra's sharp look – pulled away. "I am here to help."

"We don't need your help," Alexandra said, taking over from Harry. She was better suited to play 'bad cop' with the formidable psychic. He had a weakness for oddball characters and he couldn't help liking Dr. Gourmelon despite her nefarious schemes, a sentiment that Alexandra did not share.

"Yes, you do, my dear. Although the Visitation Room will bring joy to many, for others it will represent a threat, and they will attack its very existence. You will confront obstacles that you do not expect."

"So, we'll deal with them," Alexandra said. "I'm used to obstacles, and so is Harry."

"Yes, Alexandra, you believe that you can do anything. Despite your impressive accomplishments, you are still young and arrogant. In due course, you will discover that you are wrong, that you can benefit from my long experience communicating with spirits, and also from my contacts, both among the living and among the dear departed."

"Whatever that means," Alexandra said. "What do you want from us, in return? Or do you just want to 'help' us to succeed and nothing else for yourself?"

"I'm prepared to join with you as one of the founding partners of LifePlus."

"OK."

"And in that role, I will accept a token amount of founder's equity."

"Now finally we've gotten to the good part. Purely out of curiosity, how much equity do you have in mind?"

"Only a token amount, my dear, just one percent of the company's shares."

"Let me get this straight," Alexandra said. "We should grant you founders' equity because you know a lot of people, some living and others dead, and you will help us in a way yet to be defined but that we would value if we weren't young and arrogant."

"Alexandra, I'm so glad that we understand each other."

"Perhaps I wasn't sarcastic enough. What you've proposed is far-fetched and ridiculous."

"I understood quite well what you were trying to say, Alexandra," Dr. Gourmelon replied, apparently unfazed. "I don't take it personally."

"You should. That's how I meant it."

"My Institute for Psychical and Paranormal Research is highly respected throughout New England and my clients are very loyal. If I recommend that they reserve time slots in the LifePlus Visitation Room, they surely will. Of course I am also in communication with spirits who might appear in the Visitation Room, if circumstances are favorable."

"You mean, if you tell them not to, they won't appear?"

"I would never presume to tell the spirits what to do."

"We'll think about it," Alexandra said.

"Just be sure not to wait too long, my dear. Later, I will seek a larger equity share."

"And if 'later" turns into 'never?'" Alexandra asked.

"That would be unfortunate," Dr. Gourmelon said, in a flat matter-of-fact tone. "I will not stay idly by if you and Harry are so unwise as to put the Visitation Room at risk by refusing my help."

"Sounds like a threat, Dr. Gourmelon."

"Think of it as fair warning, my dear. I want the Visitation Room to succeed…"

"Yes, OK, we heard that."

"…but if necessary its promise can be realized without you."

At this, Alexandra pushed back from the table. "I've heard enough," she told Harry. "I'm leaving. I want nothing more to do with this woman's threats and her other nonsense. Call me later."

Dr. Gourmelon said, "No need to rush off, Alexandra. I'll go now. Keep in mind how I have been able to discover everything there is to know about LifePlus despite your Steven Cheng's efforts at security, and he's such a bright young man! I can do more, if I am forced to. Take advantage of my offer before it's too late."

"And you keep in mind that we will not sit idly by if you try anything against us," Alexandra said, getting the last word.

Thirty One

AS ANNOUNCED IN the LifePlus press release and on the LifePlus Blog:

Visitation Room To Enable Communications with Loved Ones.
People in the Boston area will recall reports last year by passengers on the Red Line that they were seeing and interacting with loved ones and with others who were important to them, who had passed on.

A research team at MIT was able to isolate the attributes of the Red Line trains that enabled these amazing events to occur. These attributes have been replicated in a "Visitation Room." Numerous tests have verified that "visits" from loved ones will occur in this room as they did on the Red Line.

LifePlus, Inc., a new company based in Cambridge, Massachusetts, will operate the Visitation Room using technology exclusively licensed from MIT.

LifePlus CEO Harry West, PhD., said, "We anticipate providing wonderful experiences to our customers who come to our Visitation Room to communicate with their loved ones. Even though we cannot explain these experiences fully, we do know that they are very real to the people who have these encounters."

Opening Day is scheduled three weeks from today. From then on, the Visitation Room in Boston's Marriott Hotel on the Waterfront will be available to the public twenty-four hours per day, seven days a week. More information about the Visitation Room and about LifePlus, Inc., and a reservation system for fifteen-minute time slots in the Visitation Room, can be found at www.VisitationRoom.com.

The Archdiocese of Boston had kept its peace during the furor about the Red Line. It had refrained from commenting publicly about the ghostly visits, about the MBTA's plan to shut them down, about the impromptu shrines of crucifixes and flowers left against the walls of Red Line stations, and about the people clutching photographs, singing hymns, and crowding the Red Line stations and trains in search of their loved ones.

While in public view, Cardinal Dermot L. O'Rourke, Archbishop of Boston, maintained a benign half-smile that was both empathetic and forgiving, as one would hope and expect from a loving Father who cared for his large and diverse flock. He customarily wore the plain, humble cassock of his religious order, eschewing the more grandiose costume of a Bishop of the Church, except for the scarlet skullcap, ring and pectoral cross that signified his exalted rank. And unless he was engaged in a religious ritual or speaking at a podium, the Cardinal's hands invariably rested tranquilly on his stomach, one hand gently and calmly touching the other. As a man of peace, he gave the appearance of wishing only the best for everyone, even for those who professed views that were contrary to the truth.

Appearances aside, Cardinal O'Rourke never hesitated to act as required to serve his Church. Concerning the Red Line visitations, he had held his tongue in public but privately, to his close confidants among the Archdiocese bishops and priests, he applauded the MBTA's determination to bring that dismaying spectacle to an end, and he had encouraged State Representative

Walter MacAuliff to pursue the matter with the MBTA which may have contributed to the MBTA's resolve to do the right thing.

Granted, it was undeniable that spirits survive the death of their physical manifestations, and that they ascend to Heaven, or descend to Hell, or transition for a time to Purgatory, depending on how they had behaved when alive. It was also an accepted truth that spirits with unfinished business on earth might, on occasion, if allowed by God, visit people they had left behind. Scripture provided examples of the dead visiting the living, notably the ghostly apparition of Moses who appeared before Jesus and three of his disciples. Certainly angels intercede to protect people from time to time. And people can become possessed by evil spirits, hence the need for exorcisms by priests trained in such arts. But it was expressly forbidden and sinful for people to seek out spirits of their loved ones. Doing so could result in people contacting not the ghosts of their departed but rather demons in disguise that might deceive the seekers and lead them away from the true faith. As clearly stated in the Catechism, 2116, *All forms of divination are to be rejected: recourse to Satan or demons, conjuring up the dead or other practices falsely supposed to "unveil" the future. Consulting horoscopes, astrology, palm reading, interpretation of omens and lots, the phenomena of clairvoyance, and recourse to mediums all conceal a desire for power over time, history, and, in the last analysis, other human beings, as well as a wish to conciliate hidden powers. They contradict the honor, respect, and loving fear that we owe to God alone.*

As Cardinal O'Rourke reminded his bishops and priests, the Church was the only acceptable venue for the faithful to venerate their dead, to contemplate their own deaths, and to prepare for the afterlife.

And now, most regrettably, after the Red Line finally had returned to normal, the same unfortunate delusion was being revived by the announced opening of a so-called Visitation Room. For people, especially the faithful, to rent time slots in a Visitation Room to communicate with the departed was an extracurricular activity that was far too "extra" to be acceptable to the Church. While financial matters were certainly not the Cardinal's primary concern, it rankled His Eminence that his parishioners would be enticed to pay money to the company that operated this Visitation Room, money that could be put to much better use if donated to the Church, especially during a time of financial stress due to the regrettable scandals involving a few wayward priests. That the Visitation Room would be open seven days a week was an additional affront. Surely at least one day could be set aside each week for the faithful to take their places in their pews hearing their priest's instruction concerning the Word of God. According to a report in the *Boston Globe*, time slots in the Marriott Visitation Room were selling out quickly, weeks prior to its Opening Day. And it was reported that the company was planning to open four more such rooms during the coming year.

Something had to be done.

Once again, Cardinal O'Rourke selected as his instrument Massachusetts State Representative Walter MacAuliff of South Boston, a loyal son of the Church although, like everyone, he suffered a few weaknesses, a fondness for drink, for one, about which the Cardinal had counseled him. In addition to his earlier intervention with the MBTA concerning the Red Line, Walter had proven his loyalty by acting to block an ill-conceived bill that would have required hospitals receiving funds from the Commonwealth to agree to perform abortions; he had co-sponsored another measure that was enacted by the legislature and signed by the Governor, that required school districts in the Commonwealth to include teaching of abstinence in their classes on family planning; and he had campaigned indefatigably for his bill to forbid health practitioners in state clinics from discussing condoms with their patients, despite stubborn opposition in the House and Senate and on the part of the Governor.

The Cardinal's assistant reached Representative MacAuliff and requested, "Please hold for Cardinal O'Rourke."

"Walter, how *are* you?" the Cardinal asked, when he came on a moment later. The Cardinal's inquiry after the Representative's well-being was infused with great warmth and concern, underscoring deep personal regard.

"I'm very well," Representative MacAuliff replied, perhaps a bit warily, because he only received these calls when the Archdiocese wanted something. "How are you, Your Eminence?"

"Well, thank you, Walter. And your family? I assume they are well."

"They also are well, Your Eminence."

After a pause, Cardinal O'Rourke said, "Walter, I have a delicate matter to discuss with you. I hope I can count on your usual discretion."

"Of course, Your Eminence."

"You've seen the stories about this Visitation Room, I assume, where people would go to encounter spirits of their loved ones."

"Yes, I have."

"It is very troubling, Walter. As we discussed earlier concerning the Red Line, seeking visits with spirits contradicts our teachings. Spiritual visits are blessings that must never be initiated by the faithful, and certainly never accompanied by any form of payment. They can only occur properly as directed by God, and only for those who live a moral life in the Church."

"I understand, Your Eminence."

"Walter, each of us has his own role to play to ensure that God's will is done. For your part, I am concerned that this Visitation Room may not be well enough understood by Government. Perhaps there are issues of health, for people who are subjected to the special conditions in this Visitation Room? I am recalling, for example, the awful fate of that poor man on the Red Line. Or fraud, if promises are being made that cannot ever be fulfilled by mortals? I worry terribly that gullible people are being taken in."

"Do you think that an investigation should be initiated to call the company's executives to account?"

"If that is what you suggest, Walter, I would support it."

"Your Eminence, as always I appreciate that you were thinking of me."

"You're in my thoughts and prayers, Walter, as is your family."

Cardinal O'Rourke was not the only notable in the Boston area to be dismayed by the LifePlus announcement. Michael Wallace brooded over the unwelcome news. In recent months there had been no more reports of strange happenings on the Red Line. Finally, once again, people who were dead were staying dead. But now, they'd be back, this time in a fucking Visitation Room, telling tales and pointing their bony fucking fingers! He failed to grasp the humor in the way the *Boston Herald* boxed the story inside black lines with a cartoon Casper-the-Ghost peering over the top right corner. Wallace crumpled the newspaper's front page into a ball and threw it angrily towards his trash basket, which he missed.

The kid who was slapping a rag against Wallace's shoes to buff them to a high gloss, who usually worked at the Davis Square T Station but was paid by Wallace to come to his office every morning to keep his shoes looking good, knew enough not to look up from his task. "You're done," Wallace said, when he could see his face mirrored on his shoes, and he handed the kid a twenty dollar bill. "You can go now. Tell Ricky and Al to come in."

"You wanted us, Mr. Wallace?" Ricky asked, in his high whispery voice, while Al looked on.

"You see the article in the *Herald* about this fucking Visitation Room?"

"Yes, sir." Ricky was actually intrigued by the story. Before he was born, his uncle Howie, Michael Wallace's older brother, had died in a car crash while being chased by police. Howie was legendary in the family for committing his first murder when he was only eight, dispatching a homeless man by whacking him repeatedly with a lead pipe. That the man was already incapacitated by drink did not detract from the myth that had grown up around the young killer. Ricky had heard about Howie's exploits, not from Michael Wallace who seldom spoke of him, but from his father before he became a long-term guest of the Commonwealth, and Ricky had considered trying out the Visitation Room to see if he might meet Howie there, but Wallace seemed down on it, so Ricky had to be careful about what he said.

"We need to deliver a message to the fuckers who are announcing this Visitation Room that it would be better for everyone if it never opened."

"Why?" Ricky couldn't help himself from asking.

"Because I say so, you fucking moron."

It was true that Ricky had a strange crazy-eyed appearance and like Al he enjoyed inflicting pain on men, women, children, and small animals, the more brutally the better, but he wasn't a moron, which was evidenced by the fact that he chose not to argue the point further.

"Also because if they open this fucking Room, the people you killed can come back to accuse you."

That gave Ricky pause. There were quite a few bodies buried in vacant lots around Somerville and he preferred that they stay quiet about how they got there. If they did come back, it wouldn't go all that well for Al, either, who was still standing stolidly by his side, nor for Michael Wallace, who had ordered the punishments meted out by him and Al.

"What do you want us to do?"

"Pay these fuckers a visit. Their office is in Cambridge, down on Memorial Drive, according to their website. Explain that their business is a bad idea."

"Should we let them know in the usual way?"

"For now, explain it to them nicely. Later on, if necessary, you can do whatever you want to make sure they listen better."

There were others, too, in the Greater Boston Area, who foresaw trouble for themselves in the news of the Visitation Room's imminent opening.

Dr. Douglas R. McDougall, a urologist who practiced at Massachusetts General Hospital and lived in historic Concord west of the city, had reported his wife missing eight months earlier. He had pleaded on TV for her assumed kidnappers to let her go, promising "No questions asked," if she were returned alive and unharmed. Unfortunately before she vanished his wife had confided to her sister about their marital troubles and the meddlesome sister had expressed suspicions to the Concord police. The sister had grown even more insistent now that McDougall was finding solace in the friendship of a physically fit young woman whom he had met through Craigslist. Not to mention the nurses at MGH who recalled his wife as a friend and colleague before she married McDougall and who, lacking any sense of humor, had complained to the MGH HR department about a few harmless gropes in the OR that he had meant only in fun. What if his wife's sister or one of these uptight nurses were to meet his wife's ghost in the Visitation Room, and thereby discover the whereabouts of her body weighted down with concrete blocks at the bottom of Walden Pond?

Also not liking the story were two teenage drug dealers in Mattapan who had left a would-be competitor sprawled dead in a playground sandbox shot execution style with a bullet behind his right ear. The victim belonged to a gang that was famous for a seriously bad attitude. What if the bloodied corpse returned to point his ill-tempered brothers in their direction?

And there was the grieving socialite in her Beacon Hill townhouse, with hair as blond as straw and medically-perfected skin, who'd finally attained fuck-you wealth from the unexpected demise of her much older husband who drowned one evening while taking his early morning swim just off their private beach on Martha's Vineyard. What if the old bastard were to come back to tell his greedy grown-up sons what really happened? She'd heard that they were planning to reserve time slots in the Visitation Room.

Unlike Michael Wallace, small-time evildoers such as these had no Ricky or Al on their payroll so their first choice was to stay low and hope for the best. Even so, for some among them, fear of discovery due to the Visitation Room might override their better judgment, such that they too would try to make the threat go away.

Thirty Two

ALL DOORS INTO the office building in which LifePlus had rented its office space were secured with coded pass-cards, thereby keeping out casual trespassers. More determined interlopers, like Ricky and Al, were not deterred. They stood casually near the front entrance pretending to take their outdoor tobacco break, a common sight in Cambridge after the City banned smoking inside public buildings. When a backpack-toting young man approached the entrance, they stubbed out their cigarettes and as a courtesy, the young man held the door open for them. Ricky whispered "thank you" to him as the three of them entered together.

The building's tenants, mostly start-ups like LifePlus, were paying rents that were far too low to cover the cost of an attendant in the lobby to check visitors' IDs, so Ricky and Al had unobstructed access to the elevators. A board beside the elevators showed the LifePlus office to be in Suite 503 and Al pushed the button for the fifth floor.

The glass door to the LifePlus office was locked. "Nobody trusts anybody anymore," Ricky muttered. He could see a young man and young woman sitting at a table inside. Ricky knocked on the glass, and the young man came to the door and opened it, asking, "How can we help you?"

Ricky held up a copy of the article in the *Boston Herald* and asked, "Is this the office of the company that has the Visitation Room?"

"We are," Steve Cheng said. "Do you need help signing up for a time slot?"

Ricky, thinking fast, said, "Yes, we are having trouble. Can you show us how?"

The two large men followed Steve into the room. Cecilia Bridges stood to be introduced and Steve said, "These two gentlemen have asked for help signing onto our website to reserve time in our Visitation Room."

When Cecilia said, "I'm Cecilia Bridges…," Ricky took her outstretched hand in one of his and squeezed hard. Cynthia winced, and said, "That hurts. Let go of my hand."

Realizing that the two men were not bewildered prospective customers as they had claimed, Steve demanded, "Who are you? What do you want?"

Al moved in close to Steve and placed his meaty hairless hands on Steve's shoulders. Ricky asked him, "Are you Harry West?"

"No, he's not here," Steve replied. "What do you want?"

Al jammed Steve down into a chair next to the table while Ricky used his grip on Cecilia's hand to lever her into another of the chairs. He let her hand go once she was seated. "If you listen carefully we will not hurt you," he said. "We have an important message for Harry West."

"What is it?" Steve asked

"We want to talk with him. Is he coming back soon?"

"I don't know when he'll return. I can deliver your message. I'll text it for you." Steve reached for his iPhone and Ricky said, "Give that here." Then he told Cecilia, "Give me yours as well."

"I want your full attention," Ricky said. "Do I have that?"

"Yes," Steve replied.

"We have been told to ask you nicely but if you are stupid about it and don't listen carefully, next time will be different. And if you give us any trouble, we will have to hurt you now. Real badly. You understand?"

"Yes. What do you want?"

"Opening Day for your Visitation Room… Cancel it."

"I can't do that," Steve said, staring up defiantly at Ricky who was leaning over him. "I don't own this business. It's not my decision. I only work here."

"Tell Harry West."

"Why do you want it cancelled?" Cecilia asked. She tried to keep her voice strong but her chest felt so squeezed that she had to struggle to get the words out.

"Are you nervous?" Ricky asked her.

"Yes."

"That's good. You should be."

"We'll pass your message to Mr. West," Steve said.

"You do that," Ricky said. "We'll be seeing you." He and Al started towards the door.

"Can we have our phones back?" Steve asked.

"You think I'm an idiot," Ricky said. He pulled a switchblade knife from an inside pocket of his suit jacket, snapped it open, and walked back towards them. Steve and Cecilia flinched when they saw the knife in the hand of the beady-eyed monster, a reaction that Ricky savored, one of the perks of his job. "Think about it," he said. "Fuck around with us and you'll see this again. That's not what you want." Then Ricky sliced the wires that connected the two office desk-phones to the phone jack on the wall and the curly wires connecting the desk-phones to their respective handsets. "We'll take your laptops as well," he said, "and your wallets." Al collected the laptops that were sitting, still open, on the table in front of Steve and Cecilia, and each of their wallets which they handed to him, silently. After a moment's reflection, Ricky added thoughtfully, more to himself than to the others in the room, "I gotta take a souvenir." He grabbed a clump of Cecilia's hair and yanked it up hard from the back.

Cecilia cried out, "What are you doing?"

"Shut up," Ricky told her, and he used his knife to saw through a handful of her hair, which he pocketed.

Steve shouted, "Leave her alone!"

Ricky swatted his arm down sideways so that his fist smacked Steve's nose. Blood streamed over Steve's mouth and chin, soaking his shirt, and dripping onto the table.

"You shut up, too," Ricky said. "Don't push your luck, Chinaman. Next time what I cut off won't grow back."

The neighboring office down the hall from LifePlus housed a start-up that was developing a mobile lottery application for smartphones. It was occupied by young entrepreneurs who were working day and night towards their dream. For sustenance, they ordered pizza and diet Pepsi delivered. They slept on cots in the office so they would waste no time commuting to their apartments. They only showered when necessary, long after others in their vicinity seemed to be holding their collective breath, and not until the pizza guy refused to come into their office because their body odor made him gag. So it was not surprising that they were in their office when Steve, with Cecilia right behind him, banged on their door and shouted to let them in, that it was an emergency.

"We've been robbed!" Steve shouted. "Can we borrow your phone?"

"Shit, man, are you hurt?" one of the entrepreneurs asked, when he saw Steve's blood-covered shirt.

"I'll live," Steve said, "but we need to make some calls."

Steve called the Cambridge police to report the theft of his and Cecilia's cellphones, PCs, and wallets, the assaults on Cecilia and himself, and the vandalism in the LifePlus office. He called a data-security service to which he had subscribed all LifePlus PCs. After giving the password for his account, and identifying the two PCs that he and Cecilia used, the service activated a message that would be transmitted to each laptop at the first instant that it was connected to the Internet. Once this message was received, it would trigger a stored program that would re-format the PC's hard-drive, erasing it completely. Cecilia requested a second cellphone from another of the guys in the office and she and Steve both called their mobile provider to report the thefts of their phones. Then Steve called Harry.

"I have bad news. Cecilia and I were robbed a few minutes ago while we were in our office. We were assaulted and threatened. We'd better talk."

"Are you both OK?"

"We're fine. We lost some stuff. The two thugs who did this were not looking for money. The police will be here shortly. Can you come over?"

"I'll be there," Harry said. "I'm with Alexandra now and she'll come with me. We're leaving now."

Twenty minutes later, two Cambridge uniformed cops arrived at the LifePlus office and Steve let them in. One of the cops, in his late 40s with short prematurely-graying hair, introduced himself as Sergeant James Murphy. His younger partner, who looked like she was in her 30s, fit, and taller than her sergeant, introduced herself as Patrol Officer Janine Daniels. "Let's start by you telling us who you are," Sergeant Murphy said.

Steve and Cecilia gave their names and positions at LifePlus, which Patrol Officer Daniels typed into a small netbook that she had opened on the meeting table.

"Can you show us your IDs?" Sergeant Murphy asked.

"Our wallets were taken," Cecilia said, "along with our cellphones and PCs, so we don't have anything here to show you."

"Alright, we'll confirm all that later." Noting the blood on Steve's shirt, Sergeant Murphy asked, "Do you need a doctor?"

"I'm OK," Steve said. "I'll change my shirt once we're done here."

"Describe the guys who did this to you."

Steve said both of the two intruders were large and both were dressed in expensive-looking suits, that only one of them talked, the one with long Jesus hair and strange beady eyes, and when he did it was in a high wispy voice, that the other one's head was completely hairless, he even had no eyebrows or eyelashes, but it didn't look like he was sick, and he had a jagged tattoo that climbed up his neck into his face.

Sergeant Murphy said, "Sounds to me like Ricky and Al."

"Who are Ricky and Al?" Cecilia asked.

"Ricky is the one with hair. Al is his hairless buddy. Never talks. Just likes to beat people up. They do their thing mainly in Somerville but also stray into Cambridge from time to time. We know them quite well. We'll check the video surveillance in the lobby around the times they arrived, and also when they left, and if we see the two guys who match your descriptions, we'll email their images to you for confirmation."

Patrol Officer Daniels said, "Tell us what happened."

Steve said, "Ricky, the one with Jesus hair, demanded that we cancel the opening of the Visitation Room or they would come back to hurt us. Then Ricky pulled out a knife and cut the phone wires and Cecilia's hair. When I complained, he popped me on my nose, to shut me up. Al collected our wallets, PCs, and cellphones, and they left."

Sergeant Murphy asked, "Are you the company described in the *Herald*, that's opening up a room where your customers will be visited by ghosts?"

"We call it a Visitation Room," Steve said. "As we tell everyone, we don't know whether they really are ghosts."

"Like on the Red Line."

"Exactly. We've reproduced the environment in the Red Line train cars so that these visits can occur in our Visitation Room."

Sergeant Murphy said, "I got a call from one of my former colleagues on the force that he had met someone on the Red Line who we had arrested and sent to prison where he was killed. According to my colleague, and he is a very reliable guy, the dead scumbag was right beside him, talking to him, even poking him a few times."

"We're hoping that not too many of our customers are visited by dead scumbags."

Patrol Officer Daniels asked, "Did Ricky and Al say why they didn't want the Visitation Room to be opened?"

"Ricky said only that we had to cancel Opening Day. They wanted that message delivered to our company CEO, Harry West."

"That would be me." The two Cambridge cops, who had been standing with their backs to the office door, swiveled to face Harry and Alexandra as they came in. "And this," Harry said, "is Alexandra Ben-Tov, who chairs our board of directors. Sorry we weren't here sooner. We were down in Boston when Steve called us."

Alexandra said, "Holy Tabasco Sauce, Steve! What happened to you?"

"Just a bloody nose. I guess I irritated one of the thugs."

"He rose to my defense," Cecilia said. "Our hero! You should have seen him before he cleaned up."

"It's nothing," Steve said, dismissing his injury as being of no consequence, channeling the resolute manliness of Harrison Ford's Indiana Jones. He introduced the two police officers. "We've been telling Officers Murphy and Daniels what happened. They may know the two men."

"Ricky and Al," Sergeant Murphy said. "Two thugs from Somerville."

"I'll get the full story later from Steve and Cecilia," Harry said, "but I did hear the part about their demand that we cancel Opening Day. Is there anything you can do to protect us?"

"As I told Steve, first thing is to confirm these two are Ricky and Al. Once that's done, based on images from the video cameras, we'll bring them in to be identified positively in a line-up. If that all works out, we can charge them."

"How long would they be off the street?"

"Maybe a few days, until their bail is posted. Then after their trial, assuming they are convicted, maybe a couple of years. If you want my opinion, it won't matter a whole lot even if these two are in jail. They only do what their boss tells them and he has other thugs to take their place."

"Who's their boss?" Alexandra asked.

"They work for Michael Wallace, a Somerville gangster. His nickname is Shiny Mikey, which he hates. No-one calls him that to his face except for police officers when we get the chance."

"Why Shiny Mikey?"

"Wallace comes from a large family in Somerville, lots of brothers and sisters and cousins, most of them well known to the police. When he was a little kid, one of his occupations while he was skipping school was to shine shoes at the Davis Square T station. He's always been a nut for staying neat and clean, so he really got into it and he did a great job with the shoes, hence Shiny Mikey."

"A heartwarming tale," Alexandra said.

"It gets better. When his customers took out their wallets to pay him, he noticed whether they were carrying a wad of cash. If they were, he'd mark them for his brothers and cousins who were always hanging about the station. They'd follow the marks and mug them and then share the loot with Shiny Mikey. He was building a good business for himself when another shoeshine kid reported him to police. That was his first personal encounter with law enforcement. He was sent to a juvenile detention center as a ward of the Department of Youth Services. He used his time there to learn how to do better in his chosen profession."

"Shining shoes?"

"How to be a successful criminal. While he was still in juvie, he discovered the identity of the kid who had reported on him. That other shoeshine kid soon disappeared and no-one saw him again."

"OK, not so heartwarming."

Sergeant Murphy continued, "Wallace is not the most brilliant bulb on the Christmas tree. In fact, he's an uneducated clod. But he's an especially vicious clod who has made a good living for himself by tormenting local merchants for extortion payoffs."

Alexandra asked, "Why don't you arrest him since you know he's a criminal, probably a murderer, and also that these thugs Ricky and Al who were here today were following his orders?"

"Because he's got very good lawyers. We won't head down that road unless we have solid evidence."

"Then how do you suggest we deal with him?" Harry asked.

"You could hire bodyguards to stay with you 24/7 in your office and in your homes."

"Sergeant, we can't afford 24/7 bodyguards and there's no way we're all going to hide behind bodyguards for the rest of our lives."

"Then you need to make Wallace change his mind so that he'll leave you alone."

"How do we do that?"

"Shiny Mikey has one overriding pre-occupation, his own self-interest. If you'll roll over without causing him too much trouble, then fine, he'll roll you over. If you make it too costly for him, then he may re-consider."

"Do you have any idea what he'd have against the Visitation Room?"

"I can't figure it," the Sergeant said. "Even Wallace has lost family members that he cared about. According to people who know, he idolized his older brother Howie who was something of a legend in his twisted family."

"What happened to Howie?" Harry asked.

"Howie was a good looking kid with an evil streak, kind of a one-kid crime wave in Somerville, including street crimes, break-ins, and muggings, especially around Davis Square, and a few suspected but unproven murders. Then one day he clubbed a woman in a Stop & Shop parking lot, and stole her purse and her car. Somerville police chased him all over town. He side-swiped a few cars and even clipped a pedestrian, probably on purpose, an old man caught in an intersection, until finally he was killed when he smashed into a garbage truck, which we all thought was a fitting conclusion to his career."

"Live stupid and die young," Patrol Office Daniels said.

"You'd think that Wallace might want to communicate with Howie again if he could," Sergeant Murphy said. "That's how I would look at it."

After the two police officers left, Steve said, "Today I learned an important lesson. Never open our office door to anyone we don't know."

"Let's get one other thing out of the way," Alexandra said. "We're not changing our plans because of a gangster named Shiny Mikey. We've come too far to give up now. This is too important to us, and to our customers. I don't care what it takes; we're going to open our Visitation Room. Do we all agree on that?"

Harry said, "That's also how I see it. We've got to see it through."

"I agree," Cecilia said.

"Me too," Steve said.

Harry said, "So we need to prepare. I want all of our staff to carry panic buttons at all times, that identify their locations and can be used to call for help. Steve, can you arrange that?"

"Yes. I'll do it right away. They can be worn on bracelets, on watches, on belts, on necklaces, almost any way you want."

"Order them for everyone," Harry said. "Now concerning your PCs and cellphones, how much of our company information has been compromised?"

"The laptops are pretty much covered," Steve said. "If they shut the cover, it puts the laptop to sleep. To restart it requires a password. Three wrong passwords produce a warning: Enter the correct password within one hour or the hard-drive will be re-formatted, erasing the memory."

"What if they keep the laptop covers open?"

"Then each laptop will be constantly looking for an unblocked WiFi connection to the Internet of which there are hundreds throughout Cambridge. As soon as I alerted our PC security service, less than ten minutes after Ricky and Al left, it sent a message to each laptop to erase the hard-drive. By now the laptops should function only as paperweights or door-stoppers."

"No more jokes about your being paranoid," Alexandra said.

"My motto is that you can't be too careful," Steve said. "I should have remembered that before letting those guys in."

"It's OK, Steve, you're allowed one mistake; you can stop beating yourself up," Harry said. "How about your cellphones?"

"I installed a security app on all of our phones. After we alerted our mobile operator that our phones were stolen, messages were transmitted that trigger the app to wipe all the data on the phone."

"So no problem either with the phones?"

"Maybe. They had ten to fifteen minutes to look at our contact lists and to read stored emails before Cecilia and I were able to get through to our mobile operator. Also if they turn off the phone's mobile radio, the mobile operator has no way to deliver the data-destroy message, which leaves exposed the files stored on the phone, both our contact lists and our emails."

"How would they know to turn off the mobile radio?"

"It's pretty widely understood by now that your cellphone location is constantly tracked by the mobile operator. I'd guess that Ricky and Al would have turned the phones off right after they grabbed them from us, and then when they turned them back on, they'd immediately disable the phones' mobile radios."

"So we have to assume they can read all of our addresses and contact information, and can probably figure out what we have been doing from the stored emails."

"Right. Sorry."

"And of course they also have your and Cecilia's home addresses from your wallets."

"Yep."

"Get those panic buttons, pronto. If you see anything strange around your apartments, don't go in. Use the panic buttons, call the police. Be careful."

Alexandra said, "Cecilia, would you like to camp out at my condo in Boston? I have plenty of room."

"Thanks, Alexandra," Cecilia said. "There's also a small matter of a husband, an eight-month-old little boy, and a cat that I can't leave behind. Anyway the bad guys will have your address as well."

Michael Wallace instructed Ricky and Al, "Tell me everything that happened. Do they understand now what they have to do?"

Ricky described the young man and woman whose iPhones and wallets were now on Wallace's desk. He didn't mention the clump of hair that he had clipped from Cecilia's head since that was his personal souvenir. He recounted that the Chinese guy said that he couldn't do anything himself but he promised to deliver the message to their CEO, Harry West. Ricky said that he and Al cut their phone lines and took their iPhones and laptops to delay their calling the police.

"Maybe you should have tied them up or knocked them unconscious, or even shot the fuckers, and make the point for this Harry West."

"I did tap the guy a little to teach him some respect. But you told us to ask nicely."

"So where are their PCs?"

"Al tossed them in a trash barrel before we left the building. I figured we wouldn't be able to use them anyway since we'd need to know the passwords and I didn't want to draw attention to ourselves, carrying them."

"You could have put them in a shopping bag."

"I'm sorry, Mr. Wallace, we were in a hurry. I told Al to dump them."

"So what do we know from these cellphones and wallets?"

"We know the home addresses of the two in the office. We also have contact information on everyone else they know, including Harry West if you want to reach him and talk to him directly."

"You did good," Wallace said. "Now I want you and Al to stay low for a while, go down to Providence. I'll tell your uncle Kevin to expect you."

Thirty Three

MASSACHUSETTS STATE REPRESENTATIVE Walter MacAuliff filed bill H04922 to require licensing of "reality-altering" services in the Commonwealth of Massachusetts, defining such services as those "offered to the public, in return for payment, in which customers perceive deceased persons, whether by sight, sound, or touch, as if such persons were present with them."

H04922 was taken up by the House and Senate's Joint Committee on Consumer Protection and Professional Licensure. The Joint Committee scheduled a public hearing on the bill and invited LifePlus, Inc., to testify.

"Don't panic," was the advice given to Harry and Alexandra by Gary Pollack, LifePlus's legal counsel, of Skiffington, Skiffington, and Mohr.

"Why wouldn't we panic?" Alexandra asked. "They're trying to put us out of business."

"They've got a long way to go before MacAuliff's bill is passed."

The public hearing on H04922 was held in Room B-2 in the Basement Annex, one of plainer hearing rooms in the State House. At the front of the room, a long slightly-curved table extended almost the entire width of the room; it was raised on a dais, and flanked at each end by US and Commonwealth of Massachusetts flags. A large mural on the wall behind the table depicted the skirmish in Lexington that started the Revolutionary War, showing smoke rising from the muskets of red-coated British soldiers, American militia men lying dead and wounded on Lexington Green, distraught women who were attempted to care for them, and a small child sitting dazed and alone on the ground.

Of the twenty one seats lined up behind the table for the members of the House and Senate Joint Committee, only seven were occupied. Apparently most of the members had more pressing business elsewhere. Walter MacAuliff, the Joint Committee's House Chair, had taken his seat and was reading a *Boston Globe*. The seats on either side of him were vacant; including those belonging to the Joint Committee's House Vice-Chair and its Senate Chair and Vice-Chair.

The *Globe* had reported the start of the Joint Committee's public hearing with a brief note on an inside page plus an editorial titled, "Waste of Time," which went on, "Representative MacAuliff's bill will serve no useful purpose. It ostensibly would license a broad category of reality-altering services but make no mistake, the bill is aimed directly at the popular Visitation Room which will be opened soon by LifePlus, Inc., a start-up based in Cambridge. According to the company, almost all of the time slots in the Visitation Room for its first three months of operation were reserved on the first day that the reservation system went online two weeks ago. The burden is on Representative MacAuliff to demonstrate that his legislation is needed to protect the public. We're not convinced."

After he gaveled the hearing to order, Representative MacAuliff waved a copy of the *Globe* editorial in the air. "As usual, they got it all wrong," he said. "Even if these reality-altering merchants were handing out LSD or cocaine, the *Globe* would say, 'that's OK, it's a lifestyle choice.' In fact, they'd be in favor of it! So they're not alarmed by use of secret technologies that might scramble the brain-waves of people who go into these rooms. It's no problem for them that people might be tricked into parting with their hard-earned cash in return for an empty promise that they will see their loved ones who have passed. It's OK with the *Globe* that this so-called Visitation Room denies the reality of God and the teachings of the Church and seduces people to search for spirits of their loved ones in a secular setting rather than through worship and prayer. It's not OK with me. It is not OK with the good people of our Commonwealth who honor family values. And I believe that my colleagues in the House and in the Senate will conclude that it's not OK with them, either."

With that, Representative MacAuliff announced that the Joint Committee was ready to hear its first witness, Ms. Alexandra Ben-Tov, Chair of the board of directors of LifePlus, Inc., accompanied by the company CEO, Harry West, and their legal counsel, Gary Pollack, Esq.

"Thank you, Mr. Chairman," Alexandra said. She raised a binder in her right hand. "We have distributed copies of the information in this binder to the Committee staff. You will see that our business has nothing to hide. We are a Massachusetts-based start-up. We already have eight full-time employees and are hiring more as we prepare for our Opening Day a week from now. We will operate our first Visitation Room in Boston and will also expand to additional locations in the Commonwealth. The data in this binder describe months of tests that demonstrate that a person's time in our Visitation Room will produce no measurable negative health effects."

Representative MacAuliff leaned towards his microphone and said, "Just a minute, Ms. Ben Tov. How do you explain the death of Mr. Rodney Williamson last year on the Red Line? A good family man with a wife and two young children, a professional, who by all accounts was driven insane by a so-called visitation that caused him to jump off the train? How do your months of tests explain that?"

"Sir, we don't know what happened with Mr. Williamson. What we do know is that during our testing, we looked for any physical or mental effects in our test partners, under the supervision of a highly respected consulting physician, and we found no measurable negative effects. Her report is included in the binder. During our pre-operational phase, we have been very sensitive to any distress that our test partners might have experienced, and none has been reported. In fact, just the opposite. Our test partners were very grateful for their experiences with us. In that regard, we can also attest that a high proportion of our test partners, almost 80% of them, did report encounters with loved ones. So despite the concerns raised in this bill, there are no health issues and there is no fraud, and therefore, no need for the bill now in front of the Committee."

Representative MacAuliff said, "We requested a commitment from you to provide identities of your Visitation Room customers, and their contact information, starting now with those who have reserved time slots, so that we will be able to conduct our own examinations of potential health effects. We have not received that commitment from you. Nor have we received the names of your test partners, which we also requested."

"Mr. MacAuliff, to protect the privacy of our customers and our test partners, it is our policy not to release their names."

"It is not up to you whether to comply with our request."

"That is our policy, sir. We have privacy obligations that we intend to honor."

"Well, if you don't cooperate voluntarily, you can expect to receive a subpoena. What is your policy on taking payments from your customers who experience nothing in your Visitation Room except for disappointment?"

"We are clear with our customers, both on our website and on their printed tickets, that an encounter with a loved one is not guaranteed. However, based on our pre-operational Visitation Room tests, we do not expect our customers to be disappointed. I have to tell you, Representative MacAuliff, that this is very personal to me. My daughter Ariel was killed ten years ago by a drunk driver. Last July, I was fortunate enough to meet her on the Red Line and I fully expect to meet her again in the Visitation Room and, in fact, I am counting on that."

Whispering rustled around the back of the room. Alexandra Ben-Tov wasn't just another business person defending her company so that she could make more money. She, herself, expected to meet the spirit of her dead child in the company's Visitation Room. "Could we have quiet back there?" Representative MacAuliff demanded.

Alexandra's reference to the drunk driver responsible for the death of her child highlighted a sensitive topic for the Representative and he was ready now to move on. "Do any other Committee members have questions or comments?" he asked. They shook their heads, since this was Walter MacAuliff's show, and he said, "Thank you Ms. Ben-Tov. We will now hear from Dr. Louis Johannsen, a noted physician in pediatrics and mental health at St. Mary's Hospital, a fine institution which is located in my district in South Boston."

Alexandra and Gary Pollack pushed back from the table but Harry put his hand on Alexandra's arm to detain her. He leaned towards the microphone and told the Committee members, "Before we leave, I would appreciate an opportunity to add a brief statement of my own to Ms. Ben-Tov's testimony."

"If you keep it brief," Representative McAuliff said. "We're trying to manage a tight schedule in this hearing and there are others who wish to speak."

"Thank you, Representative. First, to introduce myself, I am Harry West, CEO of LifePlus."

"We met earlier, I believe, when you were a consultant to the MBTA," MacAuliff said.

"Yes, sir."

A grin fluttered on MacAuliff's lips as he fashioned a witty jibe, one of his trademarks in political circles, "You were against the ghosts on the Red Line, and now you're for them."

"Circumstances change, Representative," Harry said, refusing to be drawn.

"Go ahead, then, Mr. West."

"Start-ups like LifePlus must overcome many challenges. We have done so. We have proven and tested our technology, we have raised capital, we have hired employees, we've leased spaces for our service and for our office, and we are now ready to launch a service that in just a few weeks since our res system came online has demonstrated enormous customer demand."

"We're duly impressed with all that you've achieved, Mr. West, but our job is to protect the public."

"What I'm trying to say, Representative, is that ours is not a typical business. We will provide to our customers experiences that have only been imagined over the centuries and millennia of human history. I'd ask the members of the Joint Committee to consider how amazing it is that in our Visitation Room, people will encounter their loved ones again who have passed on. Very, very few of us, including myself, would have believed this to be possible. And yet, our customers will have this incredible experience, and Ms. Ben-Tov and I hope to have it ourselves, as she has told you. Those among you who have lost a loved one, think about what the Visitation Room is offering. What value would you place on such an experience? Wouldn't it be important to you? Wouldn't you want this experience, even if only for a few minutes?" Harry paused for a moment and then continued, "At the same time, we understand the concerns that have been raised. That's why we have provided the Committee staff with our voluminous test data that refute all of these concerns."

"We'll be the judge of that, Mr. West," Representative MacAuliff said. "Although we do appreciate your inspirational speech. Are you finished?"

"Not quite. I have to tell the Committee that H04922 is not our only worry, even though, if it were passed, it would most likely destroy all that we are trying to do."

"That's not our bill's intent. Licensing will protect the public. You'll just have to comply with licensing requirements."

"The licensing regime proposed in this bill would require an impossible standard of proof, Mr. Chairman. But that is not my primary point."

"Then for heaven's sake, what is it, Mr. West?"

"I want to inform the Committee that members of our staff were threatened and assaulted by two men who demanded that we cancel the opening of our Visitation Room."

Whispering again swept through the room. MacAuliff rapped the table with his wooden gavel, "Anyone who can't resist talking is invited to leave," he said.

When quiet was restored, Harry continued, "They threatened to attack us if we do not comply. Based on descriptions provided by our staff members, Cambridge police identified them as thugs working for a notorious Boston area criminal."

"Again, Mr. West, if you are trying to make a point, please find a way to get to it more quickly."

"My point, Representative MacAuliff, is that you are probably not on the right track when your bill would produce the same result as that demanded by a well-known gangster."

"I object to that characterization. It is offensive."

"I stand by it, sir."

Another surge of whispering erupted in the Hearing Room and again MacAuliff gaveled for silence. "Surely you are not claiming that our bill is intended to benefit a gangster."

"No, Representative MacAuliff. I have no evidence that you are sponsoring your bill specifically for his benefit."

"That's quite enough, Mr. West. Are you done now, finally?"

"Yes, sir."

"Then, thank you, please make way now for Dr. Johanssen."

Dr. Johanssen took his place at the witness table. This was familiar territory for him and he spoke with confidence before his friends on the Committee. He testified frequently at the State House on matters related to family planning (pro-abstinence), and abortion (against). He and Walter MacAuliff went way back, having attended the same elementary school and having served together as altar boys. Dr. Johanssen pointed out that a reality-altering environment, such as the Visitation Rooms were reputed to be, could, in his professional opinion, cause people to become disoriented, and could produce lasting cognitive effects.

"Like what happened on the Red Line to Mr. Rodney Williamson?" asked Representative MacAuliff.

"Possibly, yes."

"What do you recommend, Dr. Johanssen?" the Representative asked.

"That the Commonwealth should develop standard tests to assess mental functioning of persons both before and after they spend time in the Visitation Room."

"Would people find such tests to be intrusive?"

"Some might object initially. I'd recommend that everyone be given a pamphlet that explains why the tests are in their best interest plus a website address where they can obtain additional information."

"We'd need the identities of these people in order to administer the standard tests, would we not?"

"Yes, of course."

"Which is why we have requested their identities from the company," Representative MacAuliff pointed out. "Dr. Johanssen, who would give these tests and evaluate the results?"

"Psychologists under the leadership of a licensing authority that would be established under your bill, Mr. Chairman."

Next up were two men and a woman who had served as test partners in the pre-operational Visitation Room. They had volunteered to testify in response to a request that was broadcast by Representative MacAuliff on a radio talk show. The two men were on script – nothing happened, it was a fraud – but the woman had a different story. Renée Curtis from Allston told the Committee members, "I met my mother in the Visitation Room. It was the most wonderful thing."

Ms. Curtis' testimony provided the headline in the next day's *Herald*, "State House Witness Saw Mom's Ghost."

The *Boston Globe* focused on a different aspect of the story, with its headline, "Gangster Threatens Visitation Room," and continued, "LifePlus, Inc., CEO Harry West told a sparsely-attended joint committee hearing chaired by Representative Walter MacAuliff, Democrat of South Boston, that a Boston-area gangster, whom he declined to name, has demanded that his company cancel next week's Opening Day for the Visitation Room located in the Marriott at the Waterfront. West said the bill (H04922) sponsored by Representative MacAuliff would similarly result in canceling the Visitation Room's opening, although he had no reason to believe that the Representative was acting on behalf of the gangster."

Michael Wallace, the gangster in question, concluded that Harry West needed more persuading. Apparently he hadn't understood the message delivered by Ricky and Al. Now he was jabbering about it in a public hearing at the State House. Most people who he dealt with were not so foolish. They did what they were told, and they knew better than to talk about it.

Maybe this Harry West, just because he had a PhD after his name, and he was close with MIT, and his fucking Visitation Room was located in a fancy Marriott in Boston, maybe he believed that Michael Wallace of Somerville did not merit his respect.

Thirty Four

A BRILLIANT WHITE light flared on Harry's bedroom windows followed an instant later by an explosive WHUMP that shook his house. Then a second explosion shattered windows downstairs and sent contents of shelves crashing onto the floor. Scrambling to his bedroom window, Harry saw his 10-year-old Toyota Camry that he'd parked on his driveway a few hours earlier engulfed in an inferno of red, yellow, and white flames. The black and white smoke billowing from the fire smelled strongly of gasoline.

Harry grabbed his cellphone that he kept next to his bed and, steadying his trembling fingers, jabbed the buttons for 911. When the 911 operator answered, he shouted, "My car has exploded! It's on fire in my driveway!"

She replied in a calming voice, "Just give me your name and address and then tell me what happened." He did so, and she said that emergency vehicles were now being dispatched. "When will they get here?" he asked. "The fire is just outside my house."

"Any moment now. They're on their way. Meanwhile get out of your house, just in case." Indeed even as they were speaking, Harry heard sirens approaching. He dressed franticly, jamming one of his legs in his trousers as he tried to shove it through. He remembered at the last moment to put on shoes to protect his feet from broken glass, dashed out of his bedroom, scrambled down his stairs, and ran outside.

A firefighter wearing a helmet with a plastic visor, a bulky yellow coat and pants with reflective stripes, and thick fire-resistive gloves, interrogated Harry, "Was anyone in the car?" "Is anyone still in the house?" Hearing "no" on both questions, he ordered Harry to stand aside while he and other similarly attired firefighters drenched the remnants of his car with water blasting from two hoses that snaked like giant pythons across his small front yard. They also soaked the wall of his house that was closest to the driveway which appeared singed by the flames and at risk of catching fire. Two ladder trucks, a fire rescue truck, an ambulance, and a police car jammed Harry's narrow residential street. Their flashing red and blue lights bounced crazily off the trees and houses, and the roar of truck engines and pumps and loud chatter on the firefighters' mobile radios filled the suburban nighttime air.

Harry's neighbors clustered on nearby lawns watching the excitement and sharing rumors. His next door neighbor, a Harvard professor wearing a nightgown, bathrobe, and slippers, approached Harry to ask if he was alright and if anyone had been hurt. Harry told her that he was fine and thanked her for asking. She said, "Let me know if you need anything," and he thanked her again and said that he would.

After the fire was extinguished, a firefighter took off his helmet and introduced himself to Harry as Arlington's Assistant Fire Chief Robert Middlebury. "Are you the owner of the vehicle?" he asked. Harry responded that he was, and provided his name and contact information.

"Can you tell me what happened here?" Middlebury asked.

"There were two explosions. I looked out of my window and saw that my car was on fire."

Once again he was asked, "Is everyone accounted for? Anyone hurt?"

"No. I live here alone. I wasn't in the car. I was in bed."

"Mr. West," Assistant Fire Chief Middlebury said, "this fire was not an accident. We'll turn this over to the police arson investigators but we know already, someone torched your car."

At 5:30 A.M., Harry called Alexandra, catching her just before she left for her morning run on the Boston Esplanade along the Charles River, and told her about his Camry.

"Are you OK?"

"Yes."

"Have you also called to warn Steve and Cecilia?"

"Not yet. I've been pretty busy here. I'll call them next. Be careful. Keep your panic button handy."

"You be careful, too, Harry. Call Steve and Cecilia now."

Steve was still groggy with sleep with Harry reached him. After he finally understood what Harry was telling him, Steve said he would text the other LifePlus staff to put them on alert. Cecilia was up and getting her son organized for day-care when Harry called. She assured Harry that she was keeping her panic button always within easy reach, and had also given one to her husband who worked as a lawyer in downtown Boston, since he drove their Volvo that currently was parked in the alley behind their condo.

Harry commuted to work each day by bus from Arlington to the Red Line station at Alewife, and then via the Red Line to Central if he was stopping at Blair West International, or to Kendall/MIT if he was going to the LifePlus office on Memorial Drive. But he needed his Camry on weekends; it had been cheap to run and was generally reliable, and now it would have to be replaced. To that end, he called his insurance company and was promised a check for the total value of the car, less the deductible, once the company received an official report on the fire signed both by Harry and by the Arlington fire department.

At 8:05 A.M., an Arlington police car pulled into Harry's driveway behind the wreck. The Arlington police officer, dressed in plain clothes, introduced himself as the department's arson investigator. A big man with white hair, he stepped over the yellow caution tape that had been placed around the car by a firefighter earlier that morning. The Camry's blackened metal frame lay tilted on the driveway since three of its tires had melted. Inside and around the frame was a mess of rubble and ashes. The arson investigator used a pole to sift through the Camry's remains and took pictures from each side, and from the front and back. He told Harry that discovering the precise cause of a car fire was difficult because everything, including the cause, was usually consumed. However, he was sure, based on Harry's report, that arson was involved: The car had been stationary on the driveway with its engine turned off when it happened; the fire had occurred during the early morning which was typical of vehicle arsons; and there were two explosions, probably the first from the accelerant tossed into the car, and the second from the gas tank.

"Do you have any idea who might want to burn your car?" he asked.

"I do," Harry said. "I'm the CEO of a start-up company. Two thugs recently came to our office and threatened my staff. Cambridge police identified them and said they usually work for a gangster in Somerville named Michael Wallace."

"Shiny Mikey," the arson investigator said. "What's your issue with him?"

"We're about to open a Visitation Room in Boston where people can communicate with their loved ones, like on the Red Line last year. Wallace wants us to cancel the opening. We don't know why."

"You're the guys offering visits from ghosts!"

"Well, something like that."

"We recently lost a police officer; cancer took him, he had a young wife, two kids, a terrible thing. Some of the guys plan to try out your Visitation Room to see if they can communicate with him."

"I hope that we'll be able to open so that they can," Harry said. "What happens next? Will you question Michael Wallace?"

"We can," the arson investigator replied. "But we don't have much evidence here and I doubt that he'll confess. We'll look for witnesses who may have seen someone near your car."

"I can give you descriptions of his two thugs, if that would help. Their names are Ricky and Al."

"Yeah, we know them. Don't get your hopes up. You live on a very quiet street so I wouldn't count on anyone seeing them at that hour of the morning."

"You're not very encouraging."

"Well, you'll get insurance money for the value of the car. But you're right, if Shiny Mikey is upset with you, I'd take care. Maybe hire a bodyguard."

It took most of the rest of the morning for Harry to pick up, sweep, and vacuum shards of glass from his broken windows, and to arrange with a carpenter who had worked on his house previously to replace the windows and the shingles on the outside wall that had been scoured off by water from the fire hose.

When he finally arrived at the LifePlus office shortly before noon, he found Steve and Cecilia there, looking glum.

"Are your faces gloomy because of me?" Harry asked.

"No, we've already forgotten about your car," Steve said. "Cecilia heard this morning from Genevieve LaPierre. She wants to terminate our lease at the Marriott."

"Did Genevieve say why?" Harry asked Cecilia, who was responsible for managing LifePlus' relationships with its partners.

"She said the hotel had been threatened," Cecilia said. "She wants to talk with you."

Genevieve LaPierre, the young and ambitious General Manager of the Boston Marriott Hotel at the Waterfront, had quickly embraced the idea of hosting a Visitation Room when it was presented to her by Harry and Alexandra. A regular commuter on the Red Line, she had witnessed other riders encountering their loved ones. She took note of the excitement, the crowds, and the higher hotel occupancy levels throughout the Boston area from a whole new category of seeker-tourists.

She foresaw that a Visitation Room would raise the Marriott's profile in Boston. Also, it would generate new revenues for the hotel. LifePlus would pay rent for otherwise-empty space in the hotel basement. LifePlus also would subsidize an attractive amenity for Marriott Hotel guests, a 10% discount for their reserved time slots in the Visitation Room. Genevieve expected that increased lobby traffic from outside the hotel would produce revenues for the hotel's restaurants and shops, more than compensating for heavier use of the restrooms just off the lobby.

When Representative Walter MacAuliff introduced his bill, Genevieve emailed Alexandra and Harry, "Don't worry. Good sense will surely prevail, even here in Massachusetts."

When parish priests, following a script handed down to them from the Archdiocese, fulminated against the Visitation Room and warned its prospective customers and everyone else who was involved, about the risk to their good standing in the Church, Genevieve told her LifePlus partners that she would not be intimidated. "I don't have time for priests or Reverends of any stripe," she said.

In short, Genevieve LaPierre had been an enthusiastic and stalwart ally.

Therefore, when Harry called her, it was disconcerting that the first thing she said after "hi-how-are-you" was, "Harry, I'm terribly sorry, but I have to terminate your lease for the Visitation Room. You'll have to cancel Opening Day."

"Cecilia told me that you'd been threatened."

"You remember your testimony at MacAuliff's hearing?"

"Of course."

"You remember the part about the gangster?"

"I do. Has something happened?"

"I got a phone call this morning. He threatened that they will damage the hotel and hurt our guests if we allow the Visitation Room to open."

"Have you called the police?"

"Not yet. The caller warned me not do. If I did, he said, they would target my hotel for sure. Anyway, before I lift the lid on that Pandora's box, I wanted to talk with you first."

"OK, thanks for that, tell me what he said."

"The call was to my unpublished cell number. That was a bad sign, right there."

"Most likely they picked that off of Steve's or Cecilia's phones."

"Jesus! How did they get Steve's and Cecilia's phones?"

"About two weeks ago, two men came to our office and threatened Steve and Cecilia who were here at the time. Said they wanted us to cancel our opening. When they left, they took the phones."

"Two weeks ago! And you're only telling me now?"

"I did mention the threat in my testimony before MacAuliff's Joint Committee, as you know, so we weren't keeping it a secret."

"You failed to mention the phones."

"I thought it was our problem to solve, not the Marriott's, and that we could manage it by increasing our security measures."

"Is there anything else you haven't told me?"

"Cambridge police have identified the two men who came to our office as thugs named Ricky and Al and according to Sergeant James Murphy, they belong to a crime family in Somerville headed by a gangster named Michael Wallace. Ricky has long hair. Al is hairless and has a big tattoo on his neck and face. We can forward their pictures to you, so that your security people will recognize them if they come to the Marriott."

"Ricky and Al."

"Yes, I don't know their last names."

"Anything else?"

"My old Toyota Camry was torched early this morning in my driveway."

There was silence on the line, and Harry continued, "That sounds bad, I know, but I hope you'll give us time to deal with this, Genevieve. It's critical for us to go forward with the opening of the Visitation Room as we've planned. Caving in to these threats now would finish us."

"I understand that, Harry. I'm really sorry."

"Can you tell me more about your phone call?"

"The man had a high whispery voice. He said, 'Listen to what I tell you. Don't let them open the Visitation Room. Otherwise we will make it very bad for your hotel.' I asked him who he was, and he said to never mind that, just do what he said. I asked why, and he repeated that I should stop asking questions, and follow instructions. I asked what he meant by 'very bad for your hotel.' He replied that things happen like fires or guests being injured in accidents. I told him that the Marriott has a binding contract with LifePlus. He said contracts can be terminated. I told him that we'd have to follow a termination process which would take some time. He said the more time it took, especially if that meant the Visitation Room were allowed to open next week, the more risk to the hotel, so I had better move fast."

"So he said 'fast,' but not immediately."

"You need to do something, Harry. Deal with it. Once I bring in the police, our parent company will get involved. There's no doubt about what they will instruct me to do, and I'll have to agree with them. I love our Visitation Room and I love you and Alexandra but I just can't put our guests in danger."

Harry's BlackBerry buzzed just after he disconnected with Genevieve. Caller ID showed "Blocked by Caller."

"Harry West," Harry said, when he took the call.

"This is Michael Wallace, Harry. Do you know who I am?" Wallace's voice sounded calm, confident and smooth like that of a businessman or indeed, a consultant, much like Harry thought that he himself might sound to others.

Harry replied, "According to Cambridge Police, you sent the two thugs who assaulted our staff, robbed us, and threatened us."

"They were asking nicely."

"You threatened our partner at the Marriott."

"You weren't listening, Harry, based on your little speech in the State House. That's a big mistake. You have a big mouth." Now Wallace sounded more like the gangster that Harry had imagined.

"And my car was torched this morning."

"So am I getting your attention finally?"

"Mr. Wallace, what do you have against our Visitation Room?"

"It's bad for my business when dead people don't stay dead. So I will make it even worse for you when you bring them back."

"We don't bring them back, Mr. Wallace. We only enable our customers to communicate with their loved ones. They are still deceased."

"I had a discussion on the Red Line with someone I know for a fact is dead. He was not a loved one. But he was there on the

Red Line dripping his fucking blood and dirt right in front of me. It was not a good conversation."

"Mr. Wallace, if you don't want another visit from this person or from anyone else who has passed on, you can avoid it by staying out of our Visitation Room. Why ruin this for everyone else?"

"Here's the thing, Harry, don't open your Visitation Room. Pack it up. That's all you need to know."

"Mr. Wallace, the police are aware that you're behind these threats. You can't just break the law like this and get away with it. You'll go to jail."

"Did the police tell you about my business interests, Harry?"

"They gave me some idea."

"So ask yourself, why am I not already in jail? What I choose to do will be your problem, not mine. Do you understand me?"

"I think so."

"Maybe you do, maybe you don't. Maybe you're brave for yourself. Your ex-wife in her condo in the Back Bay, and your Chinese guy who lives in Cambridge, and the girl you hired with her kid and husband in the South End, are they as brave, or as stupid, as you are?"

"Leave them out of it."

"Or what? Do what I say. Forget about the fucking Visitation Room. Do something else with your life."

"Mr. Wallace…"

"Yes…"

"You owe us for the two PCs and two cellphones, and we want the wallets returned that Ricky and Al took including everything that was inside them. And you owe me a used Toyota Camry."

Michael Wallace barked out a laugh and said, "Don't be an asshole, Harry," and hung up.

Cecilia Bridges and Steve Cheng pretended not to listen to Harry's end of his phone call with Wallace until Harry demanded the return of their cellphones, PCs and wallets, and a replacement for his Camry, at which point they stopped all pretense and looked at him expectantly. Harry said, "As you may have guessed, that was Shiny Mikey. I'll tell you everything once Alexandra gets here."

Five minutes later, after Alexandra arrived for their scheduled review of LifePlus' progress, Harry described the immolation of his Camry and his phone calls with Genevieve and with Michael Wallace. He told them about Wallace's implied threat to each of them.

"We assumed that he knew where we lived," Cecilia said. "His threat is not a surprise."

Harry replied, "I don't want any of you hurt on my account."

"On *our* account, Harry," Alexandra said. "Don't worry about that. We're in this together."

Steve agreed, "I'm not about to give up now."

"What about you, Cecilia?" Harry asked. "I'd understand if you decided this was more risk to you and your family than you anticipated."

"I'm not bailing out. My husband and I have discussed it."

"You're all real troopers," Harry said. "Thank you."

Alexandra said, "We've got to make Michael Wallace back off. And he has to do it in a way that convinces Genevieve that he won't be a problem."

"Alexandra, what do you suggest?" Harry asked.

"My father Beni Ben-Tov would know what to do. He'd roll his tank into Somerville, park it outside Wallace's place of business, lob a few shells, and then order in a bulldozer to remove the debris."

"So we need a tank, a bulldozer, and a deceased Israeli tank commander."

Steve said, "Meanwhile, Harry, you should call the Cambridge Police."

Alexandra said, "Tell them that it's not just Ricky and Al any more. Tell them about your car and the threats. Find out what they can do about it."

Harry called the number he had been given by Sergeant James Murphy. A woman answered, "Cambridge Police Department," and when Harry asked for Sergeant Murphy, she replied that the Sergeant was unavailable but that she would forward Harry's message. Harry said, "Please let him know that Harry West called about Michael Wallace. Tell him that we have a serious problem. If he can get back to me during the next ten minutes, have him call our office phone. Otherwise ask him to call my cell phone," and then Harry read off both numbers.

A LifePlus office desk-phone rang eight minutes later, showing "Cambridge Police Department" on Caller ID. When Harry picked up the phone, he told Sergeant Murphy that the other LifePlus executives whom the Sergeant had met earlier were in the office. The Sergeant agreed to have the call put on speakerphone.

"What's going on?" Sergeant Murphy asked.

"Michael Wallace is what's going on. Very early this morning, my car was torched in my driveway. We suspect Wallace is behind it. Also this morning, someone with a whispery voice, probably Ricky, called the manager of the Marriott in Boston that hosts our Visitation Room and threatened the hotel and its guests."

"Did the hotel manager report the threat to Boston Police?"

"Not yet. She wants to see what we can do first. Also she was warned not to."

"Tell her she should report it."

"Then Wallace called me directly and made the same demand that we heard earlier from Ricky and Al, and threatened all of us if we didn't comply."

Alexandra asked. "Sergeant Murphy, what can the police do about this?"

"Ms. Ben-Tov, we have put out an APB on Ricky and Al. No luck on that yet. Concerning Wallace, we may have enough now for probable cause to seek his arrest. You could come to the police station and file a formal report with us. Then it will be up to the district attorney's office whether to proceed with a criminal case."

"Will we get protection if we file the report?" Alexandra asked.

"Maybe it will help. Perhaps the Court will issue an injunction for him to cease his threats and to stay clear of you and your business."

"Great. That's what we want," Harry said.

"Unfortunately, Michael Wallace won't be overly worried about an injunction."

"I don't believe this!" Alexandra declared. "So we just sit back and let him destroy everything we've worked for? He burns our cars, harasses our partners, and threatens our lives? And we can't do anything about it?"

Harry said, "We'll file a formal report."

Thirty Five

THE ROBERT W. HEALY Public Safety Facility on Sixth Avenue in East Cambridge, named for a long-serving city manager, looks like a multi-layer cake with six floors of darkened-glass windows slotted between light-brown brick columns. Hanging from the tops of the columns are large light fixtures that resemble cake frosting ornaments. According to a bronze plaque set in a small garden in front of the building, the lanterns in these fixtures cast a pale blue light on the building's façade except during emergencies when they flash different colors to signify different categories of response, blue for police, red for fire, and green for medical.

A uniformed cop inside a glassed-in kiosk in the lobby watched Harry approach and waited impassively to hear his explanation of the purpose of his visit. Harry said he was meeting Sergeant James Murphy. The cop asked for his driver's license as a form of photo ID, which he said would be returned when Harry left the building. He propped Harry's license against his monitor and keyed-in his information.

Several minutes later, Sergeant Murphy appeared behind a glass door that separates the lobby from the inner building, and beckoned to Harry to come through to join him.

They occupied a small sparsely-furnished office space, equipped with only a rectangular wooden table with two wooden chairs on each side. The Sergeant placed a digital recorder on the table. "Talk in the direction of this recorder. We'll send you a transcription of your report in case there's anything you want to revise or clarify. You can also check it with your colleagues and your partner at the Marriott. We'll need your signature on the final version."

When Harry was done describing for the record all that had happened, he asked, "Will you arrest Wallace now?"

Sergeant Murphy replied, "Harry, I'll be honest with you. We've got to coordinate four police departments, in Cambridge, in Boston, in Arlington, and in Somerville; we don't have any direct evidence yet about your car; and although Wallace's threats are understandably alarming to you, we deal every day with actual serious crimes, murders, child abuse, violent muggings, home invasions, gang shootings, drug dealers in schoolyards, it's a long list."

"What are you telling me, Sergeant Murphy?"

"I'm saying that even if we arrest Wallace, unless we obtain evidence that we can use to put him away for a long time, I can't promise that the district attorney will take this case all the way to trial."

"Why not? What does it take to stop a criminal like him?"

"Probably more than we've got at the moment."

"More for what? More to put Wallace away, or more to get the police involved enough to do the job?"

"Both. Wallace has good lawyers; he intimidates jurors and even some judges; he avoids leaving evidence around; witnesses are afraid to testify against him; he donates generously to charities operated by the Church; and he's connected politically in his home town. So we're wary of moving too aggressively unless we have a solid case and a significant crime to charge him with."

"I've heard about the wheels of justice grinding slowly but this is ridiculous."

"Do you know about the 90-90 rule?"

"No."

"Ninety percent of the people who are arrested on criminal charges enter a plea of guilty in hopes of receiving a more lenient sentence. Why? Because they know that of the ten percent who do choose to go to trial, almost ninety percent of them are convicted by juries of their peers."

"So despite what you said, the odds are in our favor of putting Wallace away."

"What the 90-90 rule means is that district attorneys won't take a case to trial unless they are very sure of winning. They hate losing in Court. If they do lose, more criminals will take their chances with jury trials which will cost the justice system a lot more money and, in case you haven't heard, budgets are tight. And for the DAs, losing cases looks really bad on their résumés."

"So I've just wasted my time providing a formal report."

"No, not necessarily. Once we get the final version from you, we'll follow up with the district attorney's office. They'd like to put Wallace away and anything they can get on him helps. They may decide to go for it."

"Meanwhile, what are we supposed to do?

"The fact is, Harry, the CPD just can't devote enough resources to put a fence around you and your company that's high enough to stop Wallace's goons from climbing over. What about hiring bodyguards like I suggested earlier?"

"We told you why not."

"In case you change your mind, I know retired Cambridge cops who do that kind of work. One of them, a former sergeant here named Franklyn Brazeal, met a dead guy on the Red Line, a small-time criminal we'd arrested who was killed in prison, so he'd be interested in meeting you and learning more about your Visitation Room even if you don't take him on. I've known

Franklyn for many years and can vouch for him. He's a very solid guy. Maybe he could give you some ideas."

Harry accepted a scrap of note paper on which Sergeant Murphy had written Officer Brazeal's contact information. "I doubt that we'll call him," Harry said. "But thanks."

Alexandra reached Harry on his cell while he was walking back to the LifePlus office. "Gary Pollack just called me," she said. "MacAuliff's bill is making progress in the House and Gary is saying now that it could pass. Then the Senate will take it up and they're likely to take their lead from the House, especially with Cardinal O'Rourke in the background pulling their strings. Gary says it's time now to panic. He thinks we should meet with him to review our options. Would 3:00 P.M. at his office be OK with you?"

"I'll be there," Harry replied.

"What did you learn from Sergeant Murphy?"

"After my report is transcribed and I review and sign it, Wallace may or may not be arrested depending on whether the district attorney decides to prosecute."

"How likely is that?"

"Murphy doesn't know. He's waving his arms. He says the police can't protect us because they have other more pressing priorities. He suggested again that we hire bodyguards."

"It's awe inspiring to see our tax dollars at work," Alexandra said.

Thirty Six

FROM GARY POLLACK'S office at Skiffington, Skiffington and Mohr, on the 38th floor of the International Tower in Boston's financial district, Harry could see sailboats, yachts, ferries, and a small oil tanker plying the choppy waters of Boston Harbor, and on the other side of the harbor, passenger jets descending one after the other onto Logan Airport runways like a conga line of giant silver birds.

"Nice view," Harry said.

"If only I had more time to enjoy it," Pollack replied. "All of my time is devoted to my clients. I'm just like you were, Harry, when you were still a consultant."

"You're just trying to prepare us for a hefty legal bill," Alexandra said.

"Not at all. I think you'll find my fees to be very reasonable, in the circumstances."

"Gary, we appreciate your dedication and sacrifice," Harry said. "Alexandra told me your latest opinion that MacAuliff's bill might actually pass."

"His joint committee voted it out," Pollack said. "It passed its second reading on the House floor. If it passes its next reading, also on the House floor, it will be sent to the Senate where it will probably get through its three readings there fairly quickly. No-one is standing against it."

"Except us," Alexandra said.

"Sorry, you don't count for much," Pollack said.

"What about the people begging for time slots in the Visitation Room? Clearly, it's important to them too."

"Cardinal O'Rourke put the word out in the State House that he wants this legislation. For him, it's right up there with banning abortion and restricting availability of condoms. The politicians don't care all that much one way or the other so they'll let the Cardinal have this one. Same goes for the Governor. Once it gets to his desk, he might just sign it. He has other issues with Cardinal O'Rourke so he might decide on this one to preserve his capital."

"What do you propose that we do, Gary?" Alexandra asked.

"I've been doing research on an idea that came to me a while ago. I'm ready now to suggest it."

"Which is?"

"Call Dr. Gourmelon. She told you that she wants the Visitation Room to open as planned. She offered to help. Now is her chance."

"You're joking!" Alexandra exclaimed. "The woman is a scoundrel. She tried to hold us up."

"No, I'm definitely not joking."

"Why would we call her? What can she do?"

"Dr. Gourmelon has friends," Pollack said.

"So she told us," Alexandra said. "I have friends too. So what?"

"Amanda Menegakis is her friend."

Thirty Seven

AMANDA MENEGAKIS WAS a stylish woman. Now 57, although everyone said she could be in her early 40s, Amanda was depicted regularly on the *Boston Globe* Celebrations page at a gala benefiting one good cause or another, smiling into the camera along with other well-dressed, cheerful and amusing people holding sparkling glasses of white wine. She worked out religiously at her neighborhood sports club, and played tennis every morning at 7:30 A.M., even on Sunday.

In the early 1920s, when Amanda's mother and father were small children, they had emigrated with their respective families from different parts of Greece and settled in a Greek enclave in Boston's Italian-dominated North End. They met at school, married, and in short order produced Amanda and her four brothers.

When Amanda and her brothers became adults with good incomes, they had tried to persuade her parents to move to a more comfortable apartment. Her parents refused to move. Why would they? Their friends, their small Greek Orthodox church where they were married, their corner grocery store, and their walk-in clinic where a nurse knew them and fussed over them, were all located close by in their old neighborhood. They were still living there when Amanda's father's health declined precipitously due to congestive heart failure. Three months after he died, Amanda's mother also succumbed to the same disease. It was then that Amanda began her vegan diet which she still maintained.

Amanda kept her last name when she married Robert DeLuca, a lawyer at DeLuca, Brown, & Cipriani, a law firm based in the North End, because she was making a good living as a realtor and was already well-known in the community, both professionally and socially, as Amanda Menegakis.

Robert DeLuca aspired to do more than just craft legal language for wills, leases and contracts, so he ran for a seat to represent the North End on the Boston City Council. He lost, but his energetic campaign and courteous manner were noticed by local Democratic Party leaders and in the next election cycle, he was selected to run for a seat in the Massachusetts House of Representatives. He won that election and served in the House for twenty years while also maintaining his law practice on the side. DeLuca was well regarded by his peers, worked hard on his committee assignments, and maintained trusting relationships with the leaders in the State House, both in the House and in the Senate.

The Speaker of the Massachusetts House of Representatives exercises near-dictatorial powers over matters large and small in that body. He controls which legislation is considered for passage, to which committees the Representatives are assigned, the size and locations of Representative's offices, and their budgets for staff. A Representative who displeases the Speaker might find his furniture moved to a basement office near the State House oil-fueled furnace. One whose loyalty is in doubt might discover that the boundaries of his district have been re-drawn, with the result that his district no longer includes the neighborhoods where formerly he drew most of his support.

Occasionally, however, a Speaker goes too far, perhaps helping a friend receive a special break from a state licensing board, or playing an involuntary starring role in a *Boston Globe* "Spotlight" report about suspicious cash transactions, mysterious contracts, and barely-disguised kick-backs. When such transgressions become too egregiously blatant to be ignored, especially when they lead to an indictment, the formerly acquiescent Representatives revolt, and the erstwhile legislative dictator is toppled from his leadership post. Usually he also resigns from the House in order to focus on his legal defense, and another Representative is anointed to take his place as Speaker. It was after just such a rebellion – which forced Robert DeLuca's predecessor to depart while angrily asserting his innocence of all charges – that DeLuca was elected by his peers to become Speaker of the House.

Amanda's best friend at the Joseph N. Reilly High School in the North End was Frances Masnaghetti. They confided each other's hopes, and dreams, and secrets. They laughed wildly at each other's jokes and mourned together when either was visited by disappointments. They stayed in touch when both of them departed the North End to go to college, Amanda for Waltham, a suburb west of Boston, to take her business degree at Bentley College, and Frances for Nova Scotia to study English literature at Acadia University. Later on, when Frances met John Gourmelon during her year abroad in England after earning her doctorate in child developmental psychology at Cornell, she sent Amanda his picture – an apple-cheeked Brit – and asked whether she was crazy to consider marrying him, and Amanda replied, "If you want to do it, it's not crazy." Amanda was at Frances' side, dressed in pink, when Frances and John Gourmelon were married. Three years later, she was at her side again to console Frances when they divorced. For her part, Frances encouraged Amanda to forgive Robert DeLuca for flirting with another woman after they were engaged, and she helped to persuade Amanda's brothers not to take Robert out to a dark alley where they would "knock him around" for disrespecting their sister.

After the tragic accident at the child care center where Frances worked, Amanda insisted that Frances move into their apartment for a while to shield her from reporters. And when her father and mother died, Amanda found comfort in Dr. Frances Gourmelon's Institute for Psychical and Paranormal Research where Frances communicated with her parents' spirits and confirmed their abiding love for her.

Gary Pollack had discovered Dr. Gourmelon's relationship with Amanda Menegakis during his background research in response to Dr. Gourmelon's earlier request for founder's equity in LifePlus. He knew that Dr. Gourmelon would refuse to ask Amanda for a favor involving her husband, Speaker Robert DeLuca, unless the stakes were very high. Perhaps now, Pollack thought, they had gotten high enough.

He told Harry and Alexandra about Dr. Gourmelon and Amanda Menegakis. He also told them about the accident that closed Dr. Gourmelon's child care center. A van rented by the center for an excursion overturned while taking an exit from a highway, apparently as a result of being driven too fast. The driver and all of the six children who were riding in the van were killed. Dr. Gourmelon, who was accompanying the children, survived with minor injuries. She gave up her career in education and her professional focus on child developmental psychology and resolved instead to pursue a calling as a psychic. From then on, she would communicate with the dead so that she could provide a channel between them and those they had left behind.

"Harry, you should be the one to call Dr. Gourmelon," the lawyer said. "She likes you."

"I agree that Harry should do it," Alexandra said. "I can hardly stand the woman. She knows how I feel."

"You didn't try to hide it," Harry said. "I'll make the call."

"Call her from one of our offices where you'll have privacy," Pollack said. "We'll wait for you here."

Harry used his cellphone to call Dr. Gourmelon so that her caller ID would show his name rather than Skiffington, Skiffington and Mohr. She picked up quickly. "Hello, Harry. What can I do for you?"

"As you predicted, Dr. Gourmelon, we need your help."

"I'm so glad that you called me, dear boy."

"Can I meet with you at your Institute so that we can talk about it?"

Dr. Gourmelon agreed to meet right away, adding, "Why don't you call me Frances?"

To get to Dr. Gourmelon's Institute at 111 Essex Street, an old Boston city street that was heavily shaded on both sides by four and five story brick buildings, Harry walked by a parking garage, the offices for "D_inty Dot Hosiery," the "a" having gone missing, and a Chinese restaurant that had not yet opened for dinner. The Institute's entrance was sandwiched between an empty storefront for what used to be "Silk Stream Printing" and was now "For Lease 617-357-5700," and the "Earle Harvey Co., Purveyor of Fine Fabrics." Its full name, Institute for Psychical and Paranormal Research, was inscribed in dark red lettering across its front window.

Not seeing a doorbell, Harry slammed a heavy cast-iron lion-head knocker against its plate at the center of the Institute's shiny black wooden door. A buzzer sounded and Harry pushed the door open and entered a dark hallway.

"Down here, Harry," Dr. Gourmelon called out, from a room at the end of the hallway. She was seated at a round light-colored butcher-block table. "Hello, Harry, do come in," she said.

She gestured towards a plate heaped with chocolate chip cookies that was on the table. "Take one. I just made them."

They did smell rich and sweet, and this time Harry accepted. The cookie tasted of chocolate, and cocoa, with a hint of coffee, and butter, and brown sugar. Its texture was thickened by oats, but it was more doughy than crunchy. "Here's some hot black tea to wash it down," Dr. Gourmelon said, pouring him a cup from a porcelain tea-pot. "Would you like some milk?" Hearing 'yes,' she added a dash of milk to his cup. "Help yourself to another cookie, or two, I have plenty more. And here's a paper napkin to wipe your fingers."

The light over the table brought out the red, green and yellow swirls of color in Dr. Gourmelon's muumuu and the grey of her eyes behind her large glasses. She was the centerpiece in the room, like a sculpture placed cunningly where it would draw and hold a visitor's full attention.

"The cookie tastes wonderful," Harry said.

"And it's not even poisoned," Dr. Gourmelon said. "See what you were missing?"

"I do, and it was my loss."

"I've been expecting you, Harry. How can I help?"

"Dr. Gourmelon.."

"Frances… You'll get used to it."

"Frances, our Visitation Room is scheduled to open six days from now and almost every time slot has been reserved for its first three months. We are providing a service that people want."

"I'm looking forward to Opening Day, Harry. I've made several reservations, myself."

"Unfortunately, State Representative MacAuliff is sponsoring a bill in the House that would shut us down. We now believe that his bill might well pass the House and Senate and get signed into law."

"Before we discuss the Representative's bill, have you given more thought to my request to join LifePlus as a partner?"

"Of course. And when we talked last time, you were looking for a 1% share of the company's equity."

"I believe now that 1.5% would be reasonable, don't you agree?"

"Yes, Frances, and therefore as CEO of Lifeplus, Inc., I hereby offer you founder's equity in the amount of 1.5% of our company's shares and I will be delighted to welcome you as one of our partners."

"Will Alexandra agree?"

"She will. That's why I'm here."

"Then, Harry, I'm delighted to accept your offer," Dr. Gourmelon said, beaming at him. "Let's shake on it," she said, extending her plump hand which Harry grasped to seal their agreement. "You've made the right decision. Now, to address our problem with Representative MacAuliff's bill, you think that I can help because I know the Speaker's wife."

"We hope so. No-one wants to talk against the bill because Cardinal O'Rourke has campaigned for it."

"Tell me again, why is the bill a problem? From what I've read, it would only require licensing of Visitation Rooms. What's wrong with that?"

"We could never get a license. The requirements would be impossibly burdensome."

"In what way, Harry?"

"To start with, the licensing agency would be subject to political influence, most importantly from its primary sponsor, Representative MacAuliff. It would set the standards of proof that we are not affecting our customers' health. We'd have to reveal our customers' identities so that the agency could monitor any health effects over time. And we'd have to report each customer's experience in the Visitation Room so that the agency could verify that we are not committing fraud. Our customers would be pressured to undergo testing on their mental health before and after their sessions, implying that they are unbalanced if they're seeking to communicate with a loved one in the Visitation Room, and also implying that they might become even more deranged afterwards."

"I doubt that Representative MacAuliff would be willing to take the mental health test," Dr. Gourmelon said.

"Nor would I," Harry replied. "Nor would you. This alone would be enough to kill the Visitation Room."

"So MacAuliff's bill must be stopped in the House."

"Yes, Frances. That's what needs to happen."

"Leave it to me. Have another cookie."

Thirty Eight

WHEN AMANDA MENEGAKIS served her husband his favorite dinner, roast lamb with mint jelly, roast potatoes with sour cream, and mixed green salad, the Speaker of the Massachusetts House of Representatives Robert DeLuca anticipated that Amanda wanted something that he would hear about eventually, most likely over dessert, another of his favorites, home-made apple pie with a generous dollop of Rancatore's premium vanilla ice cream. He anticipated correctly.

"Robert, honey," Amanda said. "Would you like a cappuccino?"

"Yes, thank you."

After Amanda handed him a mug overflowing with steamed milk foam that was dusted just right with cocoa, she said, "We need to have a chat."

"Of course, my love. Let's chat."

"You know that bill that Walter MacAuliff has been pushing, about the Visitation Room..."

"Yes, Walter's very keen on it."

"You know that I would never try to influence you in doing your work in the House..."

"Of course not."

"I don't pretend to understand all of Walter's reasons for his bill, but I believe that it would do a lot of damage if it were to pass."

"He's only trying to protect the public, Amanda. There are health concerns. Also he believes there is a risk of fraud. There do need to be controls over these kinds of services."

"Honey, the Visitation Room will provide a very valuable service. I've reserved a time slot for myself. Frances is very excited about the Visitation Room. She expects that it will provide wonderful, amazing experiences."

"Aah, Frances, I thought there might be a connection."

"She's my oldest friend. You know that she was a great help to me after Mother and Father died. She says I might be able to communicate with them in the Visitation Room."

"Do you really believe that?"

"I do."

"It's not just Walter MacAuliff, Amanda. The Cardinal is also very interested. He wants something to be done to protect people."

"To protect the Church, you mean. Visitation Rooms represent competition."

"What would you like me to do, Amanda?"

"Frances says that if this bill passes, the Visitation Room won't open next week and in fact may never open since the bill imposes requirements that can't be met. There are a great many people, including myself, who will be terribly upset if this opportunity is taken from us. Can you, perhaps, delay the bill for a little while until we all have better information?"

"I'll see what I can do, Amanda."

"I know that you'll take care of it, my darling. Why don't you come up to bed early tonight?"

Representative Walter MacAuliff did not receive many invitations to visit Speaker DeLuca's office. His email from the

Speaker, "Please drop by after lunch today," left a lot to the imagination. Perhaps it was about his bill, "Protecting Consumers from Reality Altering Fraud and Injury." Perhaps he was in line for another committee assignment, or maybe the Speaker was seeking MacAuliff's support for one of his legislative priorities, support that he would give willingly, for which he would accept the Speaker's gratitude with casual good grace. Surely the Speaker wasn't inviting him in for yet another lecture about his altercation with the police after he'd been enjoying a sociable evening with his constituents in his neighborhood watering hole; he had already taken his lumps on that, including his humiliating banishment to his ground floor office out at the edge of nowhere in the East Wing.

MacAuliff left early from his office to ensure that he'd be on time for his after-lunch appointment. He stepped around the moving boxes that were still piled on his floor and walked briskly through the long State House corridors without pausing for his customary amiable chats with colleagues and staffers, with the result that he was slightly winded when he arrived with five minutes to spare.

The name, "Robert DeLuca, Speaker of the House of Representatives," was presented in small, dignified brass letters at eye-level on one of the white marble pilasters that framed the doorway to the Speaker's office. The very location of Speaker's office on the third floor of the State House, off a glistening white marble foyer a few doors down from the entrance to the Chamber of the House of Representatives, near the historic Main Staircase with its elegant wrought-iron railing, exuded authority and power, and extracted deference from all who entered.

MacAuliff turned the brass door-knob and pushed. The door swung open silently on well-oiled hinges – it wasn't locked – and he entered the Speaker's outer reception area.

DeLuca's executive assistant, Linda Rose Ciccolo, a middle-aged dark-haired woman who had worked for Robert DeLuca forever, beginning with his law practice in the North End, greeted Representative MacAuliff by name and assured him that the Speaker expected him and would not be too long.

It was much quieter here than in the marble foyer, due in part to the reception area's wall-to-wall sound-absorbing plush carpet. Phones rang discreetly, and when Linda Rose spoke on hers, MacAuliff had to strain to overhear what she was saying, something about a meeting that the Speaker would be delighted to attend with the Governor.

The inner door to Speaker DeLuca's office opened and the Speaker bounded out to shake MacAuliff's hand vigorously while apologizing for keeping him waiting. "Come on in," he said, putting his arm on MacAuliff's shoulder. "I want to catch up on what you've been doing."

As MacAuliff settled into one of the Speaker's leather easy chairs next to the fireplace in which several large oak logs were burning in a tidy, well-mannered fire. DeLuca asked, "Can we get you anything? Any refreshments? Perhaps a beer? Linda Rose will get you anything you'd like."

Had it been anyone else offering but the Speaker, MacAuliff would happily have accepted a cold beer, but he thought that abstaining might be advisable in these circumstances, so he declined with thanks.

"Well, Walter, your bill on the reality-altering services has been making good progress."

"Yes, sir, I'm very gratified that it has a lot of support."

"You've done an excellent job moving it through first and second readings."

"Thank you, sir."

"I've been impressed by the reports of your public hearings. If I'd had more time, I would have liked to sit in on some of them. You're certainly addressing an important issue and have obtained valuable inputs from everyone concerned."

"We've tried to let everyone have their say. The idea that a business would be set up that offered visits from spirits, and would charge for it; obviously that raises serious questions."

"It certainly does. What you've done is admirable and I appreciate it, Walter."

"Thank you, sir," MacAuliff replied again. "I'm proud to have your support."

"That's why I've asked you to come by," the Speaker said. "I need to ask a favor of you, Walter. Although as currently written, your bill will provide much-needed protections to the public, I still have lingering concerns about possible unintended consequences."

"I'll be glad to clarify anything you want in order to eliminate such concerns for you, sir."

"Thank you, but I believe that we'll need more time. I have decided, very reluctantly, to shelve the bill until more information can be obtained."

"Shelve it? Why?"

"Walter, this was an extremely difficult decision and I'm sure you understand that I did not make it lightly. As a great favor to me, however disappointed you may be, and I would not blame you if you were disappointed, I'm requesting that you avoid criticizing my decision in public or even privately to our colleagues in the House and Senate."

The Representative from South Boston was being cut off at the knees and it was an exceedingly unpleasant sensation. He was well aware that he was not hearing the full story from the Speaker who, he assumed, must be doing a favor for someone more significant than himself. Arguing with the Speaker, getting angry about the injustice and demanding the truth, might feel good at first, but MacAuliff had enough experience with the way things worked in the State House to realize that he'd be committing political suicide. Once he'd tagged himself as a malcontent and potential trouble-maker, he'd be consigned to a political pit so deep that he'd never again see the light of day, even deeper than his current unhappy circumstances. On the other hand, even as he struggled to manage his hurt while the lying sleazy duplicitous smug SOB sat across from him looking so sympathetic, MacAuliff sensed that he had for once been granted moral high ground, which for him was an unusual vantage point that begged to be exploited.

"Sir," he said, "you are asking a lot from me. I have worked hard for this bill. I have made commitments to colleagues to get their support. I also have made commitments to important backers, including Cardinal O'Rourke, whose strong support for this bill has been very plainly expressed to me and to others in the House and Senate. His Eminence has pointed out that a business that promises visits from the spirits may well mislead people, including the faithful, and that it conflicts with long-standing teachings of the Church."

"I will speak with Cardinal O'Rourke, Walter. I'll let him know that shelving the bill is entirely my doing and that you reminded me of his support for it."

"This is still terribly disappointing for me."

"I realize that Walter, and I am prepared to make it up to you. Is there anything I can do for you?"

"Well," MacAuliff said, "Friends of mine in South Boston who have been very loyal supporters, have been struggling to find work since they were laid off last year due to no fault of their own. They applied at the state Probation Department for positions as probation officers, for which by the way they are extremely well qualified, and I have tried to contact the Commissioner of Probation to watch out for their applications, but he's evidently not interested in hearing what I have to say. In fact, I can't even get the time of day from him."

"Would you like me to call the Commissioner on your behalf so that perhaps he will become more receptive?"

"That would help, yes sir, thank you." MacAuliff doled out an expression of gratitude that was minimally sufficient for basic courtesy. He took care not to appear more than partially mollified.

"Is there anything else I can do for you, Walter?"

"As you know, sir, my office space on the ground floor of the East Wing leaves a lot to be desired. There are security bars on my window, and it can't be opened; also it overlooks a parking lot. Would there be any chance that I could move back to a higher floor, perhaps with a view that is more appealing?"

"Walter, that is a very understandable request. I'll look into it. I'm sure we can make you much more comfortable."

"And my budget for staff was reduced to cover only one half-time person. Would it be possible to increase it up to one full-time staff, or maybe one-and-a-half?

"I'll certainly check on that as well."

Thirty Nine

"YOU'RE RUNNING OUT of time," Genevieve LaPierre told Harry.

"I know."

"What's the latest with Michael Wallace?"

"The district attorney's office is still pondering whether to arrest him, based on my report to the CPD."

"So, no progress."

"We will deal with him, Genevieve."

"I hope you're right, Harry. For now, you should assume that Opening Day is cancelled unless I hear good news about Wallace. If you don't announce the cancellation, I'll have to do it myself. I can't have people coming down to the Marriott expecting to meet their loved ones in the Visitation Room, and then blaming us when they find out that it's closed."

"I understand, Genevieve. When would you make your announcement?"

"I'll give you as long as I can, until the day before Opening Day."

"Four days from now."

"Yes, Harry, I'm sorry. I have to protect the Marriott and our guests."

Harry retrieved the scrap of paper on which Sergeant Murphy had written contact information for Franklyn Brazeal and dialed the retired Cambridge police officer's number. When Harry introduced himself, Franklyn said, "James Murphy told me that I might hear from you. He said that you've been threatened by Shiny Mikey."

"We have. Sergeant Murphy said there is not much the police can do to protect us. He suggested that we should hire bodyguards."

"But you're reluctant."

"We are. What we need now are ideas on how to deal with Wallace. You come highly recommended by Sergeant Murphy."

"He's a good friend."

"I'm hoping you can help us, perhaps as a security consultant."

"Fine with me," Franklyn said. "Let's meet at your office to discuss it and to get comfortable with each other."

"You referred to Wallace as Shiny Mikey. Do you know him?"

"We met a few times when he was pursuing his business interests in Cambridge. Just a few bumps-and-shoves to let him know the police were paying attention."

Franklyn told Harry that he would charge his standard $200 per hour consulting rate. Harry said that was acceptable, and they arranged to meet that afternoon at the LifePlus office.

Harry's first impression of Franklyn Brazeal was favorable. He looked fit, almost ascetic, with his totally bald head and tall thin frame, dressed in a buttery-smooth black leather jacket over an open-necked blue shirt, and chino slacks. Harry introduced Franklyn to Steve and Cecilia, and to Alexandra who had come to the LifePlus office specifically to meet him.

After Franklyn had taken a seat with the LifePlus team at their meeting table, he said to Steve and Cecilia, "Sergeant Murphy told me about your interaction with Ricky and Al."

"Not much of an interaction," Steve said. "We were acted upon."

"That's their usual style," Franklyn said. "They're not great listeners. They just mete out pain as instructed by Shiny Mikey. By all accounts, they enjoy their work."

"They told us that they were instructed to ask us nicely," Cecilia said.

Franklyn took off his jacket which he hung on the back of his chair. The eyes of all four members of the LifePlus team were drawn to the lead-grey grip of a handgun holstered on his belt. "Do you always carry that?" Steve asked.

"You mean my gun? Absolutely. Most retired cops do. I never go anywhere without it. There are a lot of folks out there who might bear a grudge."

"What kind of gun is it?" Alexandra asked.

"It's a compact Glock," Franklyn said. "Small enough to wear under my jacket, but highly effective. I like Glocks, as do most cops and gun guys like me. When I was on the force, I carried a Glock 22, which is larger and probably my favorite."

"Have you had to use your gun since you retired?"

"Not yet. But I wouldn't hesitate if I needed to. I'm not about to become a vic to some scuzzball – that's a professional law enforcement term – who thinks an old guy like me would be a pushover."

"What about when you were on the police force?" Cecilia asked.

"During all my years as a cop, I only had to draw my gun once and even then I didn't actually fire it, although the other cops did who I was with."

"Now you have to tell us that story," Alexandra said.

"It happened at an all-night pizza restaurant in East Cambridge. Two gang-bangers went in to rob the owner and he managed to trigger the alarm. I think we had five or six cars ringing the place. One of them came out with his hands up and he was arrested and taken away. The other one thought – well, not thought so much, he wasn't much of a thinker – he figured that he could break out if he held the owner in front of him as a hostage. The owner was a really fat Greek guy so all we could see of the gang-banger was the gun he was holding to the manager's head. Then the young cop who I was training that day got the bright idea that he could expose the gang-banger by shooting the restaurant owner, which he did; he shot him in the leg, the restaurant owner fell shouting and hollering on the ground – he was too heavy for the gang-banger to hold him up – and then the other cops were able to get a clear shot at the gang-banger."

"What happened then?" Cecilia asked.

"Quite a few of the cops fired at the same time. The gang-banger went down."

"Was he killed?"

"Yes."

"What about the restaurant owner?"

"He was very pissed off about being shot. He brought a complaint against my young trainee and received a nice settlement from the City of Cambridge for his pain and suffering."

"What happened to your trainee?"

"The Cambridge Police Department couldn't decide whether to award him for quick thinking and probably saving the restaurant owner's life, or to punish him for shooting the guy in the leg and costing the City money, so they split the difference by doing nothing. He's still on the force. You met him. Sergeant James Murphy."

After a suitably brief moment of silence to reflect upon the demise of the gang-banger, Alexandra asked, "Franklyn, what should we do about Michael Wallace?"

"I take it that you are not prepared to give in to his threats."

"No, that's out of the question."

"You're right on that. You shouldn't let him get away with it. Sometimes you've just got to stand up to these guys."

"Can we just shoot him with that Glock that you're carrying?" Alexandra asked. "I'm ex-Israeli-army so I've had plenty of experience with guns. I'd know how to use it, if you lent it to me."

"I know you're not serious, Alexandra."

"Last July when I was on the Red Line, I met our daughter and held her in my arms, ten years after she was killed by a drunk driver. No hoodlum is going to keep me from seeing her again in the Visitation Room now that we are so close. So I'm deadly serious. I'm ready, if that's the only way."

"Bad idea, Alexandra," Franklyn said. "Anyway it wouldn't be easy; Wallace is well defended."

"I can be very resourceful."

"You understand that I can't have anything to do with such a scheme."

"No-one else needs to be involved. I don't want anyone else involved," Alexandra said. And then, turning to Harry, she added emphatically, "Not even you."

"Alexandra," Harry said, "I'm with Franklyn. There has to be another way."

"I've done research on Wallace and I can tell you that he's not invincible. He spends most days in an office at his crappy Toyota dealership that he owns in Somerville. Mostly, he comes and goes in a limo that has shaded windows and pulls right to the dealership entrance, but not always. Sometimes he walks in the open up to Davis Square, maybe to check on merchants he is extorting. Also he's been seen in Cambridge, in Central Square.

He usually has bodyguards around but they're mostly for show. They'd be useless if he were shot from a distance. Everyone would assume he was killed by another gangster. Police probably wouldn't look too hard. Good riddance, they'd say, and they'd be right."

"Alexandra, if this really is your plan, I've got to leave now," Franklyn said.

"No, don't go, Franklyn," Alexandra said. "Going after Wallace myself is not my first choice. I want to hear your ideas about other ways to deal with him."

"So let's review the situation," Franklyn said. "You've filed your report with the police but the district attorney's office hasn't moved on it yet and the police have other priorities. You're not ready to hire bodyguards. And unless all else fails, you're not going to try to shoot Shiny Mikey. Have I got that right?"

"Yes," Harry said. Franklyn glanced at Alexandra and asked, "Are you on board with that?" Alexandra replied, "Umm Hmm."

"So what's left is that you need to persuade him," Franklyn said. "You can use a carrot or a stick."

"What kind of carrot?" Harry asked.

"Money. Shares in your company. Everything has a price."

"We're not going to give him money," Harry said. "Once we start down that road, he'll come back for more. We'd never get rid of him."

"Then I'd have to shoot him after all," Alexandra said, grimly. "But we'd be much poorer by the time that I finally got around to it."

"As for shares in our company, also not going to happen," Harry said. "You can't deal with people like that. It would be like riding the back of a tiger."

"We couldn't partner with the Marriott or other reputable companies if a gangster were one of our owners," Cecilia said.

"OK, so no carrots," Franklyn said, "As it happens, I agree with you. Extortion is Wallace's line of work. You don't want this kind of relationship with him."

"Now, let's talk about the stick," Alexandra said.

"Wallace needs to be persuaded that it will cost him less to live with the Visitation Room than to prevent it from opening."

"That's what Sergeant Murphy told us, as well," Harry said. "How do we deliver that kind of message?"

"For that, you'll need a credible ally."

"If only God were on our side!" Harry lamented.

"Isn't He?"

"Unfortunately God's vicar in Boston, Cardinal O'Rourke, has come out against us."

"Well, apart from divine intervention, I was thinking more along the lines of police and maybe also firefighters, our first responders."

"But we've been told repeatedly that they don't have enough resources and that they have other higher priorities," Cecilia said.

"Police departments do have other priorities. I'm talking about police officers and firefighters as individuals, the rank and file."

Cecilia said, "One of my uncles is a former Boston cop. He's told us about cops who went to the same schools as their local bad guys, attended the same churches, and some even are related, so they know each other."

"That's a fair statement," Franklyn said. "Not true of all of us, but many of the cops I worked with came from the same neighborhoods as the bad guys. They grew up together and speak the same language. If the cops from the neighborhood say 'back off!' then the local bad guys, even vicious hoods like Shiny Mikey, will pay attention."

"How do we get them on our side?" Cecilia asked.

"You could offer them time slots in the Visitation Room."

Cecilia said, getting into it now, "We'd be like the coffee shops and convenience stores that entice cops to come in and hang around so that the muggers stay away. A Dunkin Donuts near our condo in the South End always has cops inside enjoying their free donuts and hot coffees. If we give them Visitation Room time slots, they'd be camped out in our waiting room, which would discourage Wallace and his thugs from bothering us."

"I get the donuts and coffee but why would they value the Visitation Room time slots, especially?" Alexandra asked.

"To communicate with their fallen comrades," Steve said, looking at Franklyn for confirmation. "When a first responder is killed, they close the streets for parades and everyone turns out, from the top ranks on down, plus politicians and clergy, even representatives from other departments including from Canada. They really take it seriously."

"You bet we do," Franklyn affirmed.

"But there are thousands of cops and firefighters in the Boston area," Alexandra said. "It would bankrupt us to set aside time slots for all of them."

"And we're sold out during the next three months," Harry said. "We'd have to bump customers who already have reservations, assuming we get to open that is, which won't happen unless Genevieve LaPierre concludes that Wallace is no longer a threat. Whatever we come up with has to make Wallace back away during the next few days. There won't be any cops in the waiting room if the Visitation Room never opens."

"So you need to think more creatively," Franklyn said.

Alexandra replied, with a hint of testiness, "Look, Franklyn, if you already know the answer, please tell us. We could be here all day trying to figure out what's on your mind."

"Alexandra, if I knew the answer, I would have told you."

"I have an idea," Steve said. "What if we set up a lottery to win Visitation Room time slots? That way, everyone will have a shot at getting one, but we'll limit the number of winners to avoid bankrupting our company."

"A lottery for cops and firefighters?" Alexandra asked.

"Yeah, why not?"

Franklyn said, "I'm not sure I'd go for that. It feels demeaning to me, making them enter a lottery to compete for time slots. It would be undignified. And it could cause bad feelings between winners and losers. But, maybe…" He paused.

"Yes, Franklyn," Harry prodded.

Franklyn rubbed his hand vigorously back and forth on his bald head like he was revving up his brain inside. "At the memorials for cops and firefighters, and I've gone to a lot of them, it's heart-breaking to see the family members with nothing but a folded-up flag to hold onto as their loved one is laid to rest. For the rest of us, we are losing a brother or sister in uniform, but it's much worse for the family members, the wife, the kids, the parents. From personal experience, let me tell you, we'd do anything for them. We take up collections to help them pay their bills, drop by occasionally to check on how things are going, tell them how sorry we are, and that we're always there for them. But what if we could give them a way to communicate with their departed? Now that would be something!"

"So the lottery would be for family members of first responders."

"Right. For cops and firefighters, it would be another way to help the family members of our fallen comrades. Our guys would also appreciate it as a kind of insurance; when they die, they'll still be able to communicate with the folks they've left behind."

Harry said, "And it would give the first responders a stake *now* in the future availability of the Visitation Room, so they may be willing – if this works – to communicate that to Wallace."

"Right again."

"Brilliant!"

The press conference to announce the creation of the LifePlus First Responders Foundation was held in one of the smaller meeting rooms at the Boston Marriott at the Waterfront to ensure that it would be crowded and thereby create a sense of excitement. Every seat was taken. Alexandra and Harry sat facing the audience at a table at the front of the room next to a podium. Attending were reporters from the *Boston Herald* and *Boston Globe*, from the Cambridge *Chronicle*, and MIT's *Tech News*. WBZ-TV's Live at Five, Action News was there, with its camera crew and star on-air reporter, Chad Brown, who confided to Harry and Alexandra before the meeting started that he'd been assigned to cover the WBZ's 'ghost beat.' Others carrying video cameras and mics in the room included the Marriott's internal video crew, two staffers from a local origination cable channel that distributed programming to three Boston-area cable systems, and a reporter from BostonPatch.Com, an online news site.

In response to personal invitations from Franklyn Brazeal, the heads of the police unions in Boston, Cambridge, Arlington, and Somerville were present, along with their counterparts from the firefighter unions. One of the seats near the front was amply and colorfully filled by Dr. Gourmelon who'd already promised several reporters one-on-one interviews following the press conference. Off-duty cops in uniform occupied the remaining seats while others gathered in the hallway outside the room where Genevieve had mounted a TV screen and speaker that played a video feed of the proceedings. Standing at the back of the room were Genevieve, Steve, Cecilia, and Franklyn, along with a contingent from Blair West International, Jerry Seligman, Molly Lu, Ashok Chakraborty, Maureen Minion, and Janice Klein.

Alexandra took the podium. She stood silently until the room was completely quiet and then welcomed everyone to the press conference, thanked the Marriott for generously providing their meeting room, and introduced herself as Chair of the LifePlus Board of Directors and Harry West as the LifePlus CEO. She said Harry would describe the LifePlus First Responders Foundation, its purpose, and how it would operate.

Harry took the podium and explained the salient facts. The Foundation that had just been established by LifePlus, Inc., was entirely funded by the company. Its purpose was to enable family members of deceased policemen or firefighters in the greater Boston area to communicate with their departed in the Visitation Room that would open soon in the Boston Marriott on the Waterfront. A First Responders Day had been set aside for these family members approximately three months in the future since almost all time slots before then were already reserved. The math was as follows: the Visitation Room would be open for twenty-four hours on First Responders Day as it was on all other days; each time slot was fifteen minutes in duration; therefore, there would be time for ninety-four sessions allowing for minutes lost between sessions. The Foundation would pay for all these sessions. No restrictions would be imposed on which family member could apply for one of these time slots, nor any requirement that the first responder in the family had died while on duty, only that he or she had passed on within the last five years. Because many more than ninety-four applications were anticipated, LifePlus was implementing a lottery program on the LifePlus website, www.VisitationRoom.com, that would provide a randomly-generated number to each applicant. As soon as five hundred applications were received on the server, the lottery app would select the ninety-four winners. LifePlus would hold one First Responders Day per quarter, or four per year, each scheduled three months following the lottery to select the winners for that day.

The first question came from the *Globe* reporter, "When will you run the first lottery on your website?"

"Next Monday, three days from now. We're committed to providing this valuable benefit to our Boston area first responders with the least possible delay so we are dedicating all of our resources to update our website for the lottery app and I am assured by our technical team that it will be ready and fully tested by then. Again, for those who didn't write it down the first time, the First Responders Day lottery will be accessible at www.visitationroom.com."

The *Globe* reporter had a follow-up question, "How will you verify that the lottery applicants are actually members of first responder families?"

"This program is built on trust. Anyway it would be unwise for someone to apply under false pretenses and thereby deny a spot to a real family member of our Boston-area police officers or firefighters. They're probably not the best group to try to cheat." Some of the off-duty cops in the room chuckled and one said loudly enough to be heard, "Better believe it!"

Chad Brown of WBZ-TV stood to ask his question, and the 'BZ camerawoman turned her camera to focus on him, "Why are you limiting this program to family members of first responders when there are also many other worthy groups, such as family members of veterans who've lost their lives?" Harry replied with the answer that he had rehearsed with Franklyn Brazeal, "We will certainly consider ways to broaden the scope of this program in the future. Our company, LifePlus, is a start-up and we've not yet opened our first Visitation Room here in the Marriott so we need to take one step at a time to get it right. Our first responders put their lives on the line for all of us every day and we are aware of the pain suffered by their family members when tragically their lives are taken, so this is where we want to start, by giving something back to them." One of the off-duty cops sitting behind the reporters said, again loudly enough to carry throughout the room, "You got that right!" At this, the police and firefighter union leaders and the off-duty cops applauded, a reaction captured by the 'BZ camera crew.

When their applause had died down, the reporter for BostonPatch.com, a young woman wearing a denim jacket and blue jeans, stood and said, "In your earlier announcements, you have taken care not to claim that people will be visited by ghosts in the Visitation Room, only that they will have a very intense experience. Are you claiming now, in connection with this program, that first responder family members actually will be visited by spirits of deceased police officers or firefighters?"

Harry replied, "We have not changed our statement on this topic. We do not know the nature of the encounters that our customers will experience in the Visitation Room. But when these encounters do occur, we expect that our customers will believe very strongly that they have been in contact with their loved ones."

After the press conference ended, and the off-duty cops, union leaders, and most of the reporters, including the WBZ-TV crew, had filed out of the room, Dr. Gourmelon stayed behind to talk with the *Boston Herald* reporter, while the BostonPatch.com reporter hovered nearby to record her comments. The *Herald* reporter, a heavy-set man whose well-used brown and green checked sport jacket was a size or two too small for him, asked, "Do you believe that people will meet with ghosts in the Visitation Room?"

"They will, without any doubt whatsoever," Dr. Gourmelon said. "It will be wonderful for the family members and for their departed."

"But the CEO of LifePlus told us today that they don't know the nature of these encounters."

"He has to say that for legal reasons. But he knows the truth."

"Dr. Gourmelon, how do you know?"

"For many years at my Institute for Psychical and Paranormal Research, I have communicated with spirits on behalf of my clients. Since the Red Line visitations were curtailed by the MBTA, I have heard from the spirits how excited they are about the Visitation Room. It will bring spiritualist communications to a new level."

"And you are sure that you are not just imagining your contacts with spirits?"

"Oh yes, I'm quite sure."

Genevieve LaPierre told Harry and Alexandra that she had overheard the union leaders talking enthusiastically about First Responders Day. "This looks good," she said. "Let's cross our fingers that they'll let Wallace know how they feel."

After reports of LifePlus's First Responders Days were carried on TV, online, and in the newspapers, Harry called Sergeant James Murphy and asked how the plan was received by his colleagues in the CPD.

"They love it. It's all anyone wants to talk about around here."

"What about communicating that to Michael Wallace?"

"Already done. Somerville cops have let Shiny Mikey know that if anything happens to the Visitation Room, or to the Marriott, or to any of you, anything at all, they'll cut him into small pieces that they'll feed to the Canada geese which will then poop out his remains all over New England."

"How did he respond?"

"He wants to talk with you, in person."

Forty

HARRY PARKED HIS rented car at a meter on Grove Street, a side street in Somerville, about a half block from Michael Wallace's Town Toyota dealership.

According to Alexandra, who was navigating from the passenger seat, they would have a good view of the dealership from this location. "I've spent a lot of time around here," she said, without elaborating.

"Harry, we'll wait for you here in the car," Franklyn said, from the back seat behind Alexandra. "If you're not back after an hour, I'll contact Somerville police. Keep in touch."

Harry handed the car keys to Alexandra who was still sulking that Harry was going in alone without her. "You're just a civilian, Harry," she'd said. "I'm the one who's served in a military. Unlike you, I can defend myself."

Harry had agreed that between them, "you're the tough one." But Wallace had demanded to talk specifically with Harry and that he come alone. "I expect I'll be fine, and Franklyn agrees."

"You boys are just sticking together, being macho."

"The first responders have let Wallace know that they're with us so he wants to negotiate peace, not go into battle."

259

"Fine, go. But both of you are on notice. If this meeting doesn't solve our problem with Wallace, you'll need to get out of my way so that I can take care of him myself."

The cars on Town Toyota's corner lot were all used and all looked unloved. Clean enough but far from sparkling, they were not presented in a way that would attract a customer's fancy. "For Sale" signs on their windshields lacked embellishing marketing magic like "Special!" or "Promotion!" instead sticking to sparse declarations of model, year, and price. Evidently management at Town Toyota didn't much care whether customers chose to buy what was on offer.

Inside the Town Toyota showroom, there were no shiny new vehicles for customers to admire, just two desks facing the door, each occupied by a heavy-set middle-aged man. Although they were sharply dressed in business suits and ties, the men weren't doing much, just sitting and watching the door. Their desktops were bare except for black desk telephones. No computers, or papers, were anywhere in sight. The two men stared at Harry when he entered. Neither roused himself to chirp, like a motivated car salesman might, "Can I help you?" or "Which car would you like me to show you?" or even, "Hello."

Harry spoke first, "My name is Harry West. I'm here to see Michael Wallace."

"You have an appointment?" one of the men asked.

"Yes."

"Just a minute, I'll check." The man picked up his phone, pressed a button, and after a pause said, "Harry West is here, says he has an appointment." Then he hung up the phone and nodded to the other man, who stood and approached Harry, and told him to raise his arms. "I'm going to pat you down. Don't worry about it." The man started with each of his arms, then ran his hands down Harry's sides, back and chest; then up each of his legs starting at his ankles and ending high on his thighs with jabbing probes in sensitive parts in his groin.

"Easy there, partner," Harry said. "You're getting too personal."

The man who was still seated suggested, "Maybe we should do a full body cavity search."

Harry said, "Maybe you should explain to Mr. Wallace why I left before meeting him, as he requested."

"Fuck it, he's clean," the man who was doing the patting and poking said. The man who was still seated picked up his phone again and, after pressing a button, told whoever answered, "He's clean." Then he instructed Harry, "Take the stairs behind us to the second floor. You'll be met there."

The stairs were narrow and dark. At the top, another hefty man in a suit told Harry to raise his arms again, and put him through another pat-down. Then he told Harry to sit in one of the chairs next to a closed door. "Mr. Wallace won't be long," he said, taking one of the other chairs for himself.

Harry took out his BlackBerry to text Alexandra and Franklyn that he was inside and waiting to see Wallace, when the man said, "No cellphones. Put it away."

The next fifteen minutes passed with nothing for Harry to do but sit and wait, listening to the audible breathing of the man who was watching Harry out the corner of his eye. All that was missing in the gloom outside Wallace's door was a grandfather clock marking the passage of time with a hollow TICK … TOCK … TICK… TOCK. Finally, the man glanced at his cellphone and told Harry, "You can go in now" and opened the door for him to enter.

The room was cold, much colder than out in the hallway or downstairs. Although windowless, it was brightly lit by recessed indoor floodlights. At the far end of the room, Michael Wallace sat enthroned behind a large desk in an executive-size Aeron office chair. His blue double-breasted suit jacket was unbuttoned, exposing his metallic red tie which was knotted tightly at the throat of his white straight shirt collar and lay softly on his powder blue silk shirt.

Observing Harry approach his desk, Wallace puffed his cheeks, narrowed his eyes to petulant slits, and jutted out his full red lower lip, pouting like a two-year-old whose highly specific, well-reasoned demand for a chocolate candy has been arbitrarily denied. "So you're the asshole," he said, finally.

"And you're Shiny Mikey," Harry replied, adopting a similar tone.

"You can call me Mr. Wallace." Wallace gestured towards a leather-covered arm chair that faced his desk. "Sit down. Keep your hands in view where I can see them." On the desk, Harry noted two iPhones, and two leather wallets, one black, and other red with a brass clasp.

"We need to talk," Wallace said.

"I agree," Harry said. "What you've been doing has to stop."

"That's why you're here, asshole, to talk about our deal. You give me something, I give you something."

"I prefer to be called Harry, but I also answer to Dr. West," Harry replied. "Tell me more about our deal." Harry tried to suppress any hint of a triumphant smile. When Wallace capitulated as expected, Harry would specify, politely but firmly, the terms of his surrender – Wallace would notify the Marriott that he no longer objected to the Visitation Room; he would return Steve's and Cecilia's wallets and cellphones; and he would replace Harry's Camry; and for his part, Harry would agree to withdraw the complaint against Wallace that he had filed with the Cambridge police.

"Here's our deal," Wallace said. "I'll make it as clear as I can for you. You won't open your fucking Visitation Room, as I told you before. If you try to open it, despite what I'm telling you, I'll burn down the Marriott and bury you and your partners under a parking lot. You understand me now?"

Harry was too shocked to reply. Wallace leered at him, "Not what you expected, asshole?"

"No."

"You figured you could get police and firemen to scare me off?"

"We hoped you would take their wishes into account."

"You hoped wrong. They don't scare me. Never have. But assholes like you who lack proper respect, you give me a fucking headache."

Harry's first thought was 'Oh shit!' They'd been so sure that Wallace would back down. They had no back-up plan. He had to keep him talking. Perhaps something would occur to him while he was buying time.

"Mr. Wallace, what do you have against our Visitation Room?" Harry noticed a large brass crucifix that was hanging on the wall, highlighted by two small floods attached to the top of its heavy gilt-edged mahogany frame. There was a brass tag attached to the bottom of the frame. *To Michael Wallace, With Gratitude from the Boston Archdiocese for Many Generous Contributions.* "Is it because Cardinal O'Rourke and his priests have spoken against it?"

"Fucking priests don't tell me how to think."

"Why, then?"

"Because I don't need ghosts making accusations."

"But what difference would it make what anyone might see or hear in the Visitation Room? That's not evidence. No Court would accept it."

"I don't give a fuck about Courts," Wallace said, staring malevolently at Harry. "It might give some people ideas. They might try to even the score."

"Mr. Wallace, when my colleagues described the two men who threatened them in our office, the police sergeant immediately identified them as Ricky and Al, who he said worked for you."

"So?"

"Your activities are already so well-known that it won't make a difference what someone might hear in the Visitation Room."

"So I have no reason to want it shut the fuck down before it opens?"

"No, you don't," Harry said.

"That's not up to you to decide, is it?"

This was going nowhere. Harry faced a hard choice: Bow to Wallace's threats and give up on the Visitation Room, which he could never do; Ariel was his daughter too, after all, and he wouldn't be able to live with himself, when they'd come so close. Or, let Alexandra try her luck as an assassin. He couldn't stop her but he also couldn't let her go after Wallace by herself. He'd have to help in some way even though her plan would probably get them both killed. That he'd seen the inside of the dealership might prove to be useful, the layout of the showroom, the stairs to the second floor, and Wallace's office. At least he could verify Franklyn's observation that Wallace was well defended; which certainly was true inside the dealership where Wallace was sheltered behind two floors of heavies, although that would make no difference to Alexandra who'd already concluded that she'd shoot Wallace when he was outside in the open, walking up the street to Davis Square.

Davis Square. Street. Howie.

Sergeant Murphy had said that Wallace idolized his older brother.

"Tell me about your brother Howie."

"Asshole, my brother Howie is none of your fucking business."

"Mr. Wallace, I really would prefer that you address me as Harry, or Mr. West."

"Alright... Harry..." Wallace drew it out, each word dripping with scorn. "It's not real smart for you to talk about Howie."

Harry persisted, "Wouldn't you like to see him again, if you could?"

"He was cremated. Not much to see."

"You know what I mean, Mr. Wallace. To see him, and talk with him, as if he were still alive."

"Howie's dead."

"But you told me earlier that you encountered someone on the Red Line who you knew was dead, that he was standing right in front of you, and you talked with him."

"Yeah. That happened. It wasn't pleasant."

"What if you could talk with Howie?"

Wallace closed his eyes and pursed his lips, apparently pondering the idea. "So what are you proposing?"

"The Visitation Room is functional now, ready for our official opening. The technology is in place and has worked numerous times with test partners. Try it. Come to the Visitation Room. Perhaps you will see your brother."

"You guarantee that I'll see him?"

"No, I can't guarantee it," Harry said. "But think about it. What if he's there?"

"If I go down there and don't meet my brother, I will not be happy."

"OK."

"If I meet a dickhead who just wants to complain about being killed by one of my boys, I'll be even less happy. You understand?"

"Yes."

"We'll do it now. Arrange it so they'll be ready for us."

Harry said that he could make the arrangement with one phone call. With Wallace watching and listening, Harry called Steve. "Can you manage a session for a guest at the Visitation

Room in about an hour?" Harry asked. Aware that Harry was meeting Michael Wallace, and probably making the call in his presence, Steve responded simply, "No problem. See you there."

Wallace said, "You'll come with me in my car. If anything happens to me in your Visitation Room, it won't be good for you. Are we clear on that?"

"Yes."

"So your ex-wife and the bald ex-cop who are waiting for you up the street don't get too nervous, I'll send one of my guys to tell them where we're going."

"OK."

"You look surprised again. Did you really think we didn't know they were out there?"

"Of course I assumed you would know," Harry said. Actually they'd taken a detour to avoid driving by the dealership specifically so that they wouldn't be noticed.

"Anybody within a block of this place in any direction, we're watching them," Wallace boasted. "Anybody who gets close, we know about it."

Harry surmised that Wallace must have pushed a button under his desk, out of his sight, because at that moment his office door opened and the man from the hall came in. Wallace told him, "Give West the stuff off my desk. Bring him downstairs to wait by the door for my limo. Keep him out of sight until we pull up." To Harry, he said, "We'll come by in a few minutes. Don't try to use your cellphone. Got it?" Harry said that he did. The man put the iPhones and wallets in a plastic bag that he handed to Harry; he said, "let's go," and led Harry out of Wallace's office.

A black Lincoln Town Car with tinted windows glided up so close to the building that the dealership door could only be opened part-way. The man standing beside him said, "Get in fast, don't stop to look around," and Harry squeezed through the narrow doorway space and slid into the limo through a partially-open passenger door.

Two of the four seats in the limo's passenger compartment faced forward, and two faced backward. Three of the seats were already occupied. Harry took the only space that was left on a backward-facing seat, across from Wallace. Beside Harry sat a large hairless man with small red-rimmed eyes and a tattoo that zigzagged up from his neck to just in front of his ear. At Wallace's side was another large man, this one with long Jesus hair, who stared unblinkingly at Harry with beady light-grey eyes, not with overt hostility, more like he was examining a specimen that he'd dissect later.

"You must be Ricky and Al," Harry said.

Ricky replied in his breathy Marilyn Monroe voice, "The first time we had to ask nicely like we were told. Next time, we'll enjoy ourselves." Out of the corner of his eye, Harry could see Al's tongue darting out to lick his lips.

Wallace said to Ricky, "Chances are, you'll have your fun with him and the others. But for now, just keep an eye on him. You know what to do."

Harry said, "We'll be met at the entrance to the Marriott, Mr. Wallace. I'll bring you down to the Visitation Room. You'll be able to go right in. You'll be in there by yourself for a fifteen minute session."

"Yeah, except you'll stay in the car with Ricky. Al will come with me."

When Wallace's limo arrived at the Marriott, Harry could see Steve waiting for them. Al got out first and looked around, ignoring Steve, who ignored him back while preparing to greet the next person who emerged. Then Al nodded his round, hairless, tattooed head and held the limo door wider for Wallace to get out. Wallace said to Steve, "Lead us in." Al closed the limo door behind him. Harry could see that Steve was trying to check who else was inside the limo but most likely was unable to make him out through the tinted windows.

Ricky told Harry, "Stay put and keep your mouth shut. We're going to park out of sight."

The limo turned into a parking garage about a block away from the Marriott and ascended to roof level, its tires squealing as they took the tight turns in the spiral parking ramp, and then was backed into a parking space with its trunk against an outer wall, so that the limo driver could observe other cars coming onto the roof deck from the ramp.

A few moments later, the driver slid open the privacy glass separating him from the passenger compartment and called back to Ricky, "We've got company." Harry was facing towards the back and could not see who was approaching. Ricky said, "Your friends are here," and he took a handgun from his holster and held it on his lap.

There was a rap against the window and Ricky pressed a button to lower it. Alexandra and Franklyn peered inside, and Alexandra asked, "Harry, are you in there?"

"I am. Ricky has a gun."

"So do we," Alexandra said.

Franklyn said, "Hello Ricky. Haven't seen you for a while. Staying out of trouble?"

"Hello, Officer," Ricky said. "Can we help you?"

"We want Harry to get out of the car now and to come with us. Do you have a problem with that?"

"I don't care," Ricky said. "We know where to find him and the rest of you, if we need to."

Ricky unlatched the door and sat back to let Harry get out.

Wallace and Al followed Steve to an elevator in the Marriott's lobby which took them down to the basement, and then walked behind him down a corridor to the Visitation Room entrance.

Steve asked them to stay in the empty waiting area while he turned on the energy pulse transmitter.

"It needs to warm up for a few minutes before its first use," he said. "I'll be right back."

"Don't keep us too long," Wallace said.

Several minutes later, Steve returned. He stood out of the way while Al checked the inside of the Visitation Room. There wasn't much to see, just an easy chair in the center of the room, a flat video screen hanging on the wall facing the easy chair, above a bench of three attached seats from a Red Line train car, a small side table beside the easy chair, sensors that looked like dulled silver hockey pucks attached high on the wall behind the easy chair, and a small darkened glass or plastic dome – about the size of a coffee mug – suspended from the ceiling. Al pointed out the dome to Wallace who asked Steve, "Is that a video camera?"

"Yes."

"Cover it up."

Steve brought in an extension ladder and taped newspaper to the ceiling over the dome.

"OK, let's do it," Wallace said. "Al, you wait just outside. If I don't come out alive, kill this fucker and then go do the others."

Steve asked him to sit in the easy chair. "The room will be energized a few seconds after I close the door. We suggest that you remain seated but if you want to get up, that's OK. A red light over the door will come on to indicate the end of the session. If you want to end the session early, press the big red button that is under the left arm of the easy chair."

Steve left and shut the door behind him.

Wallace stared at a video playing silently on the screen of ocean waves crashing against jagged rocks. The windswept foam and dark thunderclouds in the distance looked impressive enough. He'd never seen the real thing, not having visited Maine or the more rugged parts of the Massachusetts coastline. He could afford to travel, no problem, but he preferred to stay close to home in the city where he had security and reliable creature comforts.

If the video was intended to get him in the mood it wasn't working. Nothing was happening. What a crock! He was being played for a fool. One more minute and he'd slam that button and end this shit.

The teenager slouching on the middle Red Line chair with his neatly-parted red hair, wearing a black leather biker's jacket festooned with steel zippers, tight-fitting black jeans, leather boots, and a jaunty grin that Wallace could never forget, said, "Hey, little brother!"

Harry waited in the rental car with Alexandra and Franklyn where they could watch for Wallace's limo departing the garage. If the limo was heading back to the Marriott and Steve might be in trouble, they'd do what they could to help him.

Harry's BlackBerry buzzed. The caller's number was blocked. Harry took the call.

"Harry West?" asked a wispy falsetto voice.

"Yes, Ricky, this is Harry."

"I have a message from Mr. Wallace. He says you can open the Visitation Room. Also he says to come by the dealership and tell the guys which car you want from the lot, and they'll give you the papers for it. Also he wants you to drop your complaint that you filed with the police. You got that?"

"Yes."

"So are we done?"

"I need you or Mr. Wallace to do one more thing."

"What?"

"Call Genevieve LaPierre at the Marriott to let her know Mr. Wallace's decision. You talked to her earlier. Can you do that?"

"Mr. Wallace already told me to call her."

Forty One

IN ALL THE EXCITEMENT surrounding the opening of the
Visitation Room, it was easy to overlook the instruction about
reserving time slots online. On the big day, dozens of would-be
customers who had failed to obtain reservations milled about in
the Marriott's lobby and spilled outside onto its plaza.

Large signs posted on standing billboards outside the hotel
repeated the message, "Visitation Room is Open *Only* to Holders
of Time-Slot Reservations. Please proceed to Visitation Room
Waiting Area *Only* if You Have a Time Slot Reserved During
the Next Two Hours. Time slot reservations can be obtained
Only at www.VisitationRoom.com."

Friendly LifePlus "Visitation Room Guides" – so identified
on their prominently displayed badges – mingled in the crowd.
They introduced themselves to people who looked confused and
handed out laminated cards with step-by-step instructions on
how to navigate the LifePlus website to reserve a Visitation
Room time slot.

A customer who had a confirmed reservation would print a
bar-coded ticket which, within two hours of the reserved time
slot, would unlock the door at the entrance to the Visitation
Room. Once inside, he or she would be greeted by a Visitation
Room Guide and escorted to the waiting area. Similar to airline

frequent flier clubs, the waiting area was equipped with upholstered easy chairs, a choice of magazines and newspapers, light snacks, beverages, and well-appointed restrooms. Unlike the frequent flier clubs, there were no TVs; nor were alcoholic drinks on offer. Harry didn't want to force customers in the waiting area to overhear inane TV babble while they were preparing for very personal and emotional encounters; and the Visitation Room experience would be intense enough without the added effects of alcohol.

A Commemoration Space had been designated inside the waiting area for customers to leave flowers, photographs, and other mementos. A small sign on the wall gave notice that the Commemoration Space would be cleaned out each week.

There was also a separate departure area, a smaller room with a couple of chairs, for customers who needed time to collect themselves after their encounters, before they returned to the hotel lobby and from there, to their everyday worlds.

Three minutes before the start of a customer's reserved time slot, he or she would be approached by a Visitation Room Guide and then, at the appointed moment would be led into the Visitation Room.

Each customer's time in the Visitation Room was recorded on video, as stated on a release form that customers signed prior to entering the room. The video recordings were intended, the company explained, to build a record of the visitation events for future scientific analysis and also to protect the company in case of legal or regulatory challenges. A copy of the video file was given to the customer on a flash drive. No-one observed the Visitation Room from any kind of viewing area. Although technically the room could be monitored by watching the video as it was being recorded, LifePlus staff were instructed not to do so. Harry and Alexandra decided that allowing such monitoring might encourage voyeurism and that it would be creepy to invade a customer's privacy during such personal moments. Customers were shown the red panic button attached underneath the left arm of the easy chair that could be used to summon help if an encounter became too intense or unpleasant.

On the afternoon of Opening Day, Dr. Frances Gourmelon was led into the waiting area by a Visitation Room Guide. They made an interesting pair, the Guide a tall young black woman dressed conservatively in a white blouse and tan pantsuit, towering over the stocky, grey-haired customer wearing a brilliantly patterned muumuu. The Guide asked, respectfully, "May I get you anything, Dr. Gourmelon? Any refreshments?"

"No, thank you, dear," Dr. Gourmelon replied. "Just let me know when it's time for me to go in."

Six tiny tots busied themselves around the Visitation Room. They didn't spend much time looking at Dr. Gourmelon except that occasionally one or another would check to see that she was still there and then would resume what they were doing. One, a little Chinese girl dressed in Oshkosh overalls, sat on the floor examining her toes, intently. Two boys, one red-haired and the other with long dark brown hair, were running in mad circles around Dr. Gourmelon's chair. Three other little girls, one black, one Indian, and one with light-brown hair, were seated in a circle telling each other tales that made them all cackle.

Dr. Gourmelon had laid out a basket with fresh-baked chocolate-chip cookies. The children seemed not to notice them.

"My darling babies," Dr. Gourmelon said, "do you remember me?"

"You're Frances," the little Chinese girl said, looking up at her.

"And you're MingMei," Dr. Gourmelon said.

"Yes."

"Boys! Stop chasing around the room for a moment and come over here," Dr. Gourmelon said.

The two boys approached her chair, standing beside each other at Dr. Gourmelon's right side. "Do you remember me?" she asked.

"You're Frances," the brown haired boy said, repeating MingMei's observation. He was "Malcolm," according to the name written on the stick-on badge on his coveralls.

"You look different," the red-haired boy said. His name badge identified him as "Warren."

"You mean, older and fatter?" Dr. Gourmelon asked.

"Yes," Warren said, and he and Malcolm exchanged mirthful glances.

The three girls who had been telling each other tall tales got up and stood by the other arm of Dr. Gourmelon's chair, while MingMei skooched over to sit at her feet. "You three are as silly as ever," Dr. Gourmelon said. "My little wiggle-worms."

At this, the three girls cackled again. Pamela, the black girl, began to climb onto her lap but Dr. Gourmelon pushed her off. "Even though I'm fatter than I was, I don't have enough lap for all of you," she said, "and it would be unfair to the others if you had it all to yourself."

"I want to go home now," Warren said.

"I do too," said the girl with the light brown hair, whose name was Jeannie.

"Me too," said Minal, the Indian girl, adding her voice to the chorus.

"In a short while, my darlings," Dr. Gourmelon said, noticing that a red light on the wall had turned on, which the Guide had said meant she had one minute left.

"Is it time for our walk?" MingMei asked.

"I'll take you for our walk when I return," Dr. Gourmelon said. "I'll bring the rope that we all hold onto, to stay safe."

"Warren lets go of the rope sometimes," MingMei said.

"I know, sweetheart," Dr. Gourmelon said, "that's why I watch him so very carefully."

The red light began to blink, and Dr. Gourmelon had just a moment to say "good-bye" when she heard the Guide's voice, "Dr. Gourmelon, please exit the Visitation Room using the door in front of you under the red light," and the children vanished.

The Guide handed Dr. Gourmelon a flash drive copy of the video recorded of her time in the Visitation Room, and her tin of cookies that had been left in the Visitation Room. "You can keep that," Dr. Gourmelon said.

"They smell delicious," the Guide said, "But we are not allowed to accept any kind of gift from customers."

"Give them to the other customers then. They are very good. I promise."

"Thank you, I'll be glad to do that," the Guide said. After Dr. Gourmelon left, the Guide emptied the cookies into the Marriott's trash bin. Then she placed the cookie tin, after she cleaned it, in the Commemoration Space.

That evening, as dusk overtook the pedestrian plaza outside the Marriott, the park lights switched on to pierce the deepening shadows and the day-time tourist crowd dwindled to a few stragglers. Harry could hear Alexandra's footsteps clicking on the pavement that was still damp from a late afternoon shower as she approached to join him just outside the hotel's main entrance.

Alexandra went first into the Visitation Room. As soon as she sat down and the door closed behind her, she saw Ariel standing in front of her, dressed in the same outfit as she was wearing on the Red Line, fitted blue jeans, a blue Oxford shirt, and a red cloth sash tied around her waist. They hugged, and Alexandra could feel under her hands the solidity of her daughter's strong back and shoulders, and on her cheek the feathery touch of Ariel's hair.

"I knew you'd come back," Alexandra said.

"I love you, Mom," Ariel said.

When Alexandra's session was over, she returned to the waiting area where Harry was preparing to go in.

"Ariel was there," she said. "It was worth everything."

Alexandra looked so happy, so glowing with joy, that Harry impulsively leaned towards her, grasped her shoulders, and kissed her on her forehead.

Alexandra said, "I'll wait for you here. When you come out, let's go to my place. I want company tonight."

Harry remained alone during his fifteen minutes in the Visitation Room, which gave him time to consider Alexandra's casual, offhand-sounding remark just before he'd come in.

"Ariel said I should ask you about a shower that you shared with Erin Haig."

When both Erin and Ariel had appeared to him in the 2V test room at MIT, Erin had teased about the shower that she and Harry had shared in Hong Kong and Ariel had demanded, "Daddy! What is she talking about?" Harry had never, he was almost certain, told Alexandra about that memorable event.

How, then, did the Ariel who just visited Alexandra a few minutes ago know about it, if she were no more than a figment of Alexandra's imagination?

Whatever was happening, whatever it meant, he and Alexandra were seeing their daughter again. For Harry, that was enough for now.

PART THREE

TWO MONTHS LATER

Forty Two

AN OFF-DUTY COP down on the Boston waterfront next to the Marriott noticed that a man had parked his SUV in a no-parking area near the Marriott's front entrance and then hurried away without pausing to lock his SUV's doors. He wondered why the guy would park here if he wasn't going into the Marriott? And why was he in such a rush that he'd neglect to lock his doors? The license plate was from New Hampshire which perhaps explained it; the guy might not be familiar with driving, parking, and protecting your car in Boston. However, just to be sure, the off-duty cop called in the plate number. A moment later he was told that the plate was registered not to the SUV, but to a Honda Civic in Nashua, N.H., that had been reported stolen a week earlier. Just then dense black smoke began to billow out from the vehicle.

The cop shouted into his handheld radio, "We have a vehicle here that needs to be checked out immediately! It's parked right next to the Marriott and now smoke is pouring out!"

His call shot to the top of the emergency-response list because of the Marriott's high profile as host of the Visitation Room and its sensitivity as a hotel serving many international guests. The Boston Police dispatched their bomb squad along with five police cars, sirens screaming. The Boston Fire

Department sent two ladder trucks and an emergency support van. Genevieve LaPierre was alerted about the potential emergency situation and ordered to evacuate the hotel. The hotel alarm honked ear-piercingly and incessantly as guests and staff streamed out of the hotel on the side opposite from the front entrance, which police had cordoned off. Police officers raced to each of the restaurants and stores within a one-block range of the SUV and ordered them also to be evacuated. Fire alarms blared in the nearby office buildings and these also were emptied out. The plaza in the vicinity of SUV was cleared of all pedestrians except for emergency personnel, and barricaded by yellow police caution tape.

The bomb squad maneuvered a remotely-controlled robotic vehicle to smash the side and rear windows of the SUV and look inside with a video-cam. Despite the smoke from highway flares that had ignited inside, the robot operators were able to make out two large canisters and three sacks, two alarm clocks, and wires. A chemical sensor on the robot detected signs of gasoline in the canisters and urea nitrate in the sacks.

Apparently the flares had failed to ignite the explosives as intended. However, because of the proximity of the SUV to the Marriott, the captain of the bomb squad decided that it was still too dangerous to attempt to move the vehicle or disarm the explosives by hand. Instead he deployed the BPD's "pig-stick" water-jet disrupter which had been purchased from the British Army after it was proven to be effective in neutralizing IRA car bombs. A fire hose was connected to the pigstick nozzle device that was already mounted on the remotely-controlled robot, and at the captain's order, the bomb squad technicians blasted high-intensity jets of water into the SUV to disrupt the circuitry that might cause the explosives to detonate. Bomb squad specialists then opened the SUV's back and trunk doors and disconnected the soaked circuitry from the explosives. When the bomb was declared to be disarmed, the SUV was loaded into an armored truck for transport to a safer location for forensic analysis.

It was soon determined that the SUV had been advertised for sale on Craigslist by a well-known trader in stolen cars. When interviewed by police after his arrest, the seller claimed that he never learned the name of the man who paid him cash for the SUV, but he was able to describe him as well-spoken, quite tall, blond-haired, athletic looking, and probably in his late 40s or early 50s.

The off-duty cop who first reported the suspiciously-parked SUV provided a similar description. The man's image, which had been captured by a video surveillance camera mounted outside the Marriott entrance, was broadcast on TV news. Calls flooded in from people who claimed to recognize the man as the medical doctor who, a year earlier, had appeared repeatedly on TV pleading tearfully for the return of his wife who had gone missing from their comfortable suburban home in Concord.

Then several nurses at Massachusetts General Hospital contacted the police to confirm that the man in the security video was indeed an MGH urologist with whom they worked and knew well, none other than Dr. Douglas McDougall, the distraught husband whose wife had vanished so mysteriously.

Dr. McDougall did not fit the Homeland Security profile of a terrorist who might attempt to blow up an international hotel like the Boston Marriott on the Waterfront. Although he belonged to an Episcopalian church in Concord, he seldom attended and was not known to be particularly religious. Registered to vote as an Independent, he had no apparent political affiliation. Police found no emails or website visits stored on his home or office PCs that suggested any involvement with hate groups. Nor did they find in his phone records or emails any evidence of communications with criminal organizations such as, for example, Michael Wallace's in Somerville.

However, Dr. McDougall's fingerprints were found on the steering wheel of the SUV and he was selected in multiple police line-ups by the off-duty cop, the trader in stolen cars, a fertilizer distributor in Western Massachusetts, and a gas station clerk who had observed him filling cans with gasoline at the station's self-service pump. His credit card records identified him as the purchaser of highway flares from an auto supply store, the same brand as found in the SUV.

When confronted with the evidence, Dr. McDougall confessed. Yes, he was the driver of the SUV. However, he could not recall why he tried to commit such a heinous crime. After of the disappearance of his wife, he had been under such terrible stress that he had suffered a nervous breakdown accompanied by memory loss which was exacerbated by abuse of pain-killers and of drugs to help him sleep. He said that he had no complaint against the Marriott and was grateful that the police had been able to prevent the tragedy from occurring for which he would have been responsible. He said he had no memory of leaving the SUV near the Marriott.

Dr. MacDougall's lawyer, Marvin Jones, Esq., told reporters that his client would enter rehab to battle both his addiction to pain-killer narcotics and his clinical depression. Jones also said that his client was cooperating fully with Authorities. Meanwhile, pending his trial, he would provide no additional public comments.

A reporter asked, "How does your client respond to suspicions that he was involved in the disappearance of his wife?"

"If he were here, he would respond only that he's never stopped wishing for his wife's safe return."

"Are you aware that his wife's sister claims that she met his wife's ghost in the Visitation Room in the Marriott, and that based on what she heard in the Visitation Room, the sister-in-law is now accusing Dr. McDougall of murdering his wife?"

"It would appear that Dr. McDougall's sister-in-law is a disturbed woman."

"What about the fact that the sister-in-law has now filed a formal request with the police in Concord to search Walden Pond where she says your client disposed of his wife's body, a fact that she says she learned in the Visitation Room?"

"My client would not dignify any of these questions with a response. He has been fully supportive of all efforts by law enforcement to locate his wife."

"Attorney Jones," the reporter persisted, "are you telling us that your client supports his sister-in-law's efforts to get the police to search Walden Pond?"

"I don't have anything to add concerning Dr. McDougall and his wife, whom he misses very much," Jones said. "However, speaking for myself, I must tell you that I am amazed that anyone would credit an accusation derived from meeting a ghost in the Visitation Room. What's next? Eye-witness testimony from tooth fairies? Seating werewolves on juries? Vampire judges?"

Amazon Reviews..

"A marvelously twisty thriller." *(5 stars)*

"Fascinating plot-driven story." *(4 stars)*

"Truly entertaining, very well-crafted tale that will keep you away from bedtime turning pages." *(5 stars)*

"Holds your attention as you continue reading to see how it all shakes out." *(5 stars)*

"Descriptive, fast-paced suspense novel that will keep readers on their toes guessing who is responsible for the violence and corruption at the centerpiece of this entertaining story. The author does an excellent job developing characters, a great storyline and vivid settings. It has a spellbinding quality that makes it difficult to put down. I wholeheartedly recommend this novel to those who love a great international suspense novel!" *(5 stars)*

International suspense novel...

A VILLAGE NEAR SHANGHAI is demolished to make room for the city and a young villager vows revenge on the corrupt officials who benefited. He seizes his opportunity when a shadowy Shanghai investment group is reported to be financing a huge business deal in Hong Kong.

Knowing none of this, and coping with problems of his own, consultant Harry West is engaged by the government in Hong Kong to evaluate the proposed deal.

Only after he arrives in Hong Kong does Harry discover that his assignment will be unlike anything he's done before. His task: To uncover evidence of money laundering and corruption, evidence that will expose people who will stop at nothing to protect themselves.

Along the way, Harry's journey is shaped by two women in Hong Kong, an American journalist who is investigating the same business deal and a long-lost love who comes back into his life.

A suspenseful story about intrigue, revenge, and the bonds of love and memory, *The Trail of Money* keeps the reader guessing until the end.

Released October 2012 by PenLane Press
www.thetrailofmoney.com